GET

HOW TO GET YOUR
2 FREE BOOKS AND FREE GIFT!

1. Peel off the MIRA® sticker on the front cover. Place it in the space provided at right. This automatically entitles you to receive two free books and an exciting surprise gift.

2. Send back this card and you'll get 2 "The Best of the Best™" books. These books have a combined cover price of $11.98 or more in the U.S. and $13.98 or more in Canada, but they are yours to keep absolutely FREE!

3. There's no catch. You're under no obligation to buy anything. We charge nothing – ZERO – for your first shipment. And you don't have to make any minimum number of purchases – not even one!

4. We call this line "The Best of the Best" because each month you'll receive the best books by some of today's most popular authors. These authors show up time and time again on all the major bestseller lists and their books sell out as soon as they hit the stores. You'll like the convenience of getting them delivered to your home at our special discount prices . . . and you'll love your *Heart to Heart* subscriber newsletter featuring author news, horoscopes, recipes, book reviews and much more!

5. We hope that after receiving your free books you'll want to remain a subscriber. But the choice is yours – to continue or cancel, anytime at all! So why not take us up on our invitation, with no risk of any kind. You'll be glad you did!

6. And remember…we'll send you a surprise gift ABSOLUTELY FREE just for giving THE BEST OF THE BEST a try.

SPECIAL FREE GIFT!
We'll send you a fabulous surprise gift, absolutely FREE, simply for accepting our no-risk offer!

Visit us online at
www.mirabooks.com

® and TM are registered trademarks of Harlequin Enterprises Limited.

LOVE IS
MURDER

REBECCA BRANDEWYNE
MAUREEN CHILD
LINDA WINSTEAD JONES

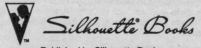
Silhouette Books

Published by Silhouette Books
America's Publisher of Contemporary Romance

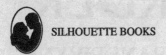 SILHOUETTE BOOKS

LOVE IS MURDER

Copyright © 2003 by Harlequin Books S.A.

ISBN 0-373-21828-1

The publisher acknowledges the copyright holders
of the individual works as follows:

TO DIE FOR
Copyright © 2003 by Rebecca Brandewyne

IN TOO DEEP
Copyright © 2003 by Maureen Child

CALLING AFTER MIDNIGHT
Copyright © 2003 by Linda Winstead Jones

Visit Silhouette at www.eHarlequin.com

Printed in U.S.A.

CONTENTS

TO DIE FOR

Rebecca Brandewyne

For Bob, Bev, Tom and Zeny.
With love.

Dear Reader,

I was very excited when my editor, Tara Gavin, at Silhouette Books, asked me to write a novella for the *Love Is Murder* anthology. As a reader, I've always enjoyed murder mysteries and have a complete collection of Agatha Christie's works. As a writer, I find murder mysteries a challenge and thought it would be especially entertaining to write one based around the Murder Mystery games that are so popular with so many people. In addition, all my family are big fans of board games like Clue and Murder on the Orient Express, and I'm no exception. So, as you may imagine, I had a great deal of fun plotting and writing my contribution, "To Die For," for this anthology! I hope you enjoy it!

Happy reading!

Rebecca Brandewyne

Love distills desire upon the eyes,
Love brings bewitching grace into the hearts
Of those he would destroy.
I pray that love may never come to me
with murderous intent,
In rhythms measureless and wild.
Not fire nor stars have stronger bolts
than those of Aphrodite sent
By the hands of Eros, Zeus's child.

Love instills doubt in the heart and mind,
Love brings enchanting days and nights into
the lives of those he finds.
He fills them with murderous passion.
Who knows where it may lead?
In rhythms measureless and wild,
Cupid shoots his arrows without
regard for the fatal deed.
Vain, heedless Aphrodite's child.

Love tills fields both fertile and barren,
Love brings spellbinding ripeness to the furrows
Of those who would eat of
Its fruits, yet leaves them hungering for more.
With murderous intent,
In rhythms measureless and wild,
Love comes with stars and strongest bolts
to slay with passion heav'n sent
By the hands of Eros, Zeus's child.

—Adapted from *Hippolytus* [428 B.C.],
by Euripides

Memories

Sweet Genevieve,
The days may come, the days may go,
But still the hands of memory weave
The blissful dreams of long ago.

Sweet Genevieve [c. 1877]
—George Cooper

Chapter 1

Savannah, Georgia
The Present—Monday

The moment that she awoke, Lily Clothier—née Harlow—knew she ought to just stay in bed and pull the covers up over her head, that it was going to be one of those days.

For one thing, having suffered insomnia last night and having slept badly when she finally had drifted into slumber, she was still so exhausted this morning that even the buzzing of her alarm clock had failed to rouse her on time. For a bleary-eyed glance at the lighted digital dial informed her that the alarm had now been sounding for well over an hour—she had not even been disturbed enough to hit the snooze button—and that she had slept straight through it. At the realization, Lily groaned.

She was stiff and sore, aching in every fiber of her being from all the long hours and heavy labor she had put in this week at Mélusine's Attic, the small shop she owned. It was named after a legendary French fairy queen and located in Savannah's historic, upscale City Market, two blocks from River Street and the waterfront. All week long, Lily had worked rearranging the store's contents, setting up new vignettes throughout its rooms, which would display her wares to their best advantage. As a result, she was now bone tired.

Briefly, she thought about just not opening up Mélusine's Attic at all today. She was already nearly an hour late as it was. But if she didn't open up the shop, nobody else would. At the moment, Lily was struggling desperately to make ends meet, and as a result, she didn't currently have any employees, although she thought that by this time next year, if she were careful, she would be able to hire back at least one or two of those she had been compelled to let go. But right now, there was no one except her—and despite how weary she was, she really couldn't afford to lose a day's business.

At that thought, with difficulty, groaning again at the effort, Lily dragged herself from bed and headed toward the small bathroom that adjoined her bedroom.

Sometimes, it was hard for her to believe that only a year ago she had been happily married and without a money care in the world. Now she was completely on her own and—in part because she had refused to accept one single penny from her estranged husband, Paul—she was teetering on the edge of financial disaster.

It had taken every last cent she possessed to get Mélusine's Attic up and running. So if she couldn't make a success of it, if it went under, Lily didn't know what she would do, what would become of her. For despite the fact that, legally, Paul was still her husband, there was no way that she could ever return to him, could ever ask for his help, after the way he had betrayed her and their marriage vows. She and Paul had still been newlyweds, not even married a year, when he had started cheating on her, embarking upon a torrid affair with Zelda Rutherford, a wealthy socialite.

Like all decent, honest, trusting, unsuspecting wives, Lily had been the last to know, finding out about Paul's infidelity through one of the worst and most public ways possible: she had read about it in one of the local newspapers, the *Savannah Spokesman,* in Freddie Fontaine's gossip column, ''The 'Delish' Dish.''

Even now, her cheeks burned with embarrassment and humiliation whenever she thought about the article. Of course, Freddie had not actually mentioned

Paul and Zelda by name, but even so, there had been no mistaking the identities of the ''Handsome Hotelier'' and the ''Hostess with the Mostest'' to whom he had referred in the paragraph he had devoted to the illicit couple. Even Lily had not been naive enough to think Freddie had been talking about Donald Trump and Donald's ex-wife, Ivana. Paul owned a chain of small, exclusive, expensive hotels throughout the South, and in Savannah, Zelda's parties were legendary, invitations to them highly coveted.

Now, as Lily turned on the taps and stepped into the shower, she felt her face unwittingly flame and her stomach churn sickeningly at the unhappy memories. No, if she lost Mélusine's Attic, she could not go to Paul. No matter how foolish it might be, her pride was such that she would rather wind up homeless and destitute than humble herself by agreeing to be Paul's wife again. The fact that she was actually still legally wedded to him was only a mere technicality, born of the fact that because of Mélusine's Attic, she had no money left with which to hire an attorney to free herself from the philandering husband who had destroyed their marriage and broken her heart.

That Paul himself, however, had never in the past year since Lily had left him filed for a divorce was a constant source of puzzlement, unease and anxiety to her. *He* certainly didn't lack for funds for a lawyer, his annual income running into seven figures.

Oh, at the start, she had understood his behavior, his fear, no doubt, that she would try to take him to the cleaners financially if he divorced her, especially since they had no prenuptial agreement and *he* was the guilty party in their marriage. Indeed, when Lily had confronted him about the affair and made it clear that she was leaving him, Paul had tried to bluff his way through their ensuing argument, steadfastly proclaiming his innocence, vowing his love and desire for her, to the point of trying to take her into his arms to make love to her right then and there, and denigrating Freddie's insinuations as nothing more than malicious gossip.

Lily had wanted desperately to believe her husband. But despite his seemingly earnest protests, deep down inside, she had known the real truth of the matter. That Paul Clothier had ever been attracted to her in the first place, much less wanted to marry her, had always seemed a fairy tale to her from the very beginning.

They had met at the art gallery where she had worked then, when Paul had come in to buy a painting. At first, aware of his reputation, Lily had refused to have anything to do with him. He was powerful, rich and handsome enough that he could have his pick of women throughout the world, and she was just a young, relatively inexperienced working girl, way out of his class and league. She had felt sure that he had little more than a short, pleasant dalliance with her in

mind when he had invited her out for drinks and supper after finally completing his purchase more than
thirty minutes after the art gallery's official closing
hour.

"Taking you to dinner is the very least I can do,"
Paul had insisted, smiling charmingly, "seeing as
how I've caused you to have to stay late."

"That's my job, Mr. Clothier," Lily had replied
primly. "I'm happy simply to have closed the sale.
Now, if you'll excuse me, I really do have to get
home. I—I have a date," she had lied, blushing, for
the truth was that she seldom went out and was un-
accustomed to telling falsehoods, besides. "Enjoy
your new painting."

She had believed that would be the extent of her
association with Paul Clothier. But much to her dismay and nervous excitement, that assumption had
soon proved wholly erroneous. Paul had returned several times to the art gallery, explaining that after years
of living in one or another of his hotels, he had finally
bought a proper house in Savannah's historic district
and was in the process of furnishing it from top to
bottom.

"Quite frankly, I'm surprised at your taking such
a personal interest in its decorating, Mr. Clothier,"
Lily had told him. "It's been my experience that
most people in your position employ an interior designer, whom they allow to present them with a se-
lection of items from which to choose for their

homes. I'm certain you must have engaged such a person or firm.''

''No, I haven't. Although several friends, acquaintances and business associates have, in fact, recommended a number of interior designers to me, and I've worked with many on my hotels, as well, the truth is that I've yet to find any whose taste genuinely meshes with my own. It is one thing to outfit a hotel, you see, and quite another to furnish one's own house. I really do much prefer that my home reflect my own personal style and flair, rather than those of somebody else, no matter how elegant and professional. If impersonal good taste were all I were after, I could have continued living in my hotels.''

''I see. But then, surely, my own opinion with regard to your choice of artwork can be of very little value to you, Mr. Clothier.''

''To the contrary. It would appear that when it comes to personal style and flair, you and I have a great deal in common, Ms. Harlow. I find your taste exquisite and completely in harmony with my own. The painting you recommended only last week, in fact, looks magnificent over the fireplace mantel in my living room. That's one of the reasons why I have continued to seek your advice and assistance. I really would be forever indebted to you if I could persuade you to come to my house and give me your thoughts on its progress and what else is still needed.

Naturally, I would pay you for your time and expertise.''

"I'm—I'm very flattered, of course, Mr. Clothier. But I'm afraid you very much mistake the matter and my own suitability for the job. I'm not an interior designer. I'm only a salesperson in an art gallery. Therefore, I'm hardly qualified—"

"Oh, but I think you are," Paul had interrupted smoothly, with a casual wave of one hand easily dismissing her protests and qualms. "I would scarcely be seeking your opinions, otherwise. What do you say to tomorrow evening, after you get off work? I'll pick you up here at the art gallery and even take you out for those drinks and supper I once promised you."

Lily had been so torn by the invitation that she hadn't known what to do. All her life, she had wanted to be an interior designer, and so far, the closest she had managed to come was landing the sales position at the art gallery. If Paul Clothier were, in fact, willing to hire her in an interior designer capacity, she would be extremely foolish to turn him down, for it was highly unlikely that she would ever again be handed such an opportunity as this!

So Lily had taken the job he had offered her, grateful not only for the chance to pursue her lifelong dream, but also for the extra income. She had worked on commission at the art gallery, and the past few months before Paul had come into her life, she had just barely managed to scrape by.

That was how her relationship with Paul had begun, to be followed by a dizzying whirlwind courtship, and their marriage just three short months later. Through it all, Lily had frequently felt as though she needed to pinch herself to be certain that everything taking place in her life was all actually happening, that it was real, rather than some dream or fairy tale. In her entire life, she had never been so happy.

Afterward, at Paul's urging, she had quit her job at the art gallery, devoting herself instead to the interior design of their own home and to the acquisition of inventory for Mélusine's Attic, the shop that, also at Paul's championing and with his backing, she planned eventually to open in Savannah's historic, upscale City Market.

Of course, her husband had paid for everything she had bought, including the small, old City Market warehouse that they had purchased to house her new store and to showcase the wares that it would offer to the public, in conjunction with Lily's own natural skill and talent as an interior designer. She had actually been well on her way to making Mélusine's Attic a success when the story about Paul's affair with Zelda Rutherford had hit the newsstands.

That was when Lily's beautiful bubble had so suddenly and horribly burst.

Now, as all these still-painful recollections flooded her mind, she felt hot tears sting her eyes, then spill over to stream down her cheeks, mingling with the steaming water that cascaded upon her from the showerhead.

She simply *had* to get hold of herself, she told herself sternly. Because all the crying in the world wasn't going to fix things—or to save Mélusine's Attic, either.

Much to Lily's distress, after she had left her husband, moving into a small town house of her own, the sales at her burgeoning shop had abruptly declined dramatically. Savannah wasn't a city so much as it was an overgrown small town, where everybody knew everybody else's business, and a coterie of powerful, wealthy people who frequented the same circles as Paul did ran everything.

Rumors about her and Paul's failed marriage had run rife, and the society women she had met through her husband and believed to be her newfound friends had instead dropped her like a hot potato. In the beginning, they had made one polite excuse after another for why they suddenly could no longer join her for brunch or buy that wonderful little antique desk that she had, at great time and expense to herself, finally managed to locate for them.

But eventually, her so-called friends had not even bothered to keep up the pretense. Instead, they had just stopped returning her telephone calls altogether, and Lily had got the cold, cruel message: She was nobody, and Paul was...well, *the* Paul Clothier, the hotel magnate. No one wanted to offend *him,* of course.

Oh, she still sold inventory from her shop and did the occasional decorating job, too. Only now, the vast majority of her customers had limited budgets that didn't even begin to run to more than a thousand dollars a yard for upholstery fabrics or a cool fifty grand for an antique French armoire. Increasingly desperate, Lily had in recent months been compelled to sell more than a few fine pieces at a considerable loss, just to keep her store open and running.

She wouldn't have had nearly as big a financial crisis if she weren't so determined to repay every single penny that Paul had ever invested in Mélusine's Attic—regardless of the fact that he had never referred to his backing in those terms. In his own words, the money for the shop had been not a business loan, but a gift to be employed in making Lily's dream of a career in interior design come true. Because they certainly hadn't needed the income. She hadn't needed to work. Even Paul, had he so desired, could have sold his chain of hotels and retired, despite the fact that, being a man in his prime, he was nowhere near retirement age.

Those first few months after Lily had left her husband and moved out into her own small town house, Paul had sent her checks to him back, uncashed, accompanied by checks of his own made out to her, along with huge bouquets in crystal vases, boxes of expensive chocolates and jewelry, and other exquisite gifts, as well as passionate love letters begging her to reconsider her decision and come home to him.

But, proud, stubborn and deeply hurt, Lily had remained adamant, returning all his checks, presents and notes, resolutely stashing all the money she felt she owed him into an escrow account, and informing him by e-mail that, as she could not afford to do so herself, she would appreciate it if he would take care of filing for their divorce, that she wanted nothing from him and would not contest whatever arrangements he made to sever their relationship.

Why Paul had yet to do what she had requested of him, she could not imagine. Still, if she were honest with herself, Lily must admit that, deep down inside, she was secretly glad that they were still married, because despite everything, she knew she was still in love with her husband—for all the good that might do her. For Paul surely cared nothing for her now—if he ever had.

At that miserable thought, her breath catching on a ragged sob, Lily finally shut off the taps and got out of the shower, shivering in her small bathroom, despite the fact that although the morning was yet early, the summer day was already hot and muggy, the yellow sunlight streaming in brightly through the window.

"Pull yourself together, Lily, damn it!" she muttered tersely to her reflection in the mirror over the pedestal sink. "Your going to pieces is *not* going to help matters!"

Knowing that to be the case, she quickly dried her shoulder-length, dark auburn hair, plaiting it into a sophisticated French braid, then, with hands that still trembled with emotion, carefully applied her makeup, once more swearing softly when she smudged her eyeliner and mascara. She really should have just stayed in bed today, she thought again, sighing heavily. She had not got off to a good start, and somehow, for whatever unknown reason, she had the strangest, most sinking feeling that things were only going to get worse!

After dressing herself in a crisp, pale lemon-yellow linen suit, Lily grabbed her handbag and car keys. As she was already late, and her stomach still felt queasy, she didn't bother with breakfast. She could make herself a cup of coffee when she reached Mélusine's Attic, she thought. Getting into the cheap, secondhand but practical automobile she had bought following her breakup with Paul, she drove to the shop, parked and then hurried to the front door, in such a rush that she didn't even notice the strange man standing to one side, studying the artistic, elegant display in one of her store windows.

"Mrs. Clothier?" he inquired, approaching her as she turned the key in the lock. "Are you Mrs. Paul Clothier, ma'am?"

"Yes, but if you're looking for my husband, I'm afraid I can't help you," she declared, a trifle breathlessly. "We're separated. So if you'll please excuse me, I'm already late opening up this morning."

Finally, Lily managed to unlock the front door and

push it open. But instead of allowing her to pass, the unfamiliar man reached into the inner pocket of his suit jacket, withdrawing a thick, ominous-looking envelope, which he handed to her.

"I'm not in search of your husband, Mrs. Clothier," he announced. "I'm a process server. Mr. Clothier has filed for a divorce from you, ma'am, and you've just been served with the papers. Have a good day."

Lily was so stunned and stricken that she could not even reply, was not even aware of the man's departure—although some dark corner of her mind dimly registered his parting words to her and, given the circumstances, their hideous irony.

Slowly, she went inside Mélusine's Attic, automatically turning on the lights as she made her way to her small office at the rear of the building. There, her knees finally giving way beneath her, she sank into the chair before her desk. With hands that now shook uncontrollably, she set her purse and keys to one side, then picked up her silver-handled letter opener to slit the envelope. It was stuffed so full and sealed so tightly that she had not proved able to tear it open herself.

Withdrawing the bundle of papers inside, she began to read. She was so distraught and uncomprehending that she had to read the petition and proposed settlement three times before she understood them.

Oh, God! she thought, horrified. *This cannot be happening! This cannot be real!*

It wasn't just the imminent dissolution of her marriage or that despite the "equitable property division" laws of Georgia, Paul didn't want to give her anything at all. It was that he was also demanding an immediate, lump-sum repayment of every last cent he had ever put into Mélusine's Attic!

Somehow—she did not know how—he had even managed to produce a copy of a business agreement purportedly made between them, detailing every single aspect of her shop and how it was to be financed and paid for. Despite how she racked her frantic brain, Lily could not remember ever even seeing such an agreement before, let alone having signed it. Yet there was her signature on the dotted line at the bottom!

There was no way she could ever come up with such a huge amount of money all at once—at least, not without shutting down the entire business and selling not only the warehouse, but also every last item of inventory she possessed. Even then, she might not be able to raise the total sum required. She would have nothing left...absolutely nothing. Her lifelong dream would be finished forever, irrevocably and completely destroyed.

It seemed that in the face of her pride and stubbornness, her determined refusal to forgive him for his unfaithfulness and give their marriage a second chance, Paul had at last decided not only to be rid of her once and for all, but also to crush her utterly in the process. She knew how wholly ruthless he could be when necessary. No one ever reached the pinnacle of success that her husband had without that capacity.

"Oh, God," Lily moaned aloud, starting to cry.

That was that, then. Her marriage was over, finished. She herself was both heartbroken and ruined. Nothing worse could possibly happen to her now, she reflected dully.

But that was before she heard the incongruously cheerful clanging of the brass bell that hung on the inside of Mélusine's Attic's front door, and then a high, effeminate, drawling voice calling her name.

"Lily…oh, Lily, dear, where are you? Yoo-hoo, Lily…? Are you here, dear?"

She really should have stayed in bed today, with the covers pulled up over her head. As long as she lived, she would never again ignore her gut instinct! For she would know that obnoxious, annoying, syrupy voice anywhere. It belonged to Freddie Fontaine—who was absolutely *the* very last person on earth whom she wanted to see right now.

Still, there was no help for it. Even as she hastily shoved the divorce papers into her desk drawer and stood, drying her eyes and hoping her mascara had not run, Lily could hear the spiteful little gossip columnist wandering through the shop's various rooms, searching for her.

He would not be deterred from entering what were clearly marked as the store's rooms for employees only, which housed not only the offices, but also a small private bath, a kitchenette and the stockrooms. Lily didn't want him back here, invading her personal sanctuary, poking and prying into matters that did not concern him. She would not put it past Freddie at all to ask her to get him a glass of water or iced tea, and then, while she was absent from her office, to rummage through her desk, discovering the divorce papers.

With hands that still trembled, she smoothed her skirt and hurried from the back rooms, pausing just briefly at the intervening doorway to catch her breath and try to compose herself, so that Freddie would not suspect there was anything wrong. He had the uncanny instincts of some slimy predator stalking its prey. Somehow, he always seemed to know how and where to ferret out the latest dirt on anybody and everybody. No one was safe from the malicious little toad!

Plastering a false but cool smile on her face, Lily advanced into the rooms open to the public at Mélusine's Attic.

"Hello, Freddie. What can I do for you?"

From where he peered nosily into the room Lily called the "Treasure Trunk," the gossip columnist turned, obviously startled. He recovered swiftly, however, smiling oilily and spreading his laden arms widely. In one hand, he carried a balloon arrangement filled, in addition to flowers, with a strange assortment of items, including a notepad and a magnifying glass. In the other hand, he bore a bottle of Dom Pérignon, vintage 1990.

"Lily, darling, how are you?"

Mincing forward, he kissed her lightly on both cheeks in greeting. Lily was barely able to repress her shudder of revulsion. She had never liked Freddie to begin with, and ever since reading his article about

Paul's extramarital affair, she had positively loathed him. She felt certain that if someone were to investigate Freddie's family tree, it would be discovered that he was, in reality, some Kewpie doll's long-lost cousin. Further, she suspected that the gossip columnist himself was not only aware of his striking resemblance to the yesteryear arcade prizes, but that he also actually actively cultivated and reinforced it. It made him seem harmless and lovable—despite the fact that he was anything but.

"I'm fine," Lily replied.

"Are you? Are you really, dear? You look as though you've been crying," Freddie observed shrewdly as his avid, beady eyes searched her pale face intently.

"It's allergies, Freddie," she lied. "My poor eyes have been streaming for days, and I don't mind telling you that I've got a raging headache, besides. In fact, the pressure's so bad at the moment that I'm worried I might even be coming down with a sinus infection. I feel so dreadful that right before you arrived, I was even thinking of closing up shop and going home. So if you'll just let me know your reason for being here…?"

"Poor darling. I *do* sympathize, for as you know, I suffer terribly from any number of allergies myself…always have, ever since I was a child. Why, I remember one year when I had *so* much trouble breathing that I had to be hospitalized and placed into an *oxygen tent!* Can you imagine? It was just awful…truly, truly *awful!* I was only six years old at the time and, so, naturally, *quite* certain I was going to die! Oh, but there, enough about me. Why am I here this morning? Well, it's because I've decided to throw a party, Lily—but not just any party, mind you. Plain old cocktail and dinner parties are all *so* very passé and boring, don't you agree?''

Without waiting for Lily to answer, Freddie pressed on excitedly.

''No, no, nothing so clichéd and old hat for Freddie Fontaine! Instead, I've hit upon the most fabulous theme, dear! I'm going to host a *Murder Mystery* party! You know, one of those affairs at which everybody present assumes a role, and a fake murder is committed by one of them, and, afterward, they all have to figure out which of them 'done it.' Oh, isn't it a positively *divine* idea? It will be wonderful...*the* event of the summer here in Savannah, Lily, I do assure you...a party *to die for!* Do say you'll come! For I warn you, I simply *won't* take no for an answer! Here is your invitation, darling.'' He abruptly thrust the balloon arrangement into her hands. ''And of course, a little something to enjoy while you're reading it.'' He gave her the bottle of champagne, as well.

''We'll have a *barrel* of fun, I promise you! Saturday night, at my house...eight o'clock sharp. Don't you *dare* be late, Lily! Oh, I can hardly wait! I feel just like a child again. Well, I must be off now to deliver the rest of my invitations. So...ta-ta for now, darling. See you Saturday evening.''

With an airy wave of one hand, Freddie exited Mélusine's Attic, leaving Lily standing there gaping-mouthed but nevertheless utterly speechless, breathing in the pungent, vaguely unpleasant scent of his cologne.

She just could not believe it! That Freddie Fontaine had actually invited her to a party at his house surely boded no good. Worse was the fact that she knew without a single doubt that if she didn't attend, he would—to get even with her for the perceived snub—think of something horrible to write about her in his spiteful gossip column. So, regardless of all her suspicions and trepidation, she simply couldn't *not* go. If she did, he would perhaps print that Paul was not only divorcing her at last, but also that she was poised on the brink of financial disaster, about to lose the only thing of value she still had left, her shop—and if even a single word about that got out, everyone in town would know she *had* to sell, and then her warehouse and inventory probably wouldn't even fetch half of what she needed. Lily's heart pounded alarmingly as she thought of that. No, she couldn't possibly stay home from Freddie's party, no matter what malicious reason he might have for inviting her.

After an interminable minute, still clutching the balloon arrangement and the Dom Pérignon, she slowly turned and made her way back to her office. There, she sat down at her desk again, plucking the gilt-edged, vellum envelope from the balloon arrangement and opening it up to remove the invitation inside.

> ## *A Party to Die For!*
>
> ❦
>
> *You are cordially invited to*
> *Fontainebleu House*
> *on Saturday,*
> *the 23rd of June*
> *at eight o'clock*
> *in the evening,*
> *for dinner and drinks.*
>
> ### *R.S.V.P.*

Further examination of the balloon arrangement revealed that what Lily had originally thought was a small notepad was, in fact, a "clue book," which contained additional information about the planned party. It was written in such a way that she had to use the magnifying glass to read it, whereupon she discovered that the murder mystery to be enacted at the party was titled *The Bookshop Caper* and that the role she had been assigned to play required her to come dressed in a Gypsy costume.

Under other circumstances, Lily would actually have looked forward to the affair, because not only was the entire invitation cleverly presented, but, also, the event itself really did sound as though it would be a great deal of fun—had anybody but Freddie Fontaine been hosting it! As it was, she could only shiver with apprehension, especially when she belatedly realized that the three silver helium balloons wafting around on the long, colorful ribbons tied to the arrangement each bore a different appropriate image: a fingerprint, a skull and crossbones, and a shadowy body lying in a pool of blood.

Still, as Lily had already recognized, she had little choice but to attend. Besides, she couldn't worry about Freddie's party right now. She had more important things on her mind.

She was just reaching into her desk to withdraw the divorce petition and proposed settlement that Paul had served on her, so that she could reread them yet again, when the telephone rang.

"Mélusine's Attic." She spoke into the receiver, her already-taut nerves nearly shattered when she discovered that the woman on the other end of the line was a potential client with whom she had scheduled an appointment for earlier this morning, and who had waited for her out in front of the closed shop for more than half an hour.

Lily, of course, had never showed up.

"I don't know how *you* are accustomed to doing business, Mrs. Clothier, but *I* can state unequivocally that *I* am not in the habit of being stood up!" the irate woman declared. "I won't be returning to your store—and I'll make sure to tell all my family and friends not to patronize it, either!" Then she rudely and violently banged the receiver down in Lily's ear.

It was the last straw. Lily buried her face in her hands and wept uncontrollably for a long while. Afterward, still distressed, she closed up Mélusine's Attic and drove home, where, after undressing, she climbed back into bed and pulled the covers up over her head, heartily wishing she were dead.

Her last thought before she drifted into a deep but troubled slumber was that with the way her luck was currently going, somebody would probably murder her at Freddie Fontaine's party to die for.

Renewing Acquaintances

Should auld acquaintance be forgot,
And never brought to min'?
Should auld acquaintance be forgot,
And days o' auld lang syne?

Auld Lang Syne [1788]
—Robert Burns

Chapter 2

The following morning, at the crack of dawn, despite how tempted she was to remain in bed again all day, Lily dragged herself from beneath the covers and into the bathroom. Some part of her realized she was depressed—probably even clinically so—and that she had been ever since she had left Paul and moved into the town house. But lying in bed, hiding under the covers, was not going to solve any of her problems and, in fact, would only make them worse. Whether she liked it or not, she simply *had* to get a grip and deal with them one way or another.

After she had showered, Lily carefully applied her makeup, then dressed in a crisp, emerald-green linen suit that matched the color of her eyes. Paul had always liked her in the ensemble, and if she were compelled to humble herself and confront him, she at least wanted to look her best, not like the poor, pathetic, lost waif she currently felt herself to be.

She drove to Mélusine's Attic, arriving early in a subconscious attempt to try to make up for yesterday. Unlocking the front door and flipping on the lights, she headed for the kitchenette, where she made herself a cup of coffee. Then Lily went into her office, where, with butterflies in her stomach and with hands that shook with emotion, she picked up the telephone receiver and quickly dialed Paul's private number at the Clothier Corporation before she could change her mind.

"Paul Clothier." His low baritone voice spoke in her ear.

For a moment, she just sat there silently and stupidly. Despite everything, she had truly not expected him to answer, had thought he would be out of the office, and she was unprepared for how just the sound of his voice alone would affect her.

"Lily? Lily…is that you?" her husband inquired, when, still, she remained mute, both her tongue and her stomach tied up in knots.

"Yes…yes, how did you know?" she murmured at last.

"I have caller identification on this line. How are you, Lily?"

"I'm—I'm...surprised, Paul. I—I received the divorce petition yesterday, along with your proposed settlement. I'm afraid I don't really know how to respond. As I informed you some months ago by e-mail, I really don't have the necessary funds even to hire an attorney, much less to repay in one immediate lump sum all the money you invested in Mélusine's Attic. As you are also aware, I *have* attempted to make payments to you, all of which checks you returned, uncashed, however. But I have put all that money into an escrow account at the bank, so I can give you that in a lump sum right away, if that would be agreeable to you.... Paul? Paul...are you still there?" she asked when he didn't respond.

"Yes...simply trying to get hold of my black temper!"

"I'm—I'm sorry you're angry, Paul. But it truly is the best I can do. Otherwise, I'll be forced to sell Mélusine's Attic lock, stock and barrel, and I'm not sure that, even then, I would be able to raise all the money."

"I see," he replied more coolly. "Well, I would be perfectly willing to discuss the matter with you, Lily. Shall we say lunch at noon? I'll pick you up at the shop."

Before she could reply, he hung up. After a long moment, Lily replaced the receiver in the cradle of the telephone, feeling as though she might faint. Paul was going to come here, to the store, and take her to lunch. And he was infuriated with her for not being able to repay all the money she owed him. That did not bode well for her at all. She could only hope that, somehow, she would be able to placate and reason with him. Otherwise, she would surely lose everything.

The rest of the morning, Lily attempted to occupy herself with finishing up the new vignettes she had created throughout Mélusine's Attic to display her stock to its best advantage. The small warehouse that housed her shop was divided into several rooms, to each of which she had given a name best suited to describe its contents. She sold a combination of goods at her store, including antiques, original artwork and reproductions, fabrics, knickknacks, and even things like candles and bath salts.

Once or twice, customers came in to browse, to one of whom she wound up selling a lovely map chest for his study. After concluding the much-needed sale, Lily chatted with the man briefly and amiably, making arrangements to have the map chest delivered to his home. She always charged extra for home delivery, since she herself had to engage a moving company to make any deliveries required.

Shortly after the man had left, Paul walked in.

As she glanced up from the cash register and spied him, Lily felt her knees go weak, and she had to grab the glass-topped counter to steady herself. He was just as tall, dark and handsome as she remembered, his broad shoulders and chest tapering to a firm, flat belly, lean hips and long legs. He wore an exquisitely tailored, black Armani suit, with a fine, crisp white shirt and a striped tie, and a pair of black leather Gucci loafers. Black brows swooped like a pair of raven's wings over his deep-set, heavily lashed, silver-gray eyes. Beneath his aquiline nose, his mouth was full and carnal, the thrust of his jaw arrogant and determined. He was the epitome of a highly successful entrepreneur and self-made multimillionaire. At the sight of him, Lily felt her pulse begin to race and her heart to hammer painfully in her breast.

"Who was that?" he queried tersely.

"Who?"

"That man…the one who just left here!"

"Oh, him…just a customer. He bought a map chest. Why do you ask?"

"I was waiting outside for the shop to be empty, watching you and him through the front windows. You seemed pretty chummy."

"I've never even met him before today, and it's my job to be friendly to customers, Paul. People would hardly want to buy anything from me or come back again if I bit their heads off."

"No, I guess not. Where are Heather, Nicole and Rhonda?"

These were Lily's former employees.

"I—I had to let them go."

"What? All three of them? Why?"

"Because I had to cut expenses somehow, and that

was one of the obvious ways," Lily explained, loath to have her husband know how poorly things were going for her. But of course, he probably already knew, anyway. He had people who researched information like that for him. So there seemed little point in trying to pretend. "I had hoped that by this time next year I would be able to hire at least one or two of them back. But now I don't know if that will be possible or not. As I told you on the telephone earlier this morning, Paul, I can't possibly even attempt to repay your investment in Mélusine's Attic in an immediate lump sum. It would mean selling the shop and everything in it, and even that might not net enough funds to cover the cost. I—I don't understand why you're being so unreasonable about this. Isn't it enough that I don't want anything from you?" She bit her lower lip anxiously.

"Why don't we wait until after lunch to discuss all this, Lily," Paul suggested smoothly. "I'm certain you wouldn't want any clients to walk in during such a personal conversation. So if you're ready to go, my car's right outside."

Once Lily had locked up the store, her husband escorted her to his powerful black Mercedes and tucked her inside, carefully fastening the seat belt around her. Then he got in beside her, turning the key in the ignition and depressing the accelerator. Presently, they were under way, weaving through the traffic around the multitude of beautiful old squares that formed the heart of Savannah. While Paul drove, he conversed easily and pleasantly with Lily, pretending not to notice how awkward and ill at ease she was as he commented on the weather, inquired about her health and her town house, and asked why Mélusine's Attic was apparently struggling now, when it had previously been doing so well.

Much to her surprise, when she told him, his mouth tightened.

"I'm sorry. I hadn't realized that was the cause," he said quietly. "I'm afraid that to some extent I've been preoccupied with business affairs. The hotel industry has had it tough this season, and business is only just now really beginning to pick up again. Ah, here we are."

"But...but this is our...*your*...house, Paul!" Lily exclaimed, startled, as she glanced out the window toward the big, beautiful, old Victorian mansion set back from the street, amid equally old, towering trees that provided welcome shade, a profusion of flower beds bursting with blooms, and a sweeping green lawn. "I thought...I thought you were taking me to lunch!"

"I am. Dinah has it all prepared and waiting for us outside on the back veranda." Dinah was their housekeeper—or, rather, Paul's housekeeper, since Lily no longer lived here anymore. "I thought that perhaps it was best if you and I dined privately, as you know how news travels here in Savannah, and since *I* know how you abhor gossip, I did not believe you would care to find yourself mentioned in that weaselly little bastard Freddie Fontaine's column.''

''No...no, I wouldn't. I wouldn't like that at all. Thank you. I hadn't considered how people would talk if we were to be seen together again, and of course, I quite understand how you would want to avoid giving the wrong impression—especially if there's...if there's someone else in your life now.''

''There isn't,'' Paul declared bluntly. ''There never was, Lily. Zelda Rutherford and I were childhood playmates. She's been my friend, yes, for years. But that's *all* she is or ever has been to me! I tried to tell you that at the time, but you wouldn't listen. But by God, you are going to listen to me now, or I am going to close down Mélusine's Attic and ensure that no interior design firm, antiques shop, art gallery, or even just a damned sidewalk cartoon artist within a radius of several hundred miles around Savannah will hire you!''

Before Lily, stricken, could sufficiently gather her wits to respond to this threat, Paul had got out of the car, come around to her side, opened the door, unfastened her seat belt and begun marching her up the sidewalk to the front door of the old Victorian mansion. Moments later, the door itself was flung open wide, and Dinah stepped outside onto the veranda, her round, black face beaming.

''Welcome, Mrs. Clothier! It sure is good to have you home again! Come in, come in. I've got lunch all ready and waiting for you...a nice, big, juicy, homegrown tomato stuffed with tuna salad—your favorite! Oh, it sure is good to see you, Mrs. Clothier! The place just ain't been the same without you, and how pretty you look in that green suit. Is that new?''

Clearly delighted by the turn of events, the housekeeper chattered on gaily, so that Lily didn't have to do much more than smile and nod in response as Dinah led her toward the back veranda, Paul following close behind them. Lily was so bewildered by everything that she didn't know what to think, for it was plain to her that the housekeeper thought she had returned home to stay, and despite that he had filed for a divorce and threatened her only moments before, still, Paul was doing nothing to correct Dinah's mistaken impression.

''I'm surprised to see that—that everything looks the same as it did when I—when I went away,'' Lily observed, when she could finally get a word in edgewise.

''Yes, indeed.'' Dinah nodded emphatically. ''Mr. Clothier wouldn't hear of our making any changes. He said it wouldn't do at all for you to come back home and find it looking like some stranger's house. Well, here we are,'' she announced as they reached the veranda. ''Would you like iced tea, Mrs. Clothier, lemonade, or something stronger?''

In truth, Lily would have been glad to have a Bloody Mary, a mint julep or a Southern Comfort with ginger ale, from which she might have at least derived some Dutch courage. But in the end, she decided it was better to try to keep her wits about her.

"Lemonade sounds lovely, Dinah. Thank you."

After the housekeeper had poured two tall glasses of lemonade and made certain that nothing else was wanted, she left Lily and Paul alone together on the veranda.

"Eat up, Lily," he ordered, not unkindly, "for despite the fact that I can see you are fairly bursting with confusion and curiosity, I know how any unpleasantness upsets you at the table, so that you can hardly swallow. So please, let us have an enjoyable lunch, and then we'll talk....hmm?"

"Yes, of course."

Of course, she reiterated dully in her mind, believing that now she understood. Paul was very fond of Dinah. He probably saw little point in hurting the housekeeper by telling her the truth: that he was divorcing Lily and that this would therefore be the very last time that she would, as his wife, ever set foot in this house that she had shared with him and tried so hard to make a home for them. How foolish she was, Lily realized, to have imagined anything else, to have even for one moment dared to hope that Paul had something on his mind other than getting rid of her at last.

With difficulty, she herself not wanting to hurt Dinah's feelings, either, Lily forced down the tuna salad. Then she salted and peppered the fresh tomato, deliberately slicing and eating it, as well as the bed of lettuce that surrounded it and for which the house-keeper, carefully remembering all of Lily's prefer-ences, had set a small pitcher of Roquefort dressing off to one side. It took every last ounce of resolution Lily possessed to choke down the so thoughtfully pre-pared lunch, but in the end, she managed to consume every single bite.

"Did you enjoy your lunch?" Paul queried. "It was good to see you eat it. You've lost weight, Lily—and you didn't have any to lose."

"I've—I've been working very hard at Mélusine's Attic, trying to keep it afloat. Paul, please don't keep me on tenterhooks this way. I thought the money for my shop was a—a gift. You never once referred to it as an investment, and I honestly don't recall ever even seeing that business agreement you sent me a copy of, much less signing it! But still, I promise that no matter how long it takes, I'll pay you back as best I can, every single penny. Only, please don't insist on having the funds all in an immediate lump sum. I'd have to sell the store, and it's all I have left. I—I know you can be a hard man, but I never believed you were a cruel one, and I'm willing to listen to whatever it is you have to say to me, if that's what it takes to save Mélusine's Attic."

"Are you now? So…is that it?" Leaning back in the white wicker chair he occupied, Paul reached into his suit jacket, withdrawing a gold case, from which he extracted a cigarette. With a matching lighter, he lit up, inhaling deeply, then blowing a cloud of smoke

into the still summer air. "Is that everything you have
to tell me?"

Lily nodded mutely, her heart pounding with apprehension.

"Good—because my patience is at an end! Now,
I know you don't believe me, Lily, but I'll say it
again, anyway! There was absolutely never anything
whatsoever except for friendship between Zelda and
me. I don't know where that miserable little worm
Freddie Fontaine ever got the idea otherwise. But if
I did, he and his source would both be extremely
sorry, let me tell you! Frankly, Freddie's lucky I
didn't break his scrawny neck for printing that piece
of malicious libel in his gossip column! In fact, I still
might! The bastard ruined our marriage—and if I
can't set that to rights, well, then the very least I in-
tend to do is to revenge myself on Freddie Fontaine!"

"Set—set our marriage to rights...? I'm afraid I—I
don't understand—"

"Damn it, Lily! I love you, and I want you back.
Is that clear enough for you?"

She was so stunned that, for a moment, she just sat
there, speechless and utterly bemused, thinking that
she had been under such a terrible strain lately that
she must finally have snapped.

"But, then...why did you file for a divorce and
send me that proposed settlement?"

"Because it was the only way I could think of to
get you to talk to me. Lily, you wouldn't listen to me.
You walked out on me. You refused to see me, to

return my telephone calls, to answer my letters and e-mails. So for months, I tried to be patient and not press you. Instead, I waited and hoped you would finally come to your senses and come home to me. But you didn't—and now I'm fed up, Lily! I'm tired of being blamed for something I never even did, tired of sleeping alone and, most of all, tired of not having my wife home with me—where she belongs! I don't want you to sell Mélusine's Attic. I don't want any money from you. The funds I gave you for the shop *were* a gift, not an investment. There was never any business agreement between us. That's why you don't remember it. I drew it up myself and forged your name to it to scare you into talking to me!''

"Oh, my God! But, Paul, your attorney *filed* all those papers with the court! That's fraud, or—or, at the very least, perjury or something!''

Much to her amazement, her husband only grinned at her sheepishly.

"My sweet, darling Lily…I'm very much afraid I have to confess that my lawyer didn't file anything. I drafted the letter you purportedly received from him, drew up the divorce petition myself, too, and got one of my hotel desk clerks to pose as a process server.''

"Good Lord, Paul!'' Lily gasped, quite shocked to hear all this. "What if—what if instead of contacting you, I'd got in touch with an attorney of my own?''

"I'd have insisted I knew absolutely nothing about any of it, that it was obviously someone playing a very mean-spirited prank. Besides, I was pretty sure you'd call me. You'd already told me that you couldn't afford to hire a lawyer.''

''I just can't believe you went to such lengths as this to force me to talk to you!''

''I was desperate. So...are you going to stop all this foolishness and come on home to me now, Lily?''

''I—I don't know. This is all so sudden and bewildering. It's taken me completely by surprise, and I need some time to think about it.''

''You still don't believe me, do you? You still think I cheated on you!''

''I don't know,'' Lily reiterated. ''I don't know what to think, I told you—except that you've certainly gone to a great deal of trouble to have this discussion with me.''

''Doesn't that count for anything?''

''Yes, I suppose so. But, Paul, surely you didn't believe that we'd just have lunch together and a chat, and that, after that, everything would be hunky-dory between us. I mean...well, we've been separated... estranged for over a year now, during which time we've hardly even spoken to each other, much less spent any time together. Why, this is the first time I've actually even seen you in months!''

''What're you saying to me, Lily?'' From beneath his thick, black lashes, his silver-gray eyes shuttered to conceal his thoughts, her husband gazed at her intently across the glass-topped, white wicker table, his earlier charming smile gone, his dark visage inscrutable. ''You're a kind, decent, honest woman. No one knows that better than I. It's one of the reasons why I love you. So tell me the truth. Are you still in love with me?''

"Oh, God, Paul...what—what kind of a question is that?''

"One I want to hear answered.''

Lily didn't know what to say to that. She wasn't normally a liar, so she wasn't very good at telling falsehoods, and her husband knew her very well. He wouldn't be fooled.

"Yes," she whispered finally, "I'm still in love with you, Paul. But so much has happened, so much time has passed, that I—I don't know if that's enough for us anymore. I still don't know what to believe about you and Zelda. Maybe you're telling the truth. You've certainly stuck to your story, professing your innocence.''

"That's because I *am* innocent, Lily—and you ought to have trusted me!''

"Maybe I should have...maybe I *would* have if I'd...if I'd been somebody like Zelda, if I'd come from an old Southern family and grown up the way she did, with money and a place in high society. But I didn't. I came from a working-class, broken home, and I've had to struggle and scratch and scrape for everything I've ever got in this life. So it was...very hard for me to believe you loved me, that you actually wanted me for your wife." Lily laughed softly, shortly, sadly. "I used to feel just like Cinderella, being swept away by Prince Charming. Sometimes, I even actually used to pinch myself, just to be sure I wasn't dreaming, hadn't somehow been magically transported into a fairy tale. I know that sounds silly and naive, but still, that's the way I felt."

She paused for a long moment, remembering. Then she continued.

"So...when I read that article in Freddie Fontaine's gossip column, I didn't doubt that it was true, that I had been nothing more to you than a—a momentary madness, and that you had come to your senses at last and realized your mistake. I didn't fit into your world."

"You fit into it just fine, Lily," Paul insisted earnestly. "Your only trouble was that you were always insecure, doubting everything about yourself...your looks, your intelligence, your talent, your own worth as a human being. I always thought it had something to do with your coming from a broken home. A divorce—especially the kind of bitter divorce that your own parents went through—invariably does one of two things to kids. It either toughens them up, imbuing them with a considerable amount of determination, grit and self-confidence, or else it leaves them wounded and vulnerable, always secretly wondering somewhere deep inside themselves if they're unlovable. But you're not unlovable, sweetheart. To the contrary. You're a very highly lovable, desirable woman, and I was proud to call you mine."

Flicking open his gold case, he withdrew another cigarette and lit up.

"However, you're right. It *has* been over a year, and I see now that it was…hopelessly wishful thinking on my own part to think that lunch and clearing the air between us would be enough. I had thought that if we talked, we could straighten everything out and go on from there. Now I belatedly realize I must, at least in some respects, seem like a total stranger to you again. We did, after all, have a whirlwind courtship and had been married for barely a year when you left me. So, if you are agreeable, Lily, I would propose that you go on living in your town house for at least a little while longer, if that is your desire, but that you allow me to call on you, to take you out, to court you, if you will. However old-fashioned that word might be in this day and age, it's still a good one. Perhaps had you known me longer and better when that stupid little cockroach Freddie published his spiteful libel about Zelda and me, you would not have doubted me, I don't know. But I would like to think so. So what do you say, darling? Would you be willing now to try again, to give me and our marriage a second chance?"

Lily's heart throbbed painfully, and the confusion she had felt ever since Paul had picked her up earlier had only increased alarmingly. Was it possible that her husband *was* telling the truth? Was it possible, as he had stated, that because she had been so insecure during their marriage, so unsure of herself and why he had loved and wanted her, she had doubted him when she ought to have trusted him?

Certainly, she despised Freddie Fontaine, had never liked him from the start. So why had she believed his gossip column over Paul's own word? Because deep down inside, all her anxieties about herself and her marriage had caused her to think that where there was smoke, there must be fire? That Freddie would not have printed such an article unless he himself had believed it to be true? But what if he had, in fact, been wrong? Surely her husband wouldn't have gone to such lengths as he had today to speak with her if he really didn't care about her! And if she truly *had* treated him unjustly and left him for no good reason, wasn't he entitled to the second chance that he had asked for?

Yes, Lily thought, he was.

"Yes...yes, Paul, I *would* be willing to try again. If I *have* judged you unfairly, left you when you didn't deserve that, then I want very much to make that up to you, to set our marriage to rights, if that's what you really want."

"It is. Thank you, Lily." Reaching forward, Paul laid his hand over hers and tightened it briefly, lovingly. "You won't be sorry, I promise you. May I see you tomorrow evening, then? Would you have supper with me here at the house...out in the gazebo? I know how you used to love that."

"Yes...yes, I did." Lily fell silent for a moment, remembering. Then she nodded. "Yes, I'll have supper with you tomorrow evening, Paul. I'll—I'll look forward to it."

"I hope so. I know I will."

After that, the hour that she allotted herself for lunch each day ended, Lily requested that her husband drive her back to Mélusine's Attic, which he did, walking her to the front door.

"I've got a business meeting in just a few minutes, Lily," he told her, glancing at his gold Cartier wristwatch as she unlocked the door. "But if it's all right with you, I'll call you at home later on tonight."

"That would be fine. Thank you for lunch, Paul. It's been...very good seeing you again."

"It's been very good to see you, too, Lily. You'll never know how many times I've thought of you since you walked out on me, how much I've missed you and longed for you."

Lifting one of her hands to his mouth, he kissed its palm gently, and as he did so, a thousand memories flooded into Lily's mind and being, setting her atremble. Since leaving her husband, she had not even looked at another man, had thought she was dead inside. But Paul still possessed the power, it seemed, to cause her breath to catch in her throat, her heart to beat fast, and her knees to weaken.

Still dazed and filled with newly wakened desire, Lily watched her husband drive away. Then, feeling as though she were floating on a cloud, she went into Mélusine's Attic. Not even on its grand-opening day had she felt so much emotion as she gazed around her shop. She was not going to lose it, after all. She was not going to be compelled to give up her lifelong dream, nor wind up broke and destitute. Most wonderful of all was the fact that Paul still loved and wanted her. She could not believe it. What a difference a few hours had made!

This morning, when she had telephoned her husband, Lily had not known what to expect. Certainly, it had never once occurred to her that he wished her to return to him. Even now, when she knew it to be true, it still seemed like a dream or a fairy tale to her, just as Paul's original courtship of her and their marriage had seemed.

But as that sobering thought crossed her mind, Lily felt some of her euphoria fade, and her doubts and insecurity began once more to plague her. No, she simply had to stop letting those get the best of her! she told herself firmly. If Paul were telling the truth, then she had mistrusted him, hurt him, walked out on him, and nearly ruined their marriage for naught... over nothing more than a vicious lie published by Freddie Fontaine! Oh, how she abhorred that prissy little weasel!

Now, more than ever, Lily wished desperately that she didn't have to attend his "party to die for" on Saturday night.

In the Still of the Night

Oft in the stilly night,
Ere Slumber's chain has bound me,
Fond Memory brings the light
Of other days around me;
The smiles, the tears,
Of boyhood's years,
The words of love then spoken;
The eyes that shone
Now dimmed and gone,
The cheerful hearts now broken.

National Airs [1815]. *Oft in the Stilly Night*
—Thomas Moore

Chapter 3

For the next three days, as good as his word, Paul
called Lily and arranged for her to have supper with
him at their house, explaining on Friday night that
while he would also like to see her on Saturday, as
well, he unfortunately had a prior engagement.

"That's all right. So do I," she replied glumly as
she sipped her drink—a tall, cool planter's punch—
in the gazebo in which they had dined together every
night this week.

She had always loved dining outside in the eve-
nings, in the old Victorian gazebo, with the trees rus-

tling in the cool night breeze, the fireflies glowing
amid the blooming flowers of the garden, the sweet,
heady, fragrant perfume of the blossoms—the magnolias, gardenias, camellias, and all the rest—filling
the silence broken only by the chirruping of the lo-
custs and the croaking of frogs in the lily pond.

"I...see." Her husband's dark, hawkish visage was
inscrutable in the darkness illuminated only by the
moonlight and the patio torches that burned all
around.

"No, I know what you're thinking, Paul, but you're
wrong. I don't have a date. There's been no one else
in my life since I left you. I've been invited to a party,
that's all. I wouldn't even go, except that it's at Freddie Fontaine's house! God only knows why he asked
me to come, but, well, he did, and I didn't believe it
would be wise to refuse."

To her surprise, her husband laughed softly, shortly
and harshly.

"That bastard! It's Freddie's party that *I* was planning on attending myself tomorrow night, too! That's
why I couldn't see you. I'll admit I was puzzled myself by his invitation. He and I haven't exactly been
on speaking terms since he printed that malicious libel
about Zelda and me. But I was going to go, anyway,
because quite frankly, I was curious about the slimy
little toad's motive for inviting me. He never does
anything without a reason, and I wondered what he
wanted from me. But now I know. He simply thought
it would provide him and his guests with a great deal
of amusement to bring you and me together totally

unexpectedly! Well, thank God, he won't get the fireworks display that he was undoubtedly looking forward to! Forewarned is forearmed, after all.''

"Well, if that's the case, then maybe I shouldn't even go. Maybe I should just stay home, the way I wanted to.''

"Lily, you must know that if you did that, Freddie would dig up something dreadful to publish about you in that spiteful gossip column of his,'' Paul pointed out. "And I feel quite sure that you don't want it bandied all over Savannah that Mélusine's Attic is having financial troubles, for instance.''

"No, of course not. Why do think I was forcing myself to attend in the first place?''

"Would you like me to escort you?'' Pushing away his dinner plate, her husband leaned back in the white, wrought-iron garden chair he occupied in the gazebo and extracted a cigarette from his gold case. Lighting up, he blew a cloud of smoke into the still night air.

"Oh, Paul…I—I don't know. I mean…I appreciate the offer. I really do. And I know that in some respects, it would be a lot easier for me if I showed up on your arm. But on the other hand, there would be a great deal of talk and speculation, people asking prying questions—especially Freddie!—wondering if you and I are getting back together again.''

"Well, people are going to find out, anyway, sooner or later, Lily.''

"Yes, but…it's just that I'd rather it were later,'' she confessed. "It was…very hard for me before… being held up to public scrutiny all the time, feeling that I didn't measure up, that all your friends thought you'd made a mistake in marrying me and would quickly tire of me.''

"That wasn't ever in anybody's mind but your own, sweetheart!" Paul insisted stoutly.

"No." Lily shook her head. "I overheard people saying things like that all the time. I was always an outsider, you see. That's part of what fueled all my insecurities during our marriage. And after I left you, those people whom I had thought actually liked me and *were* my friends…well, they didn't call or come around anymore, either." She shrugged, lightly, as though it hadn't mattered, but her husband was not deceived.

"Darling, I know how all this must have hurt you. Why didn't you tell me about any of this at the time it was happening, and afterward, when everybody stopped patronizing Mélusine's Attic and you got into such difficulties?''

"I—I didn't want to complain, to cut you off from your friends. And as for afterward, well, I understood, didn't I? People felt as though they had to choose up sides. They always do whenever a marriage fails. So they chose you. That was only natural, wasn't it? After all, they were *your* friends originally, not mine. So of course, they were loyal to you."

"I suppose so, but still, that doesn't mean it doesn't make me damned mad!" In a sharp breath, Paul exhaled a final stream of smoke, then abruptly crushed his cigarette out in the ashtray on the white, wrought-iron garden table at which they were seated. "I can promise you this, Lily, nothing like that is going to happen this *time* around! I'll see to that! So why don't you let me take you to Freddie's party tomorrow night? We'll beard the gossiping little weasel together in his hole and make him sorry for everything he ever did to us!''

"No." Reluctantly, Lily shook her head again. "Aside from all the rumors that would ensue, I'd be using you as a crutch because of my own doubts and fears, and I don't want to do that anymore. Because if we're to have any kind of a second chance at all together, Paul, I need to learn how to stand on my own two feet, to gain the self-confidence necessary for me to move in your circles. I've—I've got to get over feeling as though I'm an interloper…a working-class girl who had to struggle just to work her way up to a sales position in a local art gallery!''

"All right, Lily. If that's how you feel, then of course, I will respect your wishes. But I'll tell you what: if that miserable little worm Freddie Fontaine says or does even one single thing to hurt you tomorrow night, I'm going to kill him!''

A Party to Die For

The reason Milton wrote in fetters when he wrote of Angels and God, and at liberty when of Devils and Hell, is because he was a true poet and of the Devil's party without knowing it.

The Marriage of Heaven and Hell [1790-1793], note to *The Voice of the Devil*
—William Blake

Chapter 4

On Saturday night, Lily dressed carefully in the Gypsy costume she was supposed to wear to Freddie Fontaine's "party to die for." She had fashioned it from some of her old clothes, which she had intended to give to charity, but which now served to transform her into what popular imagination conceived of as a Gypsy wench, complete with gold hoop earrings in her ears and plenty of gold bangles on her wrists.

Although she usually wore her shoulder-length hair in a sophisticated French braid, tonight she left it loose, curling and teasing it a little, so that it looked like a wild lion's mane around her oval face. She also applied much heavier makeup than usual, outlining her emerald-green eyes all the way around with black kohl and smudging a bronze shadow across their lids, so that they seemed to slant like a cat's. Blush to emphasize her high cheekbones and lipstick to color her full, generous mouth completed the job. When she glanced at her reflection in the mirror above the pedestal sink in her bathroom, she scarcely even recognized herself.

Because she knew there would be cocktails served at Freddie's party, Lily decided to take a taxi over instead of driving herself. Also, she was so nervous that she feared she might have an accident. So she rang for a cab, and when it arrived to pick her up, she gathered up her fringed silk shawl, wrapping it around her, and grabbed her clutch purse and also the bottle of fine wine she was bringing as her host's gift. Then she got into the taxi and told the driver where to take her.

"It's a costume party," Lily explained, when she observed him eyeing her in his rearview mirror.

"I thought it must be something like that." He nodded with satisfaction. "You sure look pretty."

"Thank you."

She was almost relieved when the cab ride had ended and she had reached her destination. Coming from a broken home, with a father who had permanently absented himself following his divorce from her mother, Lily had ever since she was a child had difficulty conversing with men who were strangers to her.

She paid the driver, then got out of the taxi, pausing for a moment to take a deep breath before walking up the sidewalk to Freddie's front porch. There, Lily rang the bell.

"Good evening, Mrs. Clothier," Babbitt, the butler, greeted her politely as he opened the front door. "How nice to see you."

"Good evening, Babbitt. It's nice to see you, too. How are you?"

"Oh, getting on in years, Mrs. Clothier, I'm afraid. Getting on. Won't you please come this way? Mr. Fontaine and his guests are in the living room."

After handing the bottle of wine to the butler, Lily followed him through the expansive foyer to the tastefully and elegantly appointed living room. There, she saw that she must be the last to arrive, as the room was filled with people.

"Mrs. Clothier is here, sir," Babbitt announced to Freddie, who, turning and spying her, strode forward, his arms outstretched in greeting.

"Lily, dear, how nice of you to come! And how wonderful you look!" Grabbing hold of her, her host kissed her lightly on both cheeks. "Come in, come in. I think you know everyone else here, don't you?"

"Yes, I believe so," she said, trying to still the fluttering of the butterflies in her stomach as Freddie led her into the living room, her hand tucked under his arm, so that she could not escape.

"Everyone, Lily's here, so we're all assembled

now," he declared. "You all remember Lily, don't you? Of course, you do. Good heavens, she's still your wife, I think, isn't she, Paul?"

"Yes, she is. You don't really think I'd let such a gorgeous woman get away from me, do you?" Paul replied smoothly, stepping forward and, taking Lily's hand in his, kissing it gallantly. "You look absolutely stunning, darling."

"Thank you. You don't look too bad yourself," she managed to say calmly.

Actually, her husband looked so very handsome that he took her breath away. He had apparently been commanded to come dressed as a gangster, because he wore a dark blue pin-striped zoot suit with padded shoulders and a bright red carnation in the buttonhole of one of the wide lapels. He had a white fedora cocked over one eye, and black patent leather shoes with white spats on his feet. To Lily, Paul had always had a dangerous edge, and tonight, the way he was garbed, it seemed very pronounced, both frightening and inexplicably exciting her. She almost had to remind herself that not only was he a perfectly respectable hotel magnate and not a mobster, but also her husband.

Everybody in the living room, who appeared to have been holding their collective breath, began to talk again, either relieved or—like Freddie—disappointed that there was apparently not to be any scene between the Clothiers.

"Hello, Lily." Zelda Rutherford now moved forward to greet her. Zelda was gowned as a Southern belle, complete with corset and crinolines. "How are you, dear?"

"I'm fine, and you?"

Seeing that this meeting, too, was going to pass without incident, Freddie, suddenly clapping his hands, broke in to get everyone's attention, prissily urging them to partake of drinks and the hors d'oeuvres that Babbitt and the caterers served on sterling-silver trays, first the cocktails and then the canapés and other appetizers. For those who preferred it, there was also iced vodka and champagne with which to wash down the caviar that was offered—one dish of which, seated in a bowl of crushed ice, was plain, and the other of which had been prepared with hard-boiled eggs and chopped onions.

Since she had been compelled to come here, Lily saw no reason why she should not at least have something to eat and drink. At the very least, it would give her something to do. So she helped herself to a glass of champagne. Then, with the mother-of-pearl caviar spoon, she ladled some of the plain caviar onto a square of dry toast. Paul, she observed, was making the rounds, speaking to their host and the other guests.

"What do you think of my new acquisition?" Freddie was asking him, pointing to an exquisite marble statuette that sat upon the fireplace mantel. "It's the Greek god Hermaphroditus, who merged with the nymph Salmacis to become both male and female."

Possessing a keen interest in art of all kinds, Paul picked up the statuette to examine it more closely.

"It's quite nice…Greek, I presume…late sixth century, I should say, if I had to guess."

"Yes, that's right." Clearly, Freddie was pleased that Paul grasped the worth of the statuette, as the gossip columnist enjoyed being perceived as a connoisseur of all the finer things in life.

As she continued to study the guests assembled in the living room, Lily realized that including Freddie himself, there were thirteen of them gathered for dinner at his huge, old Victorian mansion in Savannah's historic district—a very odd and improper number for a dinner party, she thought, unwittingly shivering at the idea.

But then, everything Freddie did was peculiar and frequently indecorous. Having been born into an extremely wealthy, old Southern family, who had petted and spoiled him ever since his childhood, and having never been compelled to work to earn a living, Freddie had long done as he damned well pleased. Had he not been rich, he would probably have been homeless or even dead years ago. Had he not been eccentric, shrewd and sarcastically witty, people would not have found him outrageously entertaining, despite how much they might dislike him. Had he not written such a malicious gossip column, no one would have feared him.

But Freddie Fontaine had money, was outlandish, clever and waggish, and with his spiteful pen, he could make or break those who moved in the circles of high society.

An invitation to his house might be prized, bemoaned, distrusted or feared. But it was never refused.

Still, Lily wished she had done just that—turned Freddie's invitation down flat. She would never in a million years know why he had invited her to his party to begin with—except that Paul was probably right: Freddie had wanted to liven up the affair by bringing the two of them unexpectedly together, so that he could watch their reaction.

Too bad they had disappointed him!

Under other circumstances, Lily would have laughed at the thought of how crushed Freddie must be to have had at least one of his venomous schemes go awry. But tonight, she was much too unsettled to find any humor at all in the situation. Not only was she anxious about being here to begin with, having her relationship with Paul placed under a magnifying glass again, but, also, the guests were a motley collection not designed to put her at her ease.

In addition to her, Paul and Zelda, among those present were the famous middleweight boxer Shane Valentine, dressed as though he were preparing to step into the ring, and with him, Samantha Starr, the cute pop singer, garbed in a fifties' sweater and poodle skirt, and blowing pink bubbles with her chewing gum. Both of them had evidently come up from Atlanta to attend Freddie's party. The remainder of the guests were local movers and shakers, all with money and their own brands of notoriety.

As always, Lily felt out of her league with such people.

"How are you holding up, sweetheart?" Paul asked softly in her ear, as she munched on yet another piece of dry toast heaped high with caviar.

"I'm properly intimidated, bedazzled and probably putting on at least ten pounds—or, at least, I will if I keep on standing here, chowing down this caviar. It's absolutely fabulous! For it, I could almost be glad I came."

"Well, since you could stand to gain a few pounds, I can't be sorry about that."

There was no time for the two of them to talk further, for just then, the butler, Babbitt, announced that dinner was served, and Freddie ushered them all into the dining room across the expansive foyer.

Like the living room, the dining room was tastefully and elegantly appointed, filled with fine old furnishings and artwork. The dining table was of highly polished Honduras mahogany that gleamed beautifully beneath the soft light of the crystal chandeliers hanging from the ornate ceiling medallions, and of the dancing flames of the heavy, sterling-silver candelabra that sat at either end of the table itself. This last was elaborately set with china, crystal and silver, with place cards for each guest, their names written in calligraphy. On one wall stood a tall, glass-fronted china cabinet filled not only with china, but also with lovely, hand-painted bowls and lemonade sets. Against another wall was a matching buffet, arrayed with dishes laden with foods of all kinds to tempt the palate. Babbitt and the caterers stood ready to serve the guests.

Lily found her place at the table, secretly relieved to discover that Freddie had actually seated her next to Paul. Smiling at her encouragingly, her husband pulled out her chair for her, and when all the guests had taken their seats, the dinner commenced.

Gradually, as the evening wore on and Lily consumed more champagne, she started to grow more relaxed. Paul, to her left, conversed with her easily, giving those present cause to think neither that he was estranged from her, nor that he was secretly courting her, with the aim of setting their marriage to rights. She understood that his decorum stemmed from her own desire not to be made an object of gossip and speculation, and she was grateful for his consideration.

Nor did she observe anything in his behavior to make her suspect that he and Zelda were or ever had been anything but good friends. In fact, Zelda, seated across from them, was doing her best to be as pleasant and charming to Lily as she could. In light of that, for the very first time, Lily felt ashamed of herself. If Paul had told her the truth, then she had wronged Zelda, too, as much as she had him.

To Lily's right sat the boxer, Shane Valentine, shoveling in his food as though there were no tomorrow and, in between, loudly relating anecdotes and cracking jokes, making all the guests laugh. Despite the fact that Freddie tittered right along with everyone else, he was still annoyed, Lily could tell, because he disliked not being the center of attention, especially at his own party. So she wondered why he had invited the boxer, why, in fact, he had invited any of them, had decided to throw this party at all.

Finally, the supper ended, and as the plates were cleared away, and the brandy, amaretto, and coffee served, Babbitt handed each guest a large brown manila envelope, while Freddie rang the crystal dinner bell to get his guests' attention.

"Ladies and gentlemen," the gossip columnist began, once they had all quieted, "first of all, I want to thank you for coming this evening and tell you how delighted I am that you all could be here. Now, on to tonight's entertainment! You will notice that Babbitt has given each of you an envelope. This is your portfolio or 'character pack.' Inside, you will find your instructions for the Murder Mystery game we are going to play this evening. Do *not* show your portfolio to anyone else! Otherwise, it will spoil the game, and I will be *very* upset!"

Here, Freddie paused dramatically, as though to allow the full import of this to sink in, and Lily knew he was subtly threatening them all. She marveled that Shane Valentine didn't jump out of his chair and punch the gossip columnist in the nose.

"As you have surmised from the costumes you were requested to wear tonight, you have each been assigned to play a role in the Murder Mystery," Freddie continued. "And as you can see from my own costume—" he was dressed as a Southern colonel "—I, too, will be assuming a role, and I hope we will all do our best to play our parts *wonderfully*. Now, because this is a Murder Mystery game, one among our ranks will, of course, be the murderer, and another one of us will be the victim. The rest will be suspects, witnesses, detectives, and so on. During the game, you are each to follow the instructions you have received in your character pack. So let us now take approximately twenty or thirty minutes and each read about the parts we are to play, and then we will introduce ourselves, in character, to one another and begin the game.''

Obediently opening the envelope she had been given, Lily perused its contents, discovering that she was to be a Gypsy fortune-teller. She was not, however, she was very relieved to find out, either the murderer or the victim. Or at least, she didn't think she was. In truth, she wasn't quite sure. She had never played a Murder Mystery game before, so she wasn't certain how they worked. Maybe each one operated differently, depending on the host.

In the main, however, her part appeared to consist of making dire predictions about their futures to half the other players, along with providing the second half various reasons why each of the first half had secrets to hide and wished the victim dead.

But still, the more she read, the more uncomfortable and suspicious Lily grew. For it seemed that each of the secrets she had been assigned to reveal about the other players might, in fact, be real dirt that Freddie had dug up on them.

No, surely not, she thought uneasily. Surely even Freddie wouldn't go that far, wouldn't dare to accuse people to their face of things he frequently, in his spiteful gossip column, exposed about them merely through hints and innuendo, however destructive even that might prove. No, she tried to reassure herself again. Even Freddie knew there were limits—if for no other reason than that he would be aware of what had occurred when other notorious journalists and authors had decided to write tell-all articles or books about their famous friends. Learning of the journalists' and authors' intent, their friends had all turned on them, just as, en masse, Savannah's high society could bring down Freddie Fontaine if he, too, crossed the line where they all were concerned.

Still, despite how Lily encouraged herself, she could not wholly conquer the disquiet she felt, and so it was with a distinct sense of apprehension and even doom that, at Freddie's calling for the game to ensue, she embarked upon the role she was to play.

As she wandered through Freddie's huge, old Victorian mansion, Lily observed that while the guests had been at dinner, the rooms in which the Murder Mystery were to be played had been transformed, with vignettes and props set up throughout, and all the lights turned down very low. She found her "Gypsy tent" in the living room, where an alcove formed by the tower that ran up the front of Freddie's house had been draped with striped curtains tied back on either side to reveal a small table and two sweetheart chairs within. On the table sat a crystal ball and a single burning candlestick.

Mindful of the part she was to play and not wanting Freddie furious at her, Lily took up her position on one of the sweetheart chairs, to await her first customer. As she understood it, the "murder" would occur about halfway through the game, after which the remainder of time would present the necessary opportunity for the guests to try to figure out who "done it."

After a moment, the curtains, which were draped and tied back in such a way that one had to stoop to enter the turret, were roughly shoved aside.

"Hiya, shweetheart! What'z cookin'?"

"Oh, my God, Paul! You scared me to death!" Lily cried softly, one hand going to her breast, where her heart pounded horribly.

"My name ain't Paul, shweetheart," he chided her, grinning, as he leaned against the wall, his fedora pulled down low over one eye, a cigarette dangling from one corner of his mouth and a plastic tommy gun in hand. "It's Lefty…Lefty Gardenia, and I'ma here ta find out about that piece of scum Colonel Peaches. You're Madame Julep, ain'tcha? I understand he don'na make a move in thisa town without consultin' ya. Is thadda so?"

"Yes…thees ees so." Trying to get into the spirit of the game, Lily struck what she hoped was a mysterious pose. "What ees it zat you wish to know about heem, Meester Gardenia?"

"When's he comin' here again ta see ya?"

"Never, I hope," Lily muttered, out of character.

"Good thing you didn't have aspirations of becoming an actress, Lily," Paul observed, also out of character. "You would have failed miserably!"

He sat down in the sweetheart chair opposite her own and, reaching into his jacket, pulled out a wad of the Monopoly money that they had received in their portfolios.

"Now, looka here, shweetheart, I gotta money—"

"Hey, wise guy, take a hike!" Shane Valentine growled, as he, too, roughly shoved back the curtains. "I've got an appointment with Madame Julep, and you're cuttin' in on my time!"

"Yeah…is that so?" Paul stood. "And who do ya think ya are?"

"Who's askin'?"

"Lefty Gardenia. Who's answerin'?"

"The Brown Thrasher. Now, get lost—before I thrash *you!*"

"I tinka ya done tooka one too many blows ta the head already, punch drunk! I gotta thisa here tommy gun…see?" Paul poked his plastic weapon in the boxer's nose. "Now, scram! Before I shoota ya. I don'na take kindly ta threats."

The "Brown Thrasher" quickly departed, and after taking the wad of Monopoly money her husband handed her, Lily gave him the information he required about "Colonel Peaches," which was Freddie's role. Once Paul had vanished, Zelda, alias "Magnolia Blossom," showed up, followed by Samantha Starr, alias "Honey Bee," and then several of the other guests.

Not long after the pop singer had left, all the lights in the entire house suddenly went out, and Lily was alone in the dark tower, with only her solitary candle flickering. She understood that this must be the half-way point in the game, when the "murder" was supposed to occur, and, recalling the instructions in her character pack, she blew out the flame.

After a moment, her eyes adjusted to the dim light in the living room, now illuminated only by the silvery moonlight streaming in through the windows, and she saw a dark shape that cast a shadow in the large gilded mirror above the fireplace move silently across the floor. Briefly, she shivered unwittingly. There was someone else in the living room with her!

Oh, God! she thought, her heart in her throat. Maybe *she* was the "victim," after all!

But, no, the amorphous silhouette wasn't moving toward the turret. Instead, it was creeping toward the library, which adjoined the living room. Then, without warning, a second dark figure, wearing a hat, appeared, and as Lily watched, mesmerized, her pulse racing, the second form sneaked up behind the first, taking something from the fireplace mantel as it did so. Lifting its arm, the second shape struck the first in the back of the head. This was followed by a low groan and then a thud as the first silhouette fell.

Good Lord! Lily was horrified. It all looked so real that she was almost tempted to run out into the living room. But that would have ruined the game—and then Freddie would have been absolutely incensed at her. Besides which, belatedly, she realized that she was probably meant to be a witness to the "murder," so that Savannah's police chief, who had been as-

signed the role of "Detective Peanuts," could inter-
rogate her about the "murder."

Quickly, the second figure replaced the "weapon"
on the fireplace mantel, then disappeared. But before
Lily could determine whether or not she was supposed to leave the tower now to discover the "body,"
yet a third shadowy form appeared in the mirror. It,
too, was wearing a hat.

For an instant, the third shape paused, glancing
around. Then, abruptly, it strode toward the library.
Moments later, all the lights in the house came back
on, and deciding that signaled the end of the "murder," Lily guessed that now must be the time for her
to leave the turret and discover the "corpse."

Rising from the sweetheart chair she had occupied
in the tower, she pushed aside the low-draped curtains
to make her way into the living room, curious to learn
the identity of the "victim." As she approached the
fireplace, where the "body" lay, she observed that it
was Freddie himself, alias "Colonel Peaches."

"Freddie, if I'm not the person who's supposed to
find you, then you'd better tell me now, so that I can
return to my tent and not ruin the game," Lily whispered as she approached. "Freddie…? Damn it, Freddie! I don't think you're funny! If you don't answer
me right now, I'm going to scream, and then if that's
not what I'm supposed to do, it'll be all *your* fault if
your Murder Mystery game is ruined! Freddie…?"

Growing angry that he should try to frighten her in
this way by pretending to really be dead, she bent
over him, intending to give him a sharp shake.

"Oh, my God!" she breathed, stricken, her knees giving way without warning beneath her as she saw that the back of Freddie's head was covered with matted blood.

Somebody had smashed his skull clean in.

Lily began to scream.

Going Home

May the gods grant you all things which your heart desires, and may they give you a husband and a home and gracious concord, for there is nothing greater and better than this—when a husband and wife keep a household in oneness of mind, a great woe to their enemies and joy to their friends and win high renown.

The Odyssey
—Homer

Chapter 5

Savannah, Georgia
The Present—Sunday

Hearing Lily's screams of terror, Paul had been the first one on the grisly scene. Following hard on his heels had come Savannah's police chief, Hamilton Kiley, alias "Detective Peanuts," who, discovering Freddie Fontaine had actually been murdered for real, had immediately sealed off the living room and notified the Homicide Division.

No one had been permitted to leave the gossip columnist's Victorian mansion. Instead, they had all been herded by the police into the dining room, where they now sat anxiously, facing a police interrogation.

Even Savannah's police chief himself was being questioned, and Lily thought how embarrassing and humiliating it must be for him to have had a brutal murder committed virtually beneath his very nose.

Across the foyer, in the living room, where the police were at work, she could hear the homicide detectives and Crime Scene Unit laughing and cracking jokes about "Detective Peanuts," and she knew it would be quite a long time before Chief Kiley ever lived down this terrible night. It disturbed her that the police were making fun of their superior, with Freddie Fontaine's body still lying dead on the living room floor. She thought their gallows humor sounded terribly cold and callous...disrespectful of the victim. But then, she supposed that they were exposed to so many horrific sights on a daily basis that if they didn't learn some kind of coping mechanism, they would soon go crazy.

"Ladies and gentlemen, could I have your attention, please?" As Chief Kiley entered the dining room and spoke to the guests assembled there, they all fell silent one by one. "Thank you. These are Detectives Johnson and Adams. They're with the Homicide Division, and they'll be heading up this investigation and asking you some questions about tonight and Freddie's murder. Now, I know this has been a real shock to all of you, so please, just try to stay calm and respond as completely as you can. I've already briefed them about the party and the Murder Mystery game, so what we'd like to do now is find out about the characters you were each assigned to play, what your character was supposed to be doing, and where you were at the time of the murder. Naturally, the first thing we'd like to know is which of you was the killer.''

A round of nervous laughter greeted this announcement, and Chief Kiley, realizing how his statement could be interpreted, rolled his eyes and shook his head.

''That's not what I meant—unless, of course, anyone here would like to confess to having murdered Freddie…?''

''Oh, for heaven's sake, Ham!'' Noreen Trollope—alias Tiger Swallowtail—Savannah's district attorney, whom the police chief had escorted to the party, snapped. ''You surely can't suspect that any of us did it!''

''Well, Noreen, quite frankly, at the moment, I don't see anybody else *to* suspect. Besides Freddie's guests, there was no one else in the house at the time of his murder except for the butler, Babbitt, who's worked for him for over forty years, and the caterers—none of whom, at first glance, would appear to have had any motive for wishing to do Freddie in. Naturally, we'll check them all out. But still, more 'n likely, it was somebody sitting right here in this room who bashed Freddie's brains in. Mrs. Clothier has already told me that, based on what her character pack contained, she thought maybe Freddie had used real secrets about everyone present to put this little game of his together tonight, and you can't tell me that isn't a strong possibility, because—despite the fact that I don't want to speak ill of the dead—that's just the kind of warped slimeball Freddie was and exactly the sort of thing that would have appealed to his malicious sense of humor. Now, which one of you was supposed to kill him during the game?''

"I was," Paul said coolly, lighting up a cigarette and blowing a cloud of smoke into the air. "Colonel Peaches, Freddie's character, was supposed to have ripped off Lefty Gardenia, my own character, in a business deal. I was assigned to find out from Lily—who was Madame Julep, the fortune-teller—when Colonel Peaches came around to see her. He was alleged to be superstitious and never to make a move in this town without consulting her first. After that, I was to go around and try to locate Colonel Peaches, so that I could confront him about not paying me the money he owed me. Then, when he still refused to pay, I was to return to the fortune-telling tent, wait for him to show up, then follow him to the bookshop—that's what the library was supposed to be, hence the name of this particular Murder Mystery game, *The Bookshop Caper*—and there, I was to shoot him with my tommy gun.''

"But…Freddie had his skull cracked open—in the living room!" Noreen cried.

In truth, neither she nor Chief Kiley was the sharpest tack on the bulletin board. Before becoming Savannah's district attorney, Noreen, in fact, had been a divorce lawyer who'd had affairs with virtually the entire male half of the police force, then represented them in their divorces when their wives had found out about their infidelities. The scuttlebutt was that she'd slept her way clean up the ladder to Chief Kiley. Freddie had alternately referred to her as Noreen "Trollop" and "Never Press Charges" Noreen, because she never prosecuted a case she wasn't dead certain she could win. Over the years, her close association with the police force had taken its toll, however. She had ballooned into a real butterball from all the doughnuts and coffee.

"Well, obviously, the game didn't go as planned, did it, Noreen?" Chief Kiley pointed out impatiently.

"No, it didn't," Lily murmured, shaking her head. "Somebody crept into the living room and killed Freddie, and then after Freddie was dead, it must have been Paul who came in, looking for him, and who went into the library."

"How do we know that's what happened?" Noreen queried shrilly. "You're Paul's wife. You're probably just covering up for him!"

"You're not in a courtroom now, dear," Zelda drawled pointedly, "and you're going to need a hell of a lot more than that pitiful observation of yours as evidence if you're planning on prosecuting Paul for Freddie's murder. Why, everybody in this town knows how you drag your feet about filing charges against anybody you aren't absolutely positive you can shoot up with a lethal injection!"

The police interrogation continued, with Detectives Johnson and Adams eventually taking each guest away to talk to him or her individually in the library. But Lily was hardly cognizant of what was happening. She could see that things didn't look promising for her husband—especially since the medical examiner had declared that Freddie had been walloped with the Greek statuette of Hermaphroditus, which he had earlier that evening showed to Paul. The weapon had been bagged and tagged, then dispatched for examination by the forensics lab.

Since Paul had picked it up earlier to inspect it, his fingerprints were bound to be all over it, and Noreen had already remarked that he had doubtless handled it for just that reason—to provide himself with an explanation for his prints being on it. Lily was worried sick that the police were going to arrest her husband at any moment.

But instead, finally, just after midnight, when Freddie's corpse had been zipped into a black bag and loaded into the medical examiner's vehicle to be carried away and autopsied, the police allowed all of the guests to go home, warning them that they should all stay in town, that they would all be wanted for further questioning later on as the case progressed.

"Did you drive yourself here, Lily?" Paul inquired, as he wrapped her long, fringed shawl around her.

"No, I took a taxi."

"Good. Then come on…I'll drive you home."

"All right…yes, thank you. I would really prefer to get out of here now, rather than hanging around, waiting for a cab to come pick me up."

"I thought you might. You look all done in, darling. I know how horribly unpleasant and exhausting all this must have been for you—and while I don't want to make matters worse for you, there's a barrage of reporters out front. Their police scanners will have alerted them about the murder here this evening, even if they don't yet know who was killed—although, by now, I wouldn't even bet on that. So...come on, then,'' he reiterated.

Once they were outside, Paul shielded Lily from the reporters gathered outside the black wrought-iron fence that surrounded Freddie's property, their lights and cameras held at the ready, they themselves shouting questions as they spotted the couple. Lightbulbs flashed. Cameras and microphones were shoved in Paul's and Lily's faces as he shouldered his way through the crowd.

"No comment," he said again, and then again. "No comment."

Determinedly, he assisted Lily into his car, carefully fastening the seat belt around her. Then he went around to the other side of the automobile, opened the driver's door, slid in beside her, and turned the key in the ignition. The engine of the sleek, black Mercedes sprang to life with a roar, the headlights he now switched on adding to the illumination of the street where they were parked and of Freddie's front yard, surrounded by its wrought-iron fence, the shadows cast by its tall, old live oaks and magnolias deepened by the stark contrast with all the lights.

"Shall I take you to your town house, Lily? Or would you rather come home with me?" Paul inquired quietly. "You can sleep in one of the guest bedrooms if you like. I just thought that after what's happened here this evening, maybe you wouldn't want to be alone tonight.''

''No…no, I don't. So…yes, I'll go home with you, Paul. But I…but I hope you know I'm not promising anything by that.''

''I know, sweetheart.'' Her husband pulled slowly forward through the mass of reporters who thronged around the car, pounding on the windows and placing cameras up to the glass until hauled away by the uniformed police officers who had cordoned off the house and were directing traffic through the street.

Eventually, Paul got the automobile away from the scene, driving slowly around the old squares that formed Savannah's heart.

''The police think I did it, you know,'' he observed grimly, after a moment, a muscle pulsing in his set jaw. ''They think I murdered Freddie.''

''I—I know. I was afraid they were going to arrest you.''

''Do you believe I did it, Lily? Do you believe I murdered Freddie?''

''No.''

''But…how can you be so certain?''

''I doubted you once—about Zelda. I won't make that same mistake again.'' Lily's own face was set as resolutely as her husband's. ''I know you were angry at Freddie for printing that piece of libel about you and Zelda, and for ruining our marriage, and I know you made threats to me against him. But we're trying to give our relationship a second chance, so there was no cause for you to kill Freddie—not to mention the fact that every other guest at his party, including me, had equally good reasons for wanting to do away with him.''

She paused. Then she continued.

''Oh, how I wish I had seen who came into the living room right after Freddie did, who whacked him over the head with that statuette! Then you wouldn't have this cloud of suspicion hanging over you!''

''Don't worry about that. I'm sure that sooner or later, the police will ferret out the identity of the real killer,'' Paul asserted firmly. ''All I care about is that *you* believe me, darling! You don't know how much that means to me, especially after what happened before. I want very much to set our marriage to rights, and things seemed to be going well toward that end before tonight. I don't want Freddie's murder to spoil everything between us, everything we have together.''

''Neither do I, Paul,'' Lily said softly. ''Neither do I. Tonight has made me realize just how fleeting life really is…how it can be snuffed out in a matter of seconds. We've already wasted a year, and I'm sorry for that, sorry that I ever believed anything Freddie published about you and Zelda. I know how spiteful he was…how he liked to stir up trouble, and deep down inside, I guess I always knew you and Zelda were just friends, that you had been friends since childhood, but nothing more. I'm sorry I let my own doubts and insecurities get the better of me. I should have trusted you. I *do* trust you. I know that no matter how angry you were at Freddie, you could never have

killed him in cold blood that way. That's not the kind
of man you are. I may not know you as well as I
should, but *that,* I *do* know.''

"Thank you, Lily. Thank you for that.''

The glance Paul threw at her spoke volumes—and
made her heart beat fast. It was the way he had used
to look at her before they had made love. Until now,
Lily had determinedly kept such thoughts and memories at bay. But now they flooded her being, setting
her atremble as she remembered the way in which he
had used to kiss her, caress her, make love to her,
taking her to the heights of ecstasy and back. There
had never been anyone for her but Paul.

They finished the remainder of the drive in silence,
finally pulling up before the huge, old Victorian mansion that they had once shared.

"I always loved this house, you know,'' Lily commented quietly. "It broke my heart to think I'd lost
you to someone else, and leaving the home we had
made together was like the bitter icing on an already
unpalatable cake.''

"The door is always open, sweetheart. You can
come home any time.''

"Yes...I think I'd like that,'' Lily told him slowly,
softly. "I think I'd like that very much indeed.''

Paul's silver-gray eyes met her own emerald-green
ones, the intensity of his smoldering gaze causing her
breath to catch in her throat. She had seen that look
on his dark, hawkish visage before in the past, a look
that said he loved and desired her, wanted her now.
His eyes darkening, he leaned toward her, and for a

moment, Lily froze, her heart pounding wildly, her thoughts chaotic, until her husband drew her to him roughly, his mouth claiming hers with a hunger and an urgency that set her aflame with a love and desire that matched his own, and she ceased to think at all.

In that instant, the past year fell away as though it had never been—while, simultaneously, their months of separation imbued the kiss with a ferocity, passion and yearning that spoke more eloquently than words of their mutual, pent-up loneliness and longing, their deep love for each other, and, too, their uncertainty about their future. For they kissed as though it were for the last time, desperately, although each of them knew without speaking that their kiss was, rather, a new promise, a new beginning for their marriage and their life together.

Paul's lips moved hard and searchingly on Lily's own as he clasped her to him tightly, his fingers entangling the thick, curly cloud of her dark auburn hair and tightening, holding her still for his passionate onslaught upon her senses. And she responded in kind, her tongue meeting and twining with his as he traced the outline of her full, generous mouth, then tasted the sweetness within. Her trembling fingers burrowed through his glossy black hair, pulling him even nearer.

The sexual chemistry between them was as hot and explosive as ever, as though, during their months apart, it had only been sleeping, waiting patiently to be reawakened and reignited, knowing that its time would come again.

Paul groaned deep in his throat, his breath coming harshly as his hands roamed fervently over Lily's slender, curvaceous body. What would have happened next, however, she would never know. For just then, a lightbulb flashed at the car window, startling them both.

"Damn it!" her husband swore, abruptly leaping from the automobile.

But he was too late. The photographer who had apparently followed them from Freddie's house had already sped away on a motorcycle.

"Damned reporters!" Paul growled, as, coming around to Lily's side of the Mercedes, he opened the door for her, then hurried her up the sidewalk and into the house.

Dinah, whom Paul had called earlier on his cell phone to explain what had happened at Freddie's mansion, had waited up for them, and as they entered the foyer, she greeted them and told them that she had coffee, sweet tea, sliced ham, potato salad and fresh tomatoes waiting for them in the kitchen if they were hungry.

To their surprise, both Lily and Paul realized they were, in fact, famished, and the three of them made their way to the kitchen, where Dinah bustled about happily, laying out the light meal she had prepared.

"I declare! I just can't believe someone murdered poor old Mr. Fontaine," she said as she worked. "Well, I *can* believe it, because he really wasn't a very nice man. But you know what I mean. That anybody at his party would actually have killed him has just stunned me! I guess it'll be all over the news tomorrow morning. I wonder who did it? Do the police know yet?''

''No.'' Paul shook his head. ''However, I'm fairly certain *I* am their primary suspect!''

''*You*, Mr. Clothier?'' Dinah laughed, shaking her head. ''Good Lord. Mr. Clothier, you got a bad temper, and you don't like to be crossed, it's true…been that way ever since you was just knee-high to a grasshopper! But…murder somebody…murder Freddie Fontaine? No, that's just not your style. If you'd have wanted to get even with Mr. Fontaine, you were more likely to have pushed him into that big old pond out back in his garden…made him a laughingstock in front of his guests. He wouldn't have liked that at all, no, siree, not one little bit!'' Dinah continued to chuckle.

Paul grinned.

''Well, Dinah, I have to confess that thought actually *did* cross my mind once or twice this evening, and under different circumstances, I might have done it, too…just given old Freddie a shove right into that pond of his. But I didn't want to cause a scene with Lily there. And in the end, my restraint didn't matter, anyway. Because someone else wasn't as polite as I was. He or she picked up one of Freddie's statuettes off the fireplace mantel in the living room and conked him over the head with it.''

''I'm pretty sure it was a he,'' Lily averred as she consumed her meal. ''He was wearing a hat…the way you and Chief Kiley were.''

"Zelda was wearing a hat, too," Paul pointed out, "and Noreen had feathers in her hair."

Noreen Trollope had been compelled to attend the party as a Western saloon girl.

"Yes, but Zelda's was a Southern-belle hat, and that wasn't what I saw, and it sure as heck wasn't those towering plumes Noreen had stuck in her hair. No, this was a man's hat...the kind of Panama hat that Freddie liked to wear, actually, I think."

"Which means that anybody in the house could have grabbed it off his hat rack in the foyer," Paul commented thoughtfully.

"Why...yes...yes, they could have. I hadn't thought of that. So someone like Shane Valentine or even his girlfriend, Samantha Starr, could have done it, even though their costumes didn't have hats." Pushing away her empty plate, Lily sighed heavily. "That sure was good, Dinah. Now, all I need is to get out of this Gypsy ensemble and have a nice, long, hot soak in a bathtub to get rid of all the tension tonight's caused."

"Well, you know where the bathrooms are," her husband told her, "and if you're in need of anything to wear, all your clothes are still in your closet, where you left them."

"You mean you—you kept all my things?" Lily was not only surprised, but also deeply touched.

"Every last one of them, Mrs. Clothier," Dinah put in. "Mr. Clothier wouldn't hear of our getting rid of a single thing. He never lost faith that, one day, all the mess Mr. Fontaine caused with that article of his would get straightened out somehow, and you'd come back home.''

"And here I am. It's good to be back, Dinah.'' Lily stood and, excusing herself, made her way upstairs, to the large master suite she had used to share with Paul.

Here, as elsewhere throughout the house, everything looked just the way she had left it, as though nothing had been touched in her absence, despite the fact that she had been gone a year. Even her silver-backed hairbrush and comb were still where she had laid them on the dresser, and loose strands of her hair were still caught in the natural bristles of the brush.

Marveling, Lily touched the soft strands.

"I used to do that.'' Paul spoke from behind her. "I used to stand there just like that and imagine that you had only just left the bedroom, were in the bathroom or the closet and would return at any moment. Oh, God, Lily, how I've missed you! How I've ached for you!''

Then, somehow, she was in his arms, and his mouth was descending upon hers fiercely. Her lips yielded eagerly, sweetly, to his onslaught, a deep sigh of pleasure, which he swallowed, escaping from them as she opened them to his own. Her tongue darted forth to tease and twine with his as old, familiar passion and longing now swept through her anew. No one else had ever made her feel the way her husband did, as though all her bones were dissolving inside her, leaving her weak and supple against him, her knees trembling so that it seemed as though they would give way beneath her at any moment. In some dim corner of her mind, she was vaguely surprised to find herself still standing, rather than melting down into a quicksilver pool at his feet.

Paul's hands tunneled through her loose mane of curly hair, tangling and tightening, while Lily's own fingers crept up his broad chest to wrap around his neck, drawing him even nearer. He seemed to kiss her forever, his mouth tasting, taking, before, with a low groan, he swept her up into his powerful arms and carried her to the massive canopy bed they used to share. There, he laid her down gently, his lips and hands moving on her ardently.

Sitting down beside her, he slipped off her sandals, first one and then the other, kissing and sucking her bare toes and arches as he did so. Then, slowly, his lips traveled up to her ankles, slid up her calves to her thighs, where he pushed her Gypsy skirts up as he progressed. He tugged her lacy, French-cut panties down, tossing them aside. One hand found the soft, damp, downy swell of her, and he began to stroke her there, teasing and probing the tender, burgeoning folds of her that trembled and opened to him like a tightly furled bud unfolding beneath the warmth of the sun or the sprinkling of rain. His mouth on hers once more, he slipped one finger deeply inside her, then two, only to withdraw them as lingeringly as he had inserted them.

Arching her hips imploringly against his palm, Lily moaned low in her throat, wanting to feel him against her, inside her. She pulled off his suit jacket, then began to undo his tie and unfasten the buttons of his shirt. Presently, his bare chest was pressed against her, but still, she wanted even more.

Sensing that, Paul removed her blouse and bra, her skirts twisted about her exposed thighs. Then he cast off the remainder of his own clothing, lying down, naked, beside her and gathering her into his arms again. Flesh pressed against flesh as he bent his head to her breasts, began with his tongue to lave her pert, rosy nipples, causing waves of delight to radiate from their centers to ripple throughout her entire body.

"Lily," he murmured hoarsely in her ear, "I don't know about you, but I can't take much more of this."

"Neither can I," she breathed.

He entered her then, and together, they reached the heights of rapture.

Afterward, they soaked in a bubble-filled Jacuzzi in the bathroom, then, returning to the bedroom, made love again, taking their time.

But when Lily awakened in the morning, Paul no longer lay beside her. The police had arrived to arrest him for the murder of Freddie Fontaine.

An Agonizing Wait

Serene, I fold my hands and wait,
Nor care for wind, nor tide, nor sea;
I rave no more 'gainst time or fate,
For lo! My own shall come to me.

Waiting [1872]
—John Burroughs

Chapter 6

Savannah, Georgia
The Present—Three Months Later

Following the preliminary hearing, Paul had been indicted and bound over for trial. Bail had been set at one million dollars, which he had paid. Then he and Lily had returned home from the courthouse. Now, several weeks later, they were awaiting Paul's trial for murder. It seemed a miracle to them both that Lily had not been arrested and charged, too, as an accomplice.

The morning after Freddie's murder, a photograph of Paul and Lily in an impassioned embrace in his car had appeared in the *Savannah Spokesman,* the

newspaper that had published Freddie's gossip column, and the police had promptly decided that in order to protect her husband, Lily had invented the story
about the third man who had come into the living
room, following Freddie's brutal slaying.

Now she and Paul sat glumly at the table on the
back veranda. Had it not been for the upcoming trial
hanging over his head, the two of them would have
been very happy together, well on their way to setting
their marriage to rights. But how could they think of
a future together when, at his upcoming trial, Paul
might be found guilty of and imprisoned for a murder
he hadn't committed?

"Oh, Paul, what are we going to do?" Lily asked,
sighing heavily, so beset by anxiety that she had
scarcely touched even her morning coffee, much less
the appetizing breakfast that Dinah had so carefully
prepared for them.

"The first thing we're going to do is eat, darling,"
Paul insisted pleasantly but firmly. "You simply can't
afford to go on skipping meals, and Dinah has gone
to a lot of trouble to tempt your palate this morning.
She's worried about you—and so am I."

"I'm sorry. It's just that all this is so very upset-
ting. I'll try to do better." Picking up her fork, Lily
made a concerted effort to force the delicious food
down.

"I know, sweetheart, but sooner or later, the real
killer is bound to be discovered."

"I don't see how. Nothing new has come to light
since you were arrested, Paul, and the police don't

seem to believe they need to look anymore. They think they've got their man.''

''Well, you and I both know better—and I'm not going to take all this lying down, believe me. As you know, I've got a private-detective firm working full-time on investigating all those secrets to which 'Madame Julep' was privy about the other characters the night of Freddie's party, and Zelda's got her ear to the ground, as well.''

''I certainly do!'' Zelda herself announced as she unexpectedly appeared on the back veranda, with an older man in tow. ''Hello, Lily. I don't believe you've ever had the pleasure of meeting my husband, James Rutherford...just call him 'Jimbo.' Everybody else does.''

''How do you do, Jimbo?'' Lily greeted Zelda's husband.

''Oh, I do just fine.'' He smiled warmly at her. ''How about yourself? Or shouldn't I ask? I can't imagine it's too well under the circumstances, but I promise you, we'll soon set that to rights. Hello, Paul.'' The older man shook the younger's hand. ''I'm mighty glad to see you're bearing up all right.''

''You know me...never one to run away from a fight. It's good to see you. When did you get back home?''

''A couple of weeks ago.''

Seeing the Rutherfords, Paul had stood to welcome them. Now he resumed his wicker chair at the glass-topped wicker table and bade them be seated. Mo-

ments later, Dinah appeared, laden with more breakfast plates.

"Y'all eat up now," she urged. "There's more in
the kitchen."

Somehow, despite everything, Lily found she had
an appetite, after all, as she listened to the conversation. Jimbo had been away off and on in South America for nearly a year, something to do with the global
enterprise he owned, which was why she had never
before met him. Previously, she had even suspected
that he and Zelda were separated and estranged. But
now, watching the couple together, Lily could plainly
see that this was not the case at all, that the Rutherfords were actually very much in love. The observation made Lily feel even more ashamed of herself for
believing Freddie Fontaine's insinuations about Paul
and Zelda, especially when the latter announced that
since Jimbo's return, the two of them had been busy,
doing whatever they could to help Paul.

"And you'll never guess what we've discovered!"
Zelda exclaimed. "Why, I could hardly even believe
it myself! Do y'all remember how old Noreen was so
keen the night of poor Freddie's murder to pin it all
on Paul, even before we'd all really even got over the
shock of Freddie being dead in the first place? Well,
I thought that was pretty strange, because y'all know
everybody calls her 'Never Press Charges' Noreen,
because she never files a case unless she's absolutely
sure that she can win it...doesn't want to get a poor
conviction record. And when I called Jimbo, he

agreed. So we both decided Noreen must have some ulterior motive to want to go after Paul so quickly.''

"I hadn't really thought about it, but yes, I think you're right about that, Zelda,'' Paul remarked interestedly. ''Please go on.''

"Well, Lily said that Noreen's character, Tiger Swallowtail, was hiding a deep, dark secret about her antecedents, and that got me thinking about how old Noreen's always claimed to be an orphan. Trollope's her married name, you know. She kept it even though she's been divorced for practically aeons. I don't believe anyone's ever known her maiden name, but after a lot of digging, I finally managed to track it down. You'll never guess what it is! It's Babbitt! Old Noreen is the illegitimate daughter of Freddie's butler!''

"Good Lord!'' Paul whistled softly.

"What does it mean?'' Lily queried, confused. ''Why would Noreen want to conceal the fact that she's Babbitt's illegitimate daughter?''

"Oh, there are a lot of reasons for that, Lily,'' Jimbo told her. ''We might have come a long way since the Civil War, but bastardy's still something of a stigma these days, even so—especially for someone bent on public office and politics...not to mention that it would have been kind of difficult for Noreen to move easily in Freddie's social circles if it'd been known that his butler was her father. As much as everybody might like to claim they're politically correct nowadays and that we're all born equal, the real truth of the matter is that that's just not so. Power, fame, money, family...all these are still great divid-

ers, whether we want to admit it or not. Social classes
still exist...perhaps they always will. But what's important here is that it was Freddie Fontaine who was
murdered, and Babbitt was Freddie's butler, and Noreen is not only Babbitt's illegitimate daughter, but
also a usually lackadaisical district attorney who's
suddenly gung-ho to prosecute Paul. I don't myself
happen to believe all that's pure coincidence.''

"Nor do I," Paul stated grimly. "But if Noreen or
Babbitt or even both of them together killed Freddie,
what could their motive possibly have been? I mean,
as embarrassing as it might have been to Noreen to
be exposed as the illegitimate daughter of Freddie's
butler, that still scarcely seems a good enough reason
for either of them to have actually murdered Freddie.''

"No, probably not." Jimbo nodded in agreement.
"But you know Freddie's attorney, Lonnie Sugarbaker, is my own lawyer, too, and the moment I got
back in town after Zelda called me to come home, I
arranged to have a little chat with him. It seems that
having no kin of his own, Freddie had made a will
leaving everything he owned to Babbitt.''

"But...surely Freddie was worth millions," Lily
speculated, bemused.

"Precisely!" Zelda cried.

"Then...are you saying Noreen and Babbitt killed
Freddie for his money?" Lily asked, her brow knitted
in a puzzled frown. "But why didn't they just wait
for him to die? Then they could have collected ev-

erything without risking a murder charge being levied against one or both of them.''

''Yes, but unfortunately, as we all know, Freddie was a very malicious little toad,'' Jimbo explained, ''and he had recently quarreled with Babbitt—or so Lonnie informed me. Noreen, you see, isn't happy with being just a local district attorney. She has higher aspirations at the state level, and those require a great deal of funding. So she pressured her father to put the squeeze on Freddie. The two of them didn't have much to bargain with, of course—except for two things. One was that Noreen frequently supplied Freddie with a lot of the dirt he dished up in that spiteful gossip column of his. The other was that he didn't like change, and Babbitt, according to Lonnie, had threatened to retire if Freddie didn't make a sizable contribution to Noreen's campaign treasure chest.'' Jimbo paused, then continued.

''But while Freddie certainly enjoyed manipulating everyone else, he didn't like dancing to anybody else's tune himself, and the upshot was that he got mad at Babbitt and told him that he was going to change his will, so that if Babbitt upped and quit, he wouldn't get a dime. At first, Noreen and Babbitt might have thought Freddie was bluffing. But then Freddie called Lonnie and made an appointment to see him. I reckon that was when old Noreen and Babbitt realized that at any moment Freddie could deprive them of millions, not to mention let the cat out of the bag about Noreen and Babbitt's relationship. Naturally, Babbitt would have known all the details about

Freddie's so-called party to die for, so either he or Noreen or both of them together could have planned how to kill Freddie for real at it and blame Paul or somebody else for the dirty deed.''

"But…Jimbo, if your attorney knows all this, why hasn't he gone to the police with it?" Lily inquired.

"Because it would be a little difficult for Lonnie Sugarbaker to convince our bumbling police chief, Hamilton Kiley, that his girlfriend Noreen is the real culprit behind Freddie's murder," Paul pointed out astutely. "Ham knows Zelda and I have been friends since childhood, and that Lonnie is Jimbo's lawyer. I think we can all agree that since Ham's not the brightest kid on the block, he's more than likely simply to think that we all concocted this story to get my own neck out of the noose."

"Oh, Paul…then…what are we going to do?" Lily bit her bottom lip anxiously.

"I don't know yet," he confessed. "But at least now, thanks to Jimbo and Zelda, we've got an alternative theory to present to a jury, if necessary, to cast that all-important shadow of reasonable doubt, and that's more than we had before. Thank you both," he said to the Rutherfords.

"Don't mention it." Zelda casually brushed aside his gratitude. "What are friends for? Besides, if I hadn't been so dependent on your friendship and support during Jimbo's long absences from home because of his business, Lily might never have got the wrong idea about our relationship after that nasty little lie Freddie printed in that hateful column of his. I'm so sorry, Lily." The older woman turned to the younger. "You don't know how many times I've wanted to call you to try to clear things up. But I was afraid I would only make matters worse. Jimbo thought about calling you, too, but since you hadn't ever even met him, we didn't know if you'd believe him, either, or not. But the truth was that the reason Paul and I were spending so much time together at the time that Freddie falsely accused us of having an affair was that I was helping Paul plan a surprise first wedding anniversary party for you and him."

"Oh." Lily felt abruptly as though someone had just punched her in the stomach. "Oh, God, Zelda. Now I really feel terrible! I didn't know. All I knew was that Jimbo was gone all the time, and that you and Paul were always on the phone together or something. It's *I* who am sorry. I feel so ashamed of myself now!"

"No need to apologize, Lily," Jimbo put in kindly. "A young bride…a little shy and insecure. That slimy little worm Freddie must have thought you were a prize balloon ripe for the sticking. He was cruel that way, I'm sorry to say. I'd have called him up, given him a piece of my mind and demanded a retraction, but unfortunately, in such cases, that usually only adds fuel to the fire. So I decided it was best to ignore the whole damned thing. I knew it wasn't true. But now I regret that I *did* just let it go. Maybe if I'd spoken up at the time, you wouldn't have walked out on Paul. But I hope that's all water under the bridge now."

"It is." Lily spoke firmly, reaching over to lay her hand on Paul's own. "It is. This past year and these recent events have taught me a great deal. Freddie Fontaine isn't going to get the best of me again or destroy my and Paul's happiness a second time around—not even from the grave. Somehow, we're going to figure out a way to prove Paul's innocent of these charges against him, and that Noreen and Babbitt are guilty!"

But how they were going to do this, Lily hadn't a clue, and that night, she and Paul made love fiercely, and then again, sweetly, as though it were for the very last time.

Who Done It

Better be killed than frightened to death.

Mr. Facey Romford's Hounds [1864]
—Robert Smith Surtees

Chapter 7

Lily was so nervous that she felt as though she were going to be sick. Paul's attorney, Walker Mayfield, had finally prevailed upon Savannah's police chief, Hamilton Kiley, to re-create the events the night of Freddie Fontaine's grisly murder. So now, tonight, everyone except for the caterers was gathered once more in the dead gossip columnist's big, old Victorian mansion in the city's historic district. Even the boxer Shane Valentine and his girlfriend, the pop singer Samantha Starr, had come up from Atlanta to be present. As Freddie's fortune had been considerable and he had been murdered, his estate had yet to be settled and his will probated, so the house had been sealed up since his death, and nothing had been touched since the police's Homicide Division and Crime Scene Unit had finished their various investigations.

"I still don't see the point of all this, and I can't for the life of me imagine why you ever agreed to it, Ham!" Noreen declared shrilly at the table where they all sat again in Freddie's old dining room.

"Well, Noreen, unlike the rest of us, Walker wasn't present at Freddie's so-called party to die for," Ham replied, "and naturally, he wants to defend Paul to the very best of his ability. So of course, he wants to know exactly what happened that night, what the sequence of events was, and he felt it would be helpful to him to re-create them, so he could understand how things unfolded. I've no particular reason to object to that, and I don't know why you would, either. If you're certain your case against Paul is unassailable, then what's your worry?"

"None. I just don't see the point," Noreen reiterated mulishly. "We all know Paul's guilty!"

"We don't know any such thing!" Zelda rejoined sharply. "All we know is that Ham's arrested and charged him, and that, thanks to you, he's been bound over for trial. Whether he's guilty of Freddie's murder or not, however, has yet to be proved."

"Oh, you'd say anything to protect Paul, Zelda. We all know you've been having an affair with him for years and that Jimbo's just too good-natured and trusting to face up to it! But Lily knew better. After all, she walked out on Paul because of it, didn't she?''

"Yes, I did," Lily stated coldly, despite her anxiety. "But that was because I was foolish enough to believe Freddie printed the truth about people. However, now I know he was wrong about Paul and Zelda, that Freddie was simply a malicious, small-minded man who enjoyed causing mischief and grief for other people, and that I must have represented an irresistible target for his spite and cruel amusement. He was a very wicked man, actually. But still, no one deserves to die the way he did, and I know Paul didn't kill him.''

"Well, that's one of the things we're here to try to determine, Lily," Walker Mayfield put in smoothly. "So if you'll all please take your places, we'll get started, shall we?"

At that, obediently, Lily rose and made her way to the living room. Just the sight of it again caused her to shiver violently. It was dark outside, and the lights within were turned down low, but nevertheless, she could still see the blood that stained one edge of the Aubusson carpet and the hardwood floor upon which it lay. Shuddering once more, she turned away, entering the tower she had occupied as the Gypsy fortune-teller, Madame Julep, the night of Freddie's party. Here, everything was arranged just as it had been that fateful evening, with the curtains tied back, the table and sweetheart chairs in place, and a solitary candle burning. She sat down.

"Are you ready, Lily?" Walker called from the dining room.

"Yes," she answered, butterflies churning in her stomach and her hands trembling.

"Then the game will commence," he announced.

Everyone went through the motions then, trying to do exactly what they had done the night of Freddie's murder. Finally, the horrible moment that Lily had been awaiting occurred. All the lights went out, and the living room was plunged into darkness, save for the moonbeams that streamed in through the windows and the flicker of her candle's flame. Bending forward to blow upon it gently, she extinguished this last. Then, one by one, all the suspects paraded into the living room, approached the fireplace mantel, picked up the Greek statuette that sat there, and pretended to bash it over an imaginary victim's head. All the while, Lily watched the shadows in the mirror, just as she had that lethal evening.

"That's it! That's the figure I saw kill Freddie that night!" Lily cried when the final suspect appeared.

Immediately, Walker flicked on the living room lights to reveal Noreen standing before the hearth.

"That's ridiculous!" the district attorney snapped, as everyone came running into the living room to stare at her. "You're just saying that to protect your husband, Lily!"

"Well, that will certainly be easy enough to determine, Noreen," Walker declared grimly. "Like others of us here tonight, I knew Freddie Fontaine ever since I was a child, and one thing I know for certain about him—aside from the fact that he was a spiteful little man—is that he was very particular about his hats...had 'em cleaned and blocked regularly, and never let anybody else wear 'em. Now, we know that whoever murdered Freddie wore a hat—presumably to cast the blame on Paul, who also wore a hat that night. That's why we've had all of you put on that hat tonight." Walker indicated the Panama hat Noreen still had on her head.

Frowning furiously, she snatched it off and tossed it onto the sofa, then laughed shortly, harshly.

"That damned hat doesn't prove a blessed thing, Walker!" the district attorney sneered. "As you yourself said, *everybody* has worn it tonight."

"Yes, they have." Walker nodded, unperturbed. "But you see, Noreen, that's not Freddie's hat. That's one I bought myself this afternoon. Earlier today, I had Detectives Johnson and Adams here—" he motioned toward the two men "—collect all of Freddie's own hats from the house and bag and tag them as evidence. Forensics is examining them now—and of course, if we find traces of anyone else's hair but Freddie's few wispy strands, or of those feathers you wore that night, in any of them, well, then, I don't believe I'm going to be the only one who wonders what earthly reason you might have had for putting on one of Freddie's hats that evening...especially when it's also come to my attention that Babbitt, your father, stands to inherit all of Freddie's millions, and that you and Babbitt were pressuring Freddie for a sizable campaign contribution, and that Babbitt had quarreled with him, so Freddie had threatened to change his will.''

"Oh, God, Noreen," the butler, who stood to one side, suddenly moaned pitiably. "You never went and murdered poor Mr. Fontaine, did you now? Oh, no. Oh, no. Mr. Fontaine wouldn't really have gone and changed his will. He was always teasing me like that. But he never truly meant it. That was just his way. And he'd have given me the money for your campaign in the end, if you'd have just given me time to flatter him and sweeten him up a little. He might have been malicious, like people claim, always gossiping and causing trouble, but he wasn't cheap or stingy— not a bit. I swear, I'd have never told you all about the Murder Mystery game before that night if I'd known you intended to kill him...."

"Shut up, you doddering old fool!" Noreen growled, incensed, her nostrils pinched and white. "Just shut up, and don't say another word!"

"District Attorney Trollope, I'm afraid it's my duty to place you under arrest for the murder of Freddie Fontaine," Detective Johnson declared at that, stepping forward to handcuff her, while Detective Adams began to read Noreen her rights. Still reading her Miranda rights to her, the two detectives led the angrily protesting district attorney away, while other police officers outside tried to hold back the media, who had gathered beyond the huge, old Victorian mansion's wrought-iron fence.

"Those damned buzzard reporters!" Walker shook his head as he watched from the open front door in the foyer. "I wonder who tipped them off about tonight?"

"I don't know," Jimbo Rutherford said with feigned innocence as he hugged his wife, Zelda, affectionately. "But I wouldn't put it past Lonnie Sugarbaker, if he somehow managed to learn about this little shindig here tonight! I wonder who could have told him? I guess it must have been somebody who figured it was high time to speak up about the goings-on in this town!"

Everyone laughed, then began to depart in groups to run the media gamut outside. Paul and Lily were among the last to leave, first thanking everybody for their assistance that evening. But at last, it was time for the happy couple to go. Hand in hand, they walked outside to face the horde of microphones, cameras and flashing lightbulbs.

"Hey, you!" Paul abruptly called out, recognizing among the crowd the cheeky photographer on the motorcycle who had taken the damaging picture of his and Lily's passionate embrace that night in his Mercedes. "Here's a *real* photo op for you!" With that, Paul drew Lily fiercely into his strong arms and kissed her deeply and lingeringly. Then, raising his head, he said, "Print that—with our blessing!"

And the photographer did just that—right next to the *Savannah Spokesman*'s lead article the following morning, whose headline read: D.A. Arrested, Clothier Now Happily In Wife's Custody For Life!

IN TOO DEEP

Maureen Child

Dear Reader,

I was so excited to be invited to write one of the stories for *Love Is Murder.* Silhouette's anthologies are a treat to write and, I hope, a treat to read.

My story is really more "murder-lite," if there is such a thing. Set in a small beach town in Southern California, (since it's easy to hop in the car and research the area), "In Too Deep" is more about the aftereffects of murder.

When a mob guy is dusted by his ex-girlfriend, the town of Sunrise Beach is turned upside down—and our heroine's life will never be the same.

I really hope you enjoy reading "In Too Deep" as much as I enjoyed writing it. I'd love to hear what you think. Visit my Web site at www.maureenchild.com and drop me an e-mail.

Happy reading!

Maureen Child

Chapter 1

The funeral was more like a circus.

Floral tributes in wildly different shapes lay scattered around the cemetery like forgotten toys dropped by a spoiled child. There were lasagnas made out of carnations, playing cards sculpted from roses, and a giant slot machine made entirely of lilies and daisies. The mourners had looked like a geriatric production of *Guys and Dolls,* and ol' Blue Eyes had closed out the service, singing a tune about doing things his way.

Now, news vans surrounded the small cemetery like a wagon train preparing for an attack. Sunlight winked off the lenses of cameras following people as they left the service. Reporters clutching microphones darted in and out of the crowd, hoping for a sound bite to flash across the eleven o'clock news.

Gina Palermo glanced at them from the corner of her eye, then shut them all out and looked down at the shining brass casket as it was lowered into the waiting grave. The show was over. "Bye, Uncle Jimmy," she whispered, and tossed a single white rose atop the flowers already scattered across the lid of the casket.

Jimmy "The Weasel" Miletti, friend, honorary uncle and godfather. Pain rippled through Gina, but she battled it into submission. Jimmy had lived the way he wanted, and died…all right, maybe not the way he would have liked, but he probably hadn't been too surprised.

After all, a man who'd made his living as a mobster shouldn't have been astonished to find himself staring down the business end of a pistol. That the gun was held by his sixty-five-year-old former girlfriend might have given him a moment's pause, but in the end, did it really make a difference *whose* gun had fired the bullet that ended his life?

"How long are you gonna stay out here?"

Gina stiffened but didn't turn around. Jake Falcone. She should have expected to see him here for the funeral, but for some reason, she hadn't allowed herself to consider the possibility that he would attend. Whether that was because she was hoping he would, or wouldn't, she wasn't really sure. And she didn't want to investigate that thought any further, thanks.

She'd managed to avoid him during the brief service, but apparently, her grace period was over. Too bad, since the one thing she didn't need at the moment was to look into a pair of dark brown eyes that knew too much…saw too much. So she took the coward's way out and kept her gaze locked on the flower-bedecked coffin. "Don't you have to be somewhere?" she demanded. "Breaking a kneecap? Beheading a horse? Making an offer someone can't refuse?"

"You watch too many movies," he said. She heard amusement in his voice.

Amusement. He of all people should have known she wasn't kidding. She was being facetiously serious. If such a thing were possible.

"Movies?" she repeated, finally snapping her head around to give him a glare that would have fried a lesser man.

Naturally, it didn't phase him. There he stood, as gorgeous as some mysterious dark angel. His too-long black hair, gathered into a neat ponytail at the nape of his neck, gave him an even more dangerous air somehow. Thick black eyebrows arched high over dark brown eyes that flashed as he watched her. Sharply defined cheekbones, a strong chin and a wide mouth, now thinned into a disapproving line, all combined to make a man so damn handsome he should have been on the cover of *GQ*. Instead, he was the poster boy for Mobsters, Inc.

And her father's right-hand man.

Which was precisely why she didn't want a thing

to do with him—the thundering race of her hormones notwithstanding.

He might be able to intimidate everyone else with his stony face, but Gina was immune. She turned her back on Uncle Jimmy and took a step toward trouble.

"You think I need the *movies?*" Her index finger stabbed at his chest with enough force to snap her fingernail. She paid no attention. "This is my *life* here. The man we just buried used to sing to me and tell me stories. He drew pictures of bunny rabbits for me and then went out and did God knows what for the 'family.' So don't talk to me about movies, mister."

He shot an uneasy glance at the two or three reporters who'd hung around the edges of the cemetery when their colleagues had chased after the last of the mourners. Scowling, he shifted his gaze back to her. "You're putting on quite a show."

Gina inhaled sharply and told herself to calm down. At the moment, the news hawks didn't appear to be very interested in her and Jake, but that could change in a heartbeat. And after all, she didn't want to be watching herself on the eleven o'clock news. It was bad enough she'd have to hear about Jimmy's murder again. And the never-ending speculation on just why Jimmy had been so far from home. Why he'd come to Sunrise Beach.

She was tired of hearing the litany of Jimmy's affiliations. Tired of wincing every time the name Dominic Palermo was mentioned.

And she was so tired of being tired.

"Go away," she said, anger suddenly rushing out of her like water from a tub once the plug had been pulled.

"Can't."

"What?"

"I said, I can't go away."

"Sure you can," she countered, waving one hand and only then noticing her broken nail. Sighing, she told him, "Put one foot in front of the other until you come to that oh-so-discreet black sedan. Then get in, start the engine and drive."

"Clever."

"Hey, I went to college." Deliberately, she turned her back on him and stepped closer to the yawning black hole in front of her. All she wanted was one more minute. One minute alone to say her goodbyes.

She didn't get it.

He didn't leave. In fact, he stepped up beside her, and she fought the irritation snapping to life inside her.

"What exactly is it that you want?" she asked.

"What I want," he repeated thoughtfully. "Let's see. A place on the beach, world peace and a car that never needs a tune-up."

"Great. Jokes. Just what I need." Gina reached up

and pushed her hair out of her eyes. "I *meant* what do you want here? With me?"

"Just doing my job," he said tightly.

"Your job? I'm your job?" She shook her head. "When did that happen?"

"When Jimmy died."

Understanding clicked in her mind, and she didn't like it.

"My father sent you," she said, and it wasn't a question. Damn. She should have guessed. No way would Jake Falcone just show up, so far from Chicago. Not without direct orders from his boss. Dominic Palermo, head of the Coretti crime family.

And father of Gina Palermo, assistant district attorney in Sunrise Beach, California.

"Well," she told him stiffly, "you can head right back to my father and tell him I don't need you."

"Right," Jake said, one corner of his incredible mouth tipping up in a quirky smile. "I'll do that. I'll just tell Dom that I took orders from you instead of him. Shouldn't be a problem." His dark gaze shifted back to Jimmy's coffin and the empty plot beside it. "Maybe I could get the place next door to Jimmy. Looks like a good neighborhood."

"My father wouldn't..."

He just looked at her.

Gina sighed. She hated thinking about what her father might or might not do. For heaven's sake, how was a person supposed to go about her daily business knowing her darling daddy was a "wise guy"? The father she knew was a kind, generous, funny man who didn't like killing spiders. But there was another side to Dominic Palermo, and she knew that all too well.

Her own mother had discovered the truth about her husband a year after marrying him. As soon as she'd learned that her husband's "dry cleaning" business was really a front for the mob, she'd promptly left him, taking her baby daughter home to California, to raise Gina far from the influence—and notoriety—of Dominic Palermo's world.

Dom had never really recovered from the loss of his family. But despite being separated by thousands of miles, he'd kept in touch with Gina her whole life. With Jimmy as go-between, Dom had followed every step of his daughter's growth. He had videos of every one of her birthdays and every milestone in her life.

There'd been a few visits back and forth, but mostly Gina had steered clear of Chicago. She didn't want anything to do with Dominic's universe.

And though Gina had kept her father's identity a secret for most of her life, she loved him. In spite of the fact that he lived outside the law and she'd made a career of defending it.

"Okay, fine," she conceded. "You can't leave. But you don't have to shadow me."

He smiled again, and Gina told herself not to react. Of course, that was sort of like telling a struck match not to flame. Jake Falcone was not an easy man to ignore. Especially when every cell in her body was demanding that she pay attention.

"Look," she said, surrendering, if only for the moment. "We can talk about this later, okay? Right now I just want a minute alone."

He frowned, glanced around the old cemetery, then looked back to her. Nodding, he said, "I'll be waiting by the car."

A small victory, but at this point, she was willing to take it. Gina watched him walk away, and inhaled sharply. He walked with a sort of built-in confidence—or arrogance, she wasn't sure which. But either way, the manner in which he moved did something to her that she really couldn't explain.

With an effort, she pushed Jake out of her mind and turned back to the still-open gravesite. Across from her, solemn-eyed workers stood to one side, waiting for her to leave so they could finish up and head home for dinner.

But she paid them no attention at all. Finally, she was alone with the man she'd known all her life as a gentle, warmhearted soul. Jimmy "The Weasel" Miletti had been many things to many people. Police officers, the Federal Justice Department and no doubt the FBI had been after him at one time or another. But to Gina, he'd been simply Uncle Jimmy.

"I'll miss you," she said softly, and felt the sting of tears in her eyes. Silly. She thought she'd finished crying days ago. Besides, Jimmy wouldn't have approved of tears. If nothing else, he was a man who'd loved life—and he'd lived his precisely the way he'd wanted to. "I wish you were here right now, Jimmy." She glanced over her shoulder at the dark-haired man still watching her. "Only you would be able to get Daddy to call off his guard dog."

Jake Falcone leaned against the black sedan's front fender. Crossing his feet at the ankles, he folded his arms across his chest and kept his gaze fixed on Gina. Even from behind, she was a showstopper. Great legs, now encased in silky black stockings. She swayed slightly in three-inch black heels that did amazing things for those already pretty impressive legs. The skirt of her no-frills black business suit hit the center of her knees, and the matching jacket clung to curves he remembered all too clearly.

He couldn't see her face from here, but he didn't need to be staring at her to see it. All he had to do was close his eyes and her features appeared. Wide, round eyes the color of good cognac. Her nose was small and straight, her mouth wide and full. Her skin looked sun kissed and her shoulder-length, curly hair was at least a hundred different shades of brown. And Jake remembered all too well that it felt like silk against a man's hands.

"What the hell are you doing here, Falcone?" he muttered, then shot a glance at the last of the reporters as they gave up and drove away. Apparently they'd grown tired of waiting for Gina. Good call, he thought. The woman was stubborn enough to stand out there all night if it meant she could avoid talking to the media and to *him*. But sooner or later she would have to give in, and when she did, he would be here.

It wasn't as if he had a choice.

After all, when Dominic Palermo issued an order, it got followed.

Even Jake was in no position to say no to Gina's father.

An hour later, she was still standing at the gravesite. A sharp, cold ocean wind kicked up out of nowhere, carrying the scent of the sea with it as it dashed across the cemetery. Jake pushed away from the car and headed toward her.

Stone monuments jutted up from the earth like signposts in the city of the dead. Bedraggled flowers lay atop graves and fluttered wildly in the wind. The leaves on the trees rustled, sounding like hushed whispers from an interested crowd.

Gina was oblivious, though the wind tugged at her hair and flipped the hem of her skirt up with icy fingers.

Jake stopped alongside her, nodded to the workers still standing off to one side, and waited for them to move away before speaking.

"Gina? It's time to go."

"I'm not ready."

Stubborn. She got that from her old man. "You're gonna turn blue in another minute. It's freezing out here."

"I'm fine."

"No, you're not."

"Go away."

"We've been through that already."

She glared at him, and even in the late afternoon light, he had no trouble seeing the flash of anger in her eyes. Great. Just what he needed.

"You may take orders from my father, but I don't. I'll leave when I'm ready."

Irritation bubbled to the surface. "Then get ready," he said tightly. "I'm not standing around here all night." He jerked a thumb at the workers, who were still backing off. "And they'd probably like to call it a night, too."

"Oh well, if I'm putting everyone out…"

"Damn it, Gina," he demanded, "do you have to make everything a struggle?"

She laughed, and the sound awoke memories in Jake that he'd spent a year burying.

"I'm making this hard?"

"As always."

"Don't," she warned, and held up one hand to silence him. "You don't get to do that."

"Do what?"

"Pretend you know me."

"I do know you."

The wind pushed her hair across her eyes, and she plucked it free so she could glare at him unimpeded. "You don't know anything about me."

"I know that you're going to make me regret this," he muttered as he bent, tucked his shoulder into her middle and straightened up.

"Put me down," she ordered, bracing her hands against his back in a futile attempt to push free.

"Not likely," he said, nodding to the men, who were already scuttling toward the gravesite. Heading toward the car, Jake pinned her legs down with one arm, to keep her from kicking with the pointed shoes she wore.

Oh, yeah. This was going to be an easy assignment.

Chapter 2

"This just is *not* happening," Gina said, shooting a furious look at the man behind the wheel.

"It's not my idea of a vacation either, princess," Jake assured her as he steered the car down the narrow lane that led out of the cemetery.

Maybe not, she fumed silently, but people weren't tossing *him* over their shoulder like a sack of potatoes, were they? He hadn't given her much of a chance to escape, either. He'd just thrown her into his rental—why did these gangster types always go for black sedans?—then drove off.

Thank heaven the reporters had all left by the time he went caveman. Otherwise, the headlines in tomorrow's papers would have been charming. Mobster

Kidnaps Assistant D.A. Oh yeah, that'd be wonderful for her career.

Jake turned left onto the Pacific Coast Highway, and Gina stared out the side window at the familiar landscape. Sunrise Beach. Small, cozy, comfortable. Until *he* showed up. Now she felt as though she needed a city the size of New York just to keep from feeling crowded.

Row after row of narrow, tall beach houses raced past the window. Splotches of colorful flower gardens decorated the tiny yards fronting the busy street. Behind those houses, of course, were yet *more* houses, crawling right down to the sand, where they crouched like children waiting for high tide. Restaurants, everything from five-star dining to fast food, lined the busy highway. The sidewalks were packed with the usual summer crowd. Tourists, still cameras hanging from their necks as they clutched video cameras in sunburned fists, tried to corral children eager to get to the beach. Surfers, their boards tucked beneath their arms, headed for the water, where they were no doubt most at home. And then there were the new people in town.

Old men in snap-brim fedoras, looking like ads for a 1940s black-and-white gangster movie. Younger guys, dressed a little snappier, but no less out of place, wandered in and out of the shops, and Gina had the distinct feeling things were only going to get worse.

"Why aren't they leaving?" she wondered, and until Jake answered her, hadn't been aware she'd said it out loud.

"Leaving? They're setting up shop."

She turned her head to look at him. "Why?"

He merely glanced at her, then shifted his gaze back to the wildly merging traffic. "Are you kidding? They're all after Jimmy's treasure."

"Treasure? Jimmy didn't have a treasure." The thought was laughable. Jimmy Miletti spent money faster than he made it. Generous to a fault, he loved buying gifts for her, for his friends. And then there was the whole gambling thing. Jimmy never met a card game he didn't like. Unfortunately, the cards didn't care much for him.

Ahead, the light turned red, and Jake stopped behind a truck that was literally rocking with the blare of loud music and the crew of kids chair-dancing up front. He looked at her and shook his head. "You don't get it. Your father sent me here because he knew what would happen once Jimmy was gone."

"What are you talking about?"

Jake sighed in frustration. "Jimmy's been talking about his 'treasure' for years. Made a big secret out of it. Only said that it was here. In Sunrise Beach."

"That's nuts." Shaking her head, Gina argued, "Why would anyone who knew him believe that? Jimmy went through money like…well, fast."

He shrugged. "He was pretty convincing when he talked about the treasure. And while he was alive, nobody would have tried to cross him. But now that he's gone, the treasure is considered fair game."

"So they're all coming here to look for it?"

"You got it."

She stared out the windshield as a thug in a dark suit crossed the street. The light turned green, somebody honked and the guy looked as if he wanted to pull out a gun. Oh, perfect. This was going to be great. Her perfect little town was going to be overrun with the very gangsters she'd spent most of her life avoiding.

"Are you here for the treasure, too?" she asked.

"Nope. I told you, I'm here because Dom sent me to keep an eye on you."

"Why? I don't know where this fictional treasure is."

He stepped on the gas and didn't bother to swallow the chuckle that escaped him. "You still don't get it. Dom's not worried about Jimmy's treasure. He's afraid one of his enemies just might try to take out his baby girl."

"So you're…"

He sent her a grin that zipped straight down to her toes. "Just think of me as your own personal bodyguard."

"For how long?" she managed to ask.

"For as long as it takes."

"Swell."

The house was small.

Too damn small.

Plus it sat out on a point, overlooking the ocean. No close neighbors. No one to hear if Gina screamed for help.

Jake stalked around the outside of the place. The

soles of his shoes slid on the gravel and he told himself that was one good thing, anyway. If somebody tried to sneak up on the house, there was no way of being quiet on that damn gravel.

At least he'd be alerted before trouble actually walked in and said "howdy." But this whole situation was trouble. There wasn't a single bright spot here. His job was in Chicago, not some dinky little beach town clinging to the coast of California. What did he know about sand and seaweed? Give him the Loop, the El and real Chicago-style pizza any day.

Give him a couple thousand miles between him and Gina Palermo.

This was going way above and beyond the call of duty. Reaching into his jacket pocket, Jake pulled out his cell phone and hit speed dial. As the phone rang, he turned his face into the wind and stared out at the ocean. If he looked at it long enough, maybe he could convince himself it was really Lake Michigan.

"Hello?"

"It's me," Jake said tightly.

"How's it going?"

"It sucks, that's how it's going."

Dominic Palermo chuckled. "Relax, Falcone. How tough can this be for a man with your...qualifications?"

"Look, Dom—"

"No, you look. This is part of the deal, Falcone. You take care of my girl until Jimmy's death blows over."

"When's that gonna be?"

Dom laughed again. "As soon as those yo-yos remember that Jimmy never even had a bank account."

Wind rushed at Jake, pushing at him as though trying to shove him over the edge to the rocks four or five feet below. If he had any sense, he'd jump. But then, it wasn't high enough to kill him. Just maim him so he would have to stay here even longer.

"You owe me for this, Dom."

All amusement left the other man's voice. "You'll get what you deserve. Just watch over Gina."

"Yeah, yeah."

"Oh, and, Falcone," Dom said just before Jake could hang up.

"Yeah?"

"You lay a hand on my baby girl and I'll have you killed. *Capice?*"

The dial tone ringing in his ear told Jake that the other man had hung up without waiting to learn if his threat had been clear. But then he hadn't needed to, had he? A threat from Dom Palermo was like money in the bank. Good as gold.

And even Jake got a little cold chill thinking about it.

"So where are you staying?" Gina asked as Jake sipped the cup of coffee she'd poured him.

"The couch'll do."

"What?" She shook her head, and worked her jaw as though her ears had suddenly plugged. No way had she heard him right.

"The couch," he repeated. "It'll be fine."

"You're not staying here."

"Oh, yes, I am, and if you don't mind, I'd rather not fight about it tonight." He drained the last of his coffee, then set the cup down on the tiny, two-seater wood table under the front window. "I'm tired. Between that red-eye flight and the funeral, I'm beat. So if it's all the same to you, we'll argue about it in the morning."

Gina watched him get up and head into her living room. And suddenly her cozy little house felt about as big as a phone booth. No way was she going to have Jake Falcone stretch out on her couch. Hell, she would never be able to sit there again without thinking of him.

Uh-uh. No way.

"There's a nice motel just down the road. The Kelp Bed."

He winced and sat down on the couch. "Yeah, that sounds great."

"Damn it, Jake, you can't stay here."

"I told you, we'll argue about it tomorrow." He slipped out of his jacket, and Gina's gaze dropped to the shoulder holster he wore as easily as most men wore a belt. The shiny black stock of a pistol jutted up from the worn brown leather, and as he took the pistol out and placed it on the coffee table before him, she inhaled sharply.

"Do you have to have that thing in here?"

"Wouldn't be much of a bodyguard without one, now would I?" he asked, already stretching out on the couch and propping his heels on the arm of the sofa, since it was way too short for his tall frame. Draping one arm across his eyes, he muttered, ''Now if it's okay with you, I'm just gonna get some sleep. Wake me up if you need me.''

In seconds, his deep, even breathing told her he was asleep. How did he do that? Turn everything off and drop into slumber in a second? She had a sudden, desperate urge to stand here and kick him. Instead, she stomped off to her bedroom, slammed and locked the door, then headed for the phone.

She punched in the number and waited what felt like an eternity for someone to answer. When he did, his familiar voice hit her hard.

''Dad?''

''Gina, this is a nice surprise.''

''Tell Jake to leave.''

''Can't do that, baby,'' her father said, and she heard the reluctance in his voice. It didn't make her feel any better.

''I've been on my own a long time, Dad. I don't need a bodyguard.''

''You do right now,'' he argued. ''Jake stays. With Jimmy gone, things are a little up in the air.''

Gina plopped down onto the edge of her bed and gripped the telephone receiver tightly. Hearing her father's voice after the day she'd had was just a little more emotionally rocking than she'd thought it would be. ''I thought you might come to the funeral, too.''

''That would have only made things worse for you, Gina,'' her father said softly. ''Besides, Jimmy and me, we didn't believe in funerals.''

"Well, he had a nice one, anyway."

"I'll catch it on the news."

She nodded and plucked at a stray thread on her comforter. An ache settled in her throat, and Gina swallowed hard, pushing it down into a tight knot low in her stomach. "I'm going to miss him," she said.

"Yeah, honey. Me, too."

"Dad—"

"You do what Jake says, okay?" her father interrupted, his voice suddenly gruffer than it had been a minute ago. "He'll keep you safe."

"I don't want him here, though, and—"

"It's not forever," Dom said quickly. "Just do this for me, huh? Help an old man sleep better at night."

Gina fell backward onto the bed. She had been beaten and she knew it. Her father wasn't going to pull Jake off his assignment. And she couldn't fight him when he pulled that "old man" routine.

"Fine. He can stay."

"That's my girl."

"In the motel down the street."

"In your guest room."

"Dad—"

"Gotta go, honey. You tell Jake I said hello."

She inhaled, started to speak, then blew the wasted air out in a rush as the dial tone buzzed in her ear. Well, great. So the daughter of a Mafia don now had a hired thug sleeping on her couch. Oh yes, and did we mention the daughter was an assistant district attorney?

Gina dropped the phone and scrubbed both hands

across her face. As messy as things seemed right now, she had the distinct impression that they were only going to get worse.

Naturally, the sheriff was Gina's first visitor, bright and early the next morning. He stormed past Terry, Gina's trusted secretary, and had the older woman flapping her hands in vain as she chased him into Gina's office.

"I'm sorry, Ms. Palermo," the woman said, giving the sheriff a look that should have toasted him. "He just pushed right past me."

"It's okay, Terry," Gina said, and stood up.

"No, it's not okay," Terry told her, still glaring at the sheriff, "and he knows better. Shame on you, Todd Reynolds." Then, stiff with indignation, she marched out of the office and slammed the door behind her.

The sheriff scowled. "I feel like she's going to go out there and call my mother."

"She might."

He shifted his gaze to her. "Gina, I don't know what's going on around here, but I've about had it."

Well, she thought, that hadn't taken long. Jimmy had been dead less than a few days and already Sunrise Beach was up in arms. "What is it?"

"Jimmy Miletti's murder," he snapped, and started pacing the confines of her small office. The heels of his highly polished shoes clunked hard against the wood floor, pounding out a rhythm that seemed to throb in concert with the ache pulsing inside Gina's head. When he came to the window, he stopped, flipped the blinds out of the way and stared down into the street. "The damn FBI have taken it over." He let go of the blinds and they snapped back into place with a clatter. "They say it's a federal case now. Because of the whole gangster thing. You know," he muttered, turning on his heel to stomp in the other direction. "They've got him on interstate trafficking and tax evasion and God knows what else."

Now it was Gina's turn to wince. "They haven't 'got' him on anything, Todd. Jimmy's dead."

"Yeah, but they're tying up that murder in federal red tape. And damn it, that was my jurisdiction."

She was pretty sure she felt a tiny blood vessel pop, but maybe that was just wishful thinking. Sitting down, she rubbed at her temple and said, "I'll see what I can do, Todd. But the feds are—"

He shot her a look. "You don't have to tell me. I know what it's like to deal with the feds. Still, you're the D.A. I thought maybe you could—"

"I'm the assistant D.A., but I'll see what I can do."

He blew out a breath and smiled while he nodded like one of those little puppies in the backs of cars. "Good. Good. Okay, thanks, Gina."

"Sure." She didn't know what she could do, though. Her boss would probably love the feds being involved in a case right here in Sunrise Beach. After all, the D.A. had plans that went well beyond this little beach town. He had his sights set on the governor's mansion eventually, and working with the feds could only look good on his résumé.

"Oh and, Gina," Todd said, bringing her back from the wild tangle of thoughts pushing through her brain.

"Yeah?"

"Who's the guy sitting out in your lobby wearing a gun under his jacket?"

Chapter 3

Once Todd left, Gina got a grip on the temper that was simmering into a fine boil inside and stepped into the outer office. Her gaze shot right to Jake.

Silent, stoic, he sat in the chair closest to the door, his back to a wall. From that seat he had a perfect view out the side window and a clear picture of anyone who might come down the hall toward her office. Well, if nothing else, he did his job well, she thought. Of course, a man in his line of work was used to keeping his back to a wall and his eyes wide-open.

Slowly, he turned his head to look at her. Even from across the room the power of that steady brown stare slammed into her. And the fact that he could get to her so easily really made her furious.

"Could I speak to you for a moment?" she asked, and silently commended herself for her restraint.

One black eyebrow lifted, but he stood up and walked across the room. Nodding to Terry, he stepped past Gina into her office. She followed and closed the door behind her.

He moved straight to the windows, grabbed the plastic rod attached to the blinds and twisted it, snapping them shut. "Keep these closed, Gina. No point in taking risks, is there?"

"Great. So as long as I live in a dungeon, everything'll be fine?"

"Pays to be careful."

"Words to live by," she said, and folded her arms across her chest as she leaned back against the door.

"That's the idea." He flicked her a look. "What'd the cop want?"

"Business," she said shortly. "But he did ask about you."

"Yeah?" He smiled and perched on the corner of her desk.

"Yes. He wanted to know why there was a guy with a gun sitting in my lobby."

"What'd you tell him?"

She blew out an exasperated breath. Pushing away from the door, she walked toward her desk and stopped just opposite the man who was quickly becoming the bane of her existence. "This is so not working out."

Bad enough she'd hardly slept all night, knowing

that he was just beyond her bedroom door. Bad enough knowing that she'd have to put up with him for who knew how long. Bad enough knowing that her own father had sent him to keep her from being killed.

But she wasn't going to let him start interfering with her work. And sitting out there with his carved-in-stone face was definitely interfering. Terry was walking around looking like she half expected Jake to stand up and start shooting. The kid who delivered her café mocha had asked for an escort past the "scary guy," and Gina wasn't getting any work done because she knew he was there!

"Hey, I'm just doing my job," he said, and stepped away from the windows.

She rolled her eyes. What kind of person actually *chose* to live like that? To be wary of windows. To sit with his back to a wall. To not trust anyone, ever. But she knew the answer to that question. It was people like her father. People who lived their lives trying to dance on a razor's edge. People who woke up in the morning trying to think of ways to get *around* people like *her*.

"Fine. It's your job." She followed him with her gaze as he moved restlessly around the room. "But *my* job is the only one I'm interested in here."

"Big surprise."

She shot him a look. "What's that supposed to mean?"

"Nothing."

He stopped and held up both hands in mock surrender, and Gina couldn't help wondering if he'd ever had to assume that position for a police officer. Probably.

Oh, good God.

"That 'nothing' means 'something,'" she countered, and tapped the toe of her shiny black pump against the wooden floor.

"All it means is your job is pretty much all you talked about when you were in Chicago last year." He gave her an innocent smile, but Gina wasn't fooled. There was absolutely *nothing* innocent about Jake Falcone. Dangerous, yes. Mysterious, you bet. Sexy, oh yeah. But innocent? Not a chance.

Besides, she knew what he was doing, and she wasn't going to go along with it. "I don't want to talk about last year."

"Why not? Make you nervous?"

If she could read his eyes, she'd feel a lot better about where this conversation was headed. But he was a damn mystery. Just like always.

Just like last year, when she'd first run into him at her father's home. Then, she'd been foolish enough to let the mystery dazzle her. But the plain truth was she didn't want mystery. She wanted a regular guy. Someone who obeyed the law. Someone whose face she stood a pretty decent chance of *never* seeing on a post office wall.

"No," she said stiffly, and walked across the room to her desk. She came within arm's reach of him—

mostly to prove to herself that she could be that close to him without dissolving. Then she sat down on the uncomfortable maroon chair behind her desk. In control again, she folded her hands atop an open file folder, looked up at him and said, "I just don't see the point in opening up the past for discussion."

"You wouldn't," he said with a snort.

A sweep of hot color rushed up her throat and filled her cheeks. She felt it, so she knew he could see it, damn it. "Just because I don't want to talk about an old mistake—"

"That's not how you felt then," he reminded her.

But Gina didn't need reminding. Heck, every time she closed her eyes at night, she relived the two weeks she'd spent in Chicago last summer. And since he'd hit town, the dreams were only more vivid. Surround sound. The-hills-were-alive kind of real.

Oh, yeah.

Her memory was perfect, unfortunately.

"Jake, what are you trying to do?"

He stared into her eyes for a long, heart-fluttering minute. Sixty seconds never ticked past so slowly. She heard a fly buzzing against the windowpane behind her. She heard the creak of the floorboards as her chair rolled a half inch. She could have sworn she heard the second hand on her wristwatch ticking, and she was pretty sure she heard the staccato beat of her own heart.

He leaned closer.

She took a breath and held it.

His gaze moved over her features.

Gina's stomach pitched wildly.

Then he blinked and the moment was over. Pushing away from her desk, he shoved his hands into his pants pockets and walked the room. Letting his gaze slide across the framed diplomas and commendations, he said, "Sorry. Guess I'm a little restless."

Air whooshed out of her and she sucked in another deep breath to try to steady herself again. Oh, this was not a good thing. She'd thought Jake was behind her. Those wild, racing feelings she'd discovered on her last trip to Chicago had scared her enough that she'd cut short her visit with her father and raced back to California. One night with Jake and she'd almost been willing to forget all about her scruples. Forget the fact that she was an attorney. Forget the fact that he was, like her father, a mob guy.

And she couldn't let that happen. She'd had to run before her hormones had overcome her common sense.

But now here he was again, and just looking at him was enough to stir old feelings. To entice her with thoughts of what might have been.

"This is a good picture of you."

"Hmm? What?" She came up out of her thoughts gratefully and looked across the room. Jake was staring at one of the framed newspaper articles, leaning in until his nose practically pressed against the glass.

"Impressive," he said, and the word was whispered, almost as if he didn't really want her to hear him. "You nailed a guy who'd committed forty bank jobs?"

A flicker of pride shot through her, but Gina didn't let it show. "It was a team effort," she said, although she couldn't help remembering all of the hours she'd put into that case. How many nights she'd spent here, in her office, alone with the case files and a bag of Chinese takeout! But it had been worth it. The case had gone to trial airtight, and the Panty Hose Bandit was now doing a sentence of twenty-five to thirty years.

"The guy doesn't look real happy with you in this picture," Jake commented.

"I guess not," she admitted. "Actually, he was my first threat."

Jake swiveled his head slowly. "What?"

"Him," Gina said. "The Panty Hose Bandit was the first guy to threaten me from prison."

"You say that as if it's no big deal," he said.

"Well," she pointed out, "he *is* in prison."

"He could have friends."

Now she laughed shortly. "Not likely."

"Guys willing to do him a favor, then," Jake said, and straightened up, turning to face her with an unreadable expression on his face.

She opened her mouth to argue, thought better of it and asked instead, "Is there a point to this?"

"Sure, but you won't like it."

"Haven't liked much in the last few days," Gina said. "Try me."

"Okay. Maybe your dad sending me here was a better idea than you think."

"Oh, now I'm fascinated," she lied. "Go on."

One corner of Jake's mouth quirked into a brief shadow of a smile, then flattened out again in a humorless line. "Think about it. You've got a little town in the middle of nowhere—"

"Southern California is hardly the middle of nowhere," she argued.

"It ain't Chicago," he snapped. "Anyway, you've got this little town suddenly crawling with…" He paused. "How do I put this? Colorful characters…"

Gina choked out a laugh.

"What better time," he said, his voice dropping to a near growl, "for some clown doing his time in prison to take a shot at the D.A. who put him there?"

"Nice attempt at scaring me," Gina said, and stood up. "But it won't work. How would the guys in the lockup know about Jimmy and…?" Her voice trailed off. Okay, that was a dumb question.

"Uh-huh," Jake said, nodding as comprehension dawned on her features. "These days, most prisons are better equipped than some hotels. Color TV, with satellite dish. Gyms, saunas—you name it, a guy in the joint can find it. Even if it's only a way to get even from behind bars."

Gina swallowed hard, but it didn't dissolve the sudden knot in her stomach.

"So I'm guessing," Jake continued as he walked back toward her, "that all of the guys you sent up over the years know exactly what's going on around here. And just who to call to ask a favor."

"You *are* trying to scare me."

"How am I doing?"

"Pretty good," she admitted quietly. "Okay, fine. I didn't really think about any of what you just said. But even if you're right, I can't have a bodyguard forever." As she spoke, she stiffened her spine and straightened her shoulders. She'd known when she took this job that there were risks. After all, they didn't call them "bad guys" for nothing. "I won't live the rest of my life afraid to do my job."

"Good for you."

"Huh?"

Jake shrugged, gave her a brief, tight smile and said, "You're stubborn. I like that. You've got nerves of steel. I like that, too." He gave her a slow once-over that set off sparklerlike sizzles of heat inside her. "In fact, you're a lot like your old man."

Gina scowled at him. "I love my father, but I'm not like him."

"You might be surprised."

"I don't think so," she said, and heard the ice in her voice. Dominic Palermo was her dad. She loved him. She couldn't change that and wouldn't want to. But their worlds were two very different places—and it was best if Jake remembered that.

"Your dad's a good guy," Jake said softly.

Her gaze snapped up to his. "Of course you would say that. You work for him. But he's not one of the good guys. As much as I wish he were...." Her voice trailed off wistfully.

She'd spent a lot of time over the years wishing that her dad was more like her friends' fathers. But then she'd had to grow up and accept the fact that Dom wasn't going to change. He was who he was, and she either had to accept that and love him anyway or cut him out of her life.

"He sent me here to you, didn't he?"

"Yes," she said, and smiled in spite of the fact that only a few minutes ago she'd been furious about her father's interference. "That doesn't change anything, though. He sent you here because I'm his daughter. But he's still..."

"The enemy?"

"Not mine," she said quickly, thankful that she lived thousands of miles from Dom's empire. It was the main reason she'd never considered moving to Chicago. She didn't want to put herself in the position of having to face her own father across a courtroom.

As it was, every time one of the old-time gangsters was taken to court, Gina fought her own private demons. As a D.A., she supported and defended the law. As a daughter, she was terrified to think that one day she might be going to visit her dad in prison.

Oh, in the world of crime, Dom was probably a small fish compared to some of his colleagues. But size didn't matter to the Justice Department. And sooner or later, they'd be going after Dom, just as they'd gone after all the rest.

"You worry too much," Jake said suddenly, and Gina inhaled sharply. He was much closer than he had been a minute ago. He'd moved in on her—silently, stealthily—and his nearness now nearly cut off her breath.

He lifted one hand and smoothed the spot between her eyebrows. "There's a line here that wasn't there last year."

"Gee, thanks," she said. Nothing like having Adonis point out your wrinkles.

He smiled again and in that one flashing, brilliant second, she was pathetically grateful that he smiled so seldom. Otherwise, she'd be in real trouble.

"Don't worry about that," he said, his voice a low, throaty whisper that made her think of all sorts of things that she really shouldn't be thinking. "You still look great, Gina."

"Jake…"

"Hey, what am I, blind?" he asked, letting his hand drop and taking a step back. "Just because I can't touch doesn't mean I don't look."

One heartbeat, then two, passed before she said, "Jake, we can't do this."

"*We're* not doing anything, Gina."

"This is just too hard. Too weird."

"Maybe, but it's necessary. Hell, you just admitted I was right about a possible threat to you."

"Yes, but that's part of my job."

"And watching out for you is part of mine."

Okey dokey. That mind-splitting headache was

back and it had brought friends this time. Rubbing her temple with the tips of her fingers, Gina told herself to try logic.

"You're a distraction, Jake. One I don't need."

"I'll stay out of your way."

"Just sitting out there, you're causing trouble." She waved one hand toward the outer office, where he'd spent the morning sitting like some carved-out-of-stone dark avenger. "I had to tell the sheriff that you're a private investigator."

He laughed. "Yeah? Did he buy it?"

Remembering the look on Todd's face, she shook her head. "I don't think so."

"Not surprising."

"And you make Terry nervous."

Irritation dashed across Jake's features. "I'll have a talk with her."

"She won't like that, either."

"I don't know what to tell you, Gina. But I'm not going away."

Head pounding, she nodded, accepting defeat, for the moment. She would try to come up with something later. For right now, she just wanted about sixty aspirin and a tall glass of water.

"You're too tense," he muttered, and reaching out, he spun her around until her back was to him.

She stiffened instinctively and tried to pull away from him. But as she had reason to know, Jake was too strong to let her get away if he didn't want her to.

"What are you doing?"

"Can you just relax for a second?"

"Oh, sure," she said snidely. "No problem. Let me make a note to myself. Jake says *relax*."

"Man, what a mouth you have on you."

"You're one to talk." She made a break for it again and grumbled under her breath when she didn't move an inch. His fingers were like a vise grip on her upper arms. And until he got tired of playing Neanderthal, she was stuck. Of course, she could just stomp one of her three-inch heels into the arch of his foot....

His hands moved, slapping down on her shoulders. "Tense," he muttered again.

"Gee, wonder why?" she snapped. "You've spent the last several minutes pointing out to me what an excellent target I am. The sheriff's going nuts because the FBI is playing in his sandbox. My father sent a hired gun to baby-sit me... *Ow*."

His strong fingers dug into the too-tight muscles of her shoulders, and Gina wanted to weep. Pain shimmered brightly behind her closed eyes, but at the same time, a weird sense of relief washed over her, too. As his hands worked at the knots in her muscles, she felt herself slowly loosening up. Relaxing. Tension drained away and puddled at her feet. Maybe it would be all right. Maybe she could survive Jake being here without doing something stupid like sleeping with him. Again. Maybe this would all blow over and she could get back to her normal, everyday, humdrum life—

Suddenly a rock smashed through the window. It just missed Gina and shards of glass tinkled to the floor like some demented set of wind chimes.

Chapter 4

"**G**et down!" Jake grabbed Gina and threw her to the floor. Falling on top of her, he tossed a quick glance at the fist-size chunk of rock skittering across the gleaming wood floor.

Damn it.

"What happened?" Gina asked, her voice muffled against his chest.

Before he could answer, the door opened. "Ms. Palermo? Are you all right?" Terry hurried into the room and skidded to a stop when she saw the two people huddled on the floor.

"Get out!" Jake shouted, and to give the woman her due, shocked or not, she did just that, slamming the door behind her.

Good. He didn't need to have his attention diverted. Raising himself slightly, he looked down at Gina and whispered, "Just stay put for a minute, okay? I want to check things out."

She nodded, and it was almost enough to convince him of miracles. Almost. But knowing Gina, she wouldn't be still for long, so he had to take advantage of the stunned surprise keeping her quiet. Slowly, he lifted his head to look at the window. The blinds were twisted, hanging weirdly from the cords, and jagged pieces of glass lay scattered across the top of Gina's desk and the floor below.

A close call. Too damn close. Gritting his teeth, he moved off of her and crawled toward the window.

"Do you see anything?"

"Not yet," he muttered with a quick look at her. Hadn't taken her long to work past the shock. "Now stay put."

She rolled over, braced herself on her elbows and flipped her hair out of her eyes. He saw defiance written in their depths, and almost groaned.

Scowling at him, Gina said, "I'm not going to stay crouched on my floor like—"

"You damn sure are," he said tightly. That hard jolt of panic that had shot through him at the same speed as the damn rock was still with him. The projectile had just missed her, and he couldn't help thinking about what might have happened if he hadn't been in her office. If she'd been sitting at her desk working rather than standing up arguing with him, or if it had been a bullet that had come through the window instead.

A cold, black rage suddenly poured through him, overwhelming the fear, shoving it down into the pit of his stomach where he knew it would live a long life. Getting to his feet, he kept his back flat against the wall and used his fingertips to move the blinds aside. His practiced gaze swept the parking lot and surrounding area.

Not a soul to be seen. The sun was shining, palm trees swaying in a gentle breeze. Whoever had tossed that rock had done the job and then split. They could be anywhere by now. Dropping the blinds again, he turned back to Gina and wasn't even surprised to see her standing beside her desk.

Glaring down at the bits of glass dotting her paperwork like diamonds sparkling in the sunlight, she said, "Who would do this?"

"The list is pretty much endless," he said. But he'd try to narrow it down. Talk to people. See if anyone had seen something. Chances were slim, but it was worth a shot. He wasn't about to let this incident slide by. He couldn't afford to. Rocks could escalate to something more deadly.

The office door opened a crack and Terry stuck her face in. "All clear?"

Gina gave her a tight smile. "It's okay, Terry. Just a broken window. No serious damage."

The older woman's glance flicked between Gina and Jake. Her expression told him she wasn't buying that explanation, but all she said was, "I'll call maintenance," before she slipped out again.

"Not serious, huh?" Jake demanded, feeling the swell of anger building inside him again.

"It was a rock." Gina bent to pick it up and clutched it tightly, her fingers digging into its rough edges. Small chunks crumbled off and dropped to the floor.

"This time," he snarled. He stared hard into her eyes before he added, "But it could just as easily have been a bullet."

That word hung in the air between them for a long second before it hit home with her.

"God." She looked at the rock again, as if imagining it a lot smaller and a lot more pointed. Then she suddenly dropped it. "Fingerprints. Damn it, I should have known better."

Jake shook his head. He'd already thought of that and discounted it. "Can't get prints off a rock. Too rough. Uneven."

"Of course. You're right. I knew that." She closed her eyes briefly and took several long, deep breaths. He knew what that was like. She was fighting the adrenaline surge, trying to get her system back into line. It wasn't easy, but Gina was a strong woman. She would make it.

Jake walked past her, snatched up the rock again and tossed it up and down as he would a baseball.

Heavy.

Solid.

He looked at Gina. Her hair was a wild tangle of curls framing her pale face. Her eyes were wide, and despite her air of bravado, there were shadows in those golden-brown depths. And he wanted to go find the bastard who'd put them there and beat the hell out of him. It wouldn't do her any good, but it'd make him feel a hell of a lot better.

"I'll, uh, call the sheriff," she said, but made no move to grab the phone.

"I'll do some looking around, too," Jake told her, and fisted his hands at his sides to keep from reaching for her. Caring for her wasn't in the game plan. This was just another assignment. *She* was just another assignment. It had to be that way.

Hell, he'd learned his lesson last year, when she'd visited her father in Chicago. Images he'd spent the last year trying to bury skittered through his mind in rapid succession. Attraction had sizzled between them from the first time they'd laid eyes on each other. And over the course of a few days, Jake had just about forgotten everything. His career. His position in the Palermo "family." Even about old Dom himself. All he'd been able to think about was Gina.

It had been the same for her. He'd seen it in her eyes. She hadn't expected what they'd found together any more than he had. But the morning after their one amazing night of lovemaking a year ago, she'd grabbed her suitcase and headed for the airport. At the time, he'd been furious. But when his hormones dropped to a normal level and his brain had taken over…he'd realized she was right.

The sex was amazing, but it didn't change the facts. She was on one side of a fence and he was on the other.

Still, being with her again was harder than he'd thought it would be. They hadn't seen each other in more than a year. He'd expected that wild rush of need to have disappeared. Yet here it was again, as strong as ever and just as demanding.

"No, don't." She spoke up, and Jake let the memories slide into the past, where he planned to keep them. Gina shook her head and looked at him. "I mean, let the sheriff take care of this. You shouldn't be getting noticed anyway, right?"

"Worried about me?" He slid magically back into the ironic, lazy attitude he wore like a shield.

"No." She laughed shortly. "Worrying about you would be pointless in your line of work, wouldn't it? It's just—" Gina reached up to scoop one hand through her hair and hissed in a breath. She winced and drew her hand down to look at it. Blood seeped from a tiny wound in the center of her palm. "Glass," she whispered. "Must have glass in my hair."

A fresh bolt of anger blasted through him, but Jake battled it down. He couldn't give in to the rage. He had to be calm. Cool.

Dispassionate.

Right.

"What about your eyes? They okay?"

She nodded, still staring down at the stain of blood, dripping along her life line like some crazed omen of impending doom.

A cold, tight fist squeezed his heart. He didn't like seeing that wounded look on Gina. It didn't suit her. She was a fighter. As he had plenty of reason to know. And by God, he would make sure she was all right. Nobody was going to hurt her. Because to get to her, they would have to get past him first. And that wasn't going to happen.

"Come on," he said, his voice gruff and harsher than he'd planned as he took her arm. "I'll take you home. You can wash out the glass."

"I have to work."

"It'll keep."

She lifted her head to meet his gaze, and Jake's heart stumbled. Damn it. Since he'd known her, he'd seen Gina furious, he'd heard her laughter and watched her eyes go hazy with passion.

But he'd never seen her hurt.

He didn't like it.

"You were right," she muttered, with a backward glance at the twisted blinds. "I wish you weren't, but you were right."

He forced a smile he didn't feel. "Ordinarily, I'd enjoy hearing those words from you. Hell, I'd probably make you repeat 'em into a tape recorder. But right now I've got other things on my mind."

She nodded. "Like who did it, for instance?"

"For instance." He would find out who was behind that rock. And when he did... "Let's go."

Back at her house, Gina stripped in her bedroom and carefully put her dark blue power suit into a white trash bag. At least that way, no little specks of stray glass would escape before she had the chance to take it to the cleaners.

None of this felt real. Even while she wore her dark, forest-green robe and stuck her head under the kitchen faucet, she felt as though it wasn't really happening. For goodness sake, she'd never been the target of...well, anyone, before. Warm water rushed over her head, pushing through her hair, rinsing away whatever tiny pieces of glass were still lodged in her thick curls. She stared at the water swirling around the drain in the white porcelain sink and was almost hypnotized by the movement.

Mind racing, she found her imagination cooking up images of what might have been. Had she been sitting at her desk, as usual, that rock would surely have hit her. And even if it had missed, she would have been covered by a shower of glass rather than the few stray specks she was worried about now.

"Let me check," Jake said from his position alongside her. His fingers moved through her hair, scraping across her scalp, and tingles of awareness lit up and burst inside her like soap bubbles full of dynamite. His touch was gentle as he carefully searched through her hair for anything she might have missed.

She closed her eyes and let herself remember another time when he'd threaded his hands through her hair. That hot, muggy night in Chicago. When they'd lain together in his bed, at his apartment. The French doors were open to the night, despite the heat. A small table, scattered with the remains of the very romantic dinner he'd had delivered, sat forgotten beneath the stars while Jake entered her body and showed her a whole new set of stars.

The hum of traffic from six stories below had sounded almost like a sigh. Wind off Lake Michigan breezed through the room, but couldn't fight the heat clinging to the city—or the sexual heat shimmering between the two of them. Tangled together on the sheets, they moved in an intimate dance. Breath mingling, bodies pressed together, they discovered something neither of them had counted on. Something neither of them could claim.

And still, a year later, Gina was haunted by the feel of his hands on her skin, by the memory of his body sliding into hers.

"Looks good," he said brusquely, and moved away, snatching up a towel from the lemon-yellow tile counter. "You can go take a shower now. Shouldn't be any more glass for you to step on."

Breath caught in her chest, Gina reached up and turned off the faucet. She didn't move for a second or two. She couldn't. Just remembering being with Jake had turned her knees to jelly, and she needed a little time to let them harden up again.

Oh, this was sad.

"Hello?" he asked. "You awake?"

Wide-awake and still lost in dreams. Perfect. She shifted a sideways look at him, snatched the towel out of his hands and said, "Yes. I'm awake. And wet. And mad and—" Oh man, women did *not* admit to being horny. Especially to the *one* man they couldn't have.

Okay, best to just shut up, she told herself. If she kept talking, she might say something they'd both end up regretting.

"Good." Jake moved farther away from her, as if maybe he was fighting his own memory demons. "I'm gonna make a couple calls while you're in the shower, then I'll take you back to the office."

Instinctively, she argued, "I don't need—"

He erupted. "If you try to tell me you don't need a bodyguard, I'll—"

"What?" she demanded, twisting the towel onto the top of her head. Jamming both hands on her hips, she squared off and faced him. What had been between them was over. In the past. What she was fighting for here was her future.

"Damn it, Gina," he snapped, "you could have been killed today."

"Killed?" She remembered the rock, the glass, but still shook her head. "Hardly killed. Hurt, perhaps. But—"

"And that's okay with you?"

"Of course not, but I'm not going to change the

way I live just because I'm afraid someone somewhere might try to hurt me."

"You are for right now," he said, and his tone left
no room for arguments.

"Hiding out's not going to help, Jake. Heck, having my own personal bodyguard didn't help. You
can't protect me from everything." She saw him
wince at her words and almost wished she could take
them back. Instead, she tried to keep a nice, even,
logical tone in her voice as she said, "I can be as
careful as I like, but if someone wants at me badly
enough, they'll find a way."

"Not while I'm here," he assured her.

She could have pointed out that he was in the room
when the rock came crashing in, but he knew that
already. And it wasn't setting well with him. His body
was tight as a wire, his eyes narrowed. Fury pumped
through him at such a rate she could almost *see* him
vibrating with the urge to go out and pummel something.

Her own personal white knight. Any other time that
might have set off a warm little glow inside her. Hey,
women's liberation aside, there was something to be
said for a tall, dark, manly man sweeping in to defeat
your enemies.

Unfortunately, *her* white knight was being paid by
her daddy to keep her safe. There was nothing personal here. Just one man trying to keep his boss
happy. She ignored the tiny pang of disappointment
that echoed within her. After all, it would be foolish

to wish things were different, when they so clearly weren't.

Jake was still her father's trusted associate—and she was still Jake's natural enemy...the law. She'd run from Chicago a year ago because of her rampaging feelings for him. She couldn't give in to them *now*.

Inhaling sharply, she said, "It's your job to keep me safe, right?"

"Right."

"Fine. Then you do your job so I can do mine." She turned and left the kitchen, headed for the bathroom and a nice, hot shower. Or maybe, she told herself grimly, a *cold* one.

No sign of anything.

No witnesses.

No suspects.

A teenager with long blond hair and a dark tan went by on a skateboard, shouted, "Heads up!" and zipped past Jake with no more than an inch to spare.

He glared at the kid's back and muttered, "I hate California." Back home in Chicago he would have had access to sources. People he could go to. Talk to. *Bribe*.

Here he had the beach and the sun and stupid teenagers and no damn clue what to do about some rock-throwing sociopath.

Jake stood outside City Hall and looked back over his shoulder at the adobe-style building with the

Spanish tile roof. Looked like a damn postcard, with its palm trees out front and bright splotches of yellow flowers in neat cement containers.

"Where's the graffiti?" he muttered. "Where's the soot? Where's the *character?*"

"Yeah," a deep, gravelly voice from behind him agreed. "Too much sun ain't good for a man."

Hell.

Jake's chin hit his chest. His day had just gone from miserable to downright crap. Turning around slowly, he looked down into the shifty blue eyes of a man he'd thought to be safely back in Joliet, Illinois.

The *prison* in Joliet.

"Freddie," Jake muttered, suddenly feeling very tired, "what the hell are you doing here?"

Freddie "The Lip" Baldini winced as if hurt. He lifted his less than pristine hanky to wipe his oversize bottom lip, then looked first to one side then the other, making sure no one was listening.

No one was.

"Hey," the short, skinny man in the bad suit whined, "I got a right to look for the treasure, just like everybody else."

The treasure. Naturally.

"There's no treasure," Jake told him.

Freddie snorted. "'Course you're gonna say that. *You* want it. That's why Dom sent you here. I ain't stupid."

The little guy was usually harmless. He was a small fish in Chicago and looked even more out of place in

sunny California than Jake felt. Sighing, he asked,
"When'd you get out of Joliet?"

Freddie shrugged. "Couple weeks ago." He
laughed and his whole body seemed to shiver, clothes
rippling on his bony frame like sheets on a clothes-
line. "Good timing, huh?"

"Great." Disgusted, Jake scraped one hand across
his face. Just as he was thinking that things couldn't
get worse, something dawned on him. Hell, he wasn't
in Chicago, but a hell of a lot of Chicago was *here*.
Might as well use them. Dropping one arm around
the shorter man's narrow shoulders, Jake said, "Freddie, how'd you like to do Dom—and me—a favor?"

Chapter 5

The next few days passed in a blur.

At work, Gina did her job with Jake at her heels. Like a trained guard dog, he was constantly by her side. He practically snarled when anyone came too close. Which made life at City Hall a little more difficult than usual.

Jake intercepted her messages, stood between her and the public defender, and every day frisked the kid making her mocha delivery. She'd even heard that the employees at Java World were now drawing straws, with the loser being the one forced to deliver her coffee.

Terry and Jake had reached what seemed like an armed truce. Each of them keeping a wary eye on the other, they worked in tag-team protection. One of them was near Gina at all times, which left her nerves more frazzled than they would have been if she were on her own.

Gina felt as though she was trapped in a lockbox. She couldn't take two steps without a shadow. Every minute of every day was monitored.

And every minute of every night was haunted.

Propping her elbows on her desktop, Gina buried her head in her hands. Her hair fell down on either side of her face like a thick, dark brown curtain.

"Maybe all of this would be easier to take if I was getting some sleep." But how could she be expected to sleep soundly when she knew that Jake was in her guest room? Separated from her by nothing more than a little cheap drywall and a few two-by-fours?

Every night she lay awake in her bed, listening to him move restlessly around his room. And every night she had to force herself to keep from getting up and going to him. It was ridiculous. Nothing could come of them being together. She knew that. She'd *always* known. She'd already run from the implications once. And nothing had changed. He was the only man she'd ever known who could turn her body into a carnival—and the one man she shouldn't... couldn't have.

The office door opened and she pushed her hair out of her face and looked up.

"Ms. Palermo?" Terry said, "did you forget? You're due in court in fifteen minutes."

Guilt slammed home with a sharp, quick jab. Her

job, the one she'd worked so hard to get, the one that was so important to her, was definitely suffering.

Gina sucked in a breath and pushed herself to her feet. "I did forget. God, where's my mind?"

Terry tipped her head backward, toward the waiting room where Jake no doubt sat, like the guardian at the gates of hell. "Oh," the older woman said with a knowing half smile on her face, "I think I know where your mind has been. And can't say as I blame you." She sighed and added in a strained whisper, "Heck, if I was twenty years younger, I'd be thinking the same thing."

Gina blinked at her. "Terry!"

"Hey, I'm old. I'm not dead." She stepped farther into the office and let her voice drop to a whisper that wouldn't carry to the outer office. "Although, I've got to say, I don't really trust him. He's a little too—"

"I know," Gina said, thinking of the word she'd heard from so many people lately. "Scary."

"Well, I was going to go for *intense,* but scary works."

"I know he seems that way, but—"

"If it walks like a duck…" Terry stopped abruptly and held up one hand before shaking her head. "None of my business, Ms. Palermo. Just be careful."

What Terry wasn't saying came through loud and clear. She and a few others knew about Gina's father. Most people never made the connection. After all, Palermo was just a name. And no one expected the upright, hardworking D.A. to actually be related to a mob boss. Those who did know, thankfully, were able to separate her from her infamous father.

Well, until lately. Now Gina saw curiosity in the sheriff's eyes. And the worry in Terry's eyes, and she appreciated it. She really did. But worry wouldn't help anything. She just had to find a way to get through her life unscathed until the idiots searching for a treasure that didn't exist gave up and went home—or back under their rocks.

Until then... Gina flipped open her briefcase and quickly looked through the manila envelopes tucked inside. There weren't many. Which meant a short court day. Good.

As tired as she was, falling asleep at the prosecutor's table was a real possibility.

Snapping her briefcase closed again, she picked it up, smiled at Terry and headed to the outer office. Her gaze went directly to Jake, sitting in the spot he'd claimed as his own.

Gina paused in the doorway just to look at him. She had the distinct feeling that long after he left, long after Jake went home to Chicago, she would still be seeing him in that chair. It was as if he'd imprinted in her life and on the beige walls, making them somehow more vibrant. Even the air in the office felt different with him in it. More *alive* somehow.

And that thought only proved just how tired she was.

Jake unfolded his long, lean body from the too-small chair, and for the first time, Gina realized he had to be *very* uncomfortable out here on "Gina

Watch.'' Those office chairs were designed to keep visitors moving right along, and no one would be happy in one for more than half an hour.

Yet Jake had been there for hours at a time, every day.

If nothing else, the man had staying power.

"Court," she said unnecessarily. After all, he probably knew her schedule as well as—or better than—she did now.

He nodded, stepped toward the door and walked through it, into the hall. No silly pretense at chivalry here, Gina thought. He wouldn't hold the door open for her to precede him. However, he *was* willing to go into the hall and get shot first.

Keeping his gaze fixed on the hallway, he stretched out one hand behind him and crooked a finger. Gina's fingers tightened around the handle of her briefcase. She sucked in a deep breath and reminded herself that no one had been killed at City Hall in years. With any luck at all, that record would hold.

Squaring her shoulders, she walked through the door, made a sharp left turn and headed down the glistening, linoleum pathway toward courtroom 6. Her heels tapped out a rhythm that sounded skittish, anxious. She listened to the solid thump of Jake's footsteps right behind her and realized that she *enjoyed* knowing he was near. It was comforting, somehow.

Yet knowing that, admitting that, if only to herself, was absolutely *terrifying*.

"Wait up." Jake's voice seemed to echo in the

long corridor, bouncing off the walls, ricocheting off the gleaming floor, to finally settle along her spine like a warm touch. She stopped and half turned, looking at him.

He stepped past her, pushed the heavy swinging door open, then entered the courtroom, as usual, a step ahead of her. Attila the Hun meets Lancelot. A pushy white knight. Every girl's dream.

Shaking her head, Gina walked into the courtroom and immediately checked out the surroundings. She was getting almost as good as Jake at this.

There were only a handful of cases to wrap up today. So there were very few people in the pewlike bleachers. A couple of older teenagers, one with very long blond hair that looked nearly white against his tan, sat in the back row and didn't even move as she passed. Mrs. Ryan and Mr. Hobson, two elderly people who whiled away their retirement boredom by trial watching, were right up front, in their usual seats, behind and to the right of the prosecutor's table. Off on the left, one middle-aged woman sat alone, crying softly into a tissue that looked more than used up. Ahead, just beyond the two-foot-tall wooden barricade, were the judge's bench, a uniformed, armed bailiff, the P.D. assigned to today's docket, and her own table, empty but for a pitcher of water and a spotty-but-clean glass.

Normal.

She let out a breath she hadn't realized she'd been holding, and swiveled her head to look up at Jake. "Short day today."

"Glad to hear it," he muttered with a half smile. "Courtrooms give me hives."

"I'll bet," she said, smiling in turn, then moved toward her spot in the day's proceedings.

The bailiff called the court to order, and when the judge walked in, they got down to business.

Jake enjoyed watching Gina in her element. Damn it, he just plain enjoyed watching her. As that thought danced through his brain, he flinched and gave an uncomfortable glance around. Damn good thing there were no mind readers in here.

Scowling to himself, he tried to concentrate on listening to Gina's arguments to the judge. Unfortunately, his gaze *and* his concentration kept slipping to the silky columns of her legs. He was in bad shape here. If things didn't get straightened out soon, this would get ugly.

Still, he pulled his brain away from thoughts of Gina naked to thoughts of Fate. How was it that a mob boss's daughter became a D.A.? Was that just her destiny? Had she been wired to stand for the very law that Dom had spent a lifetime circumventing? Or was it because her mother had whisked her out of Chicago and away from her father's influence at such a young age?

Would Gina have chosen this career path if she'd grown up around Dom? Or would she be a part of the "family" Jake had joined two years ago?

These were questions made to drive a man nuts, he thought. And besides, was it really important? She'd made her choice. The situation was what it was. No point in wondering about what-ifs.

The proceedings went along in a mind-staggeringly boring rut. He said, she said, then the judge said and that was that.

One after the other, cases were brought up, then shut down, and only the faces of the accused changed. Jake watched them all. His sharp-eyed, experienced gaze studied the faces, the eyes, the body language, looking for something…anything…that might help him figure out if any one of them was behind that rock aimed at Gina.

It wasn't so much the rock bothering him as it was the aim. For God's sake, if whoever had done this could get a rock that close to her head, how far off would the bullet sent down the same path have come?

The room held more than a couple familiar faces from Chicago. Frankie "Two Toes" Chiara, retired muscle, was sentenced to five days community service for running his metal detector in backyards—with no one's permission. Genevieve Hall, Frankie's fiancée for the last twenty-five years, got two weeks for trying to steal historical reference books from the library. And Tony "Tipsy" Baretti got assigned a week of cleaning the highway for tearing apart Jimmy Miletti's hotel room, looking for the key to the ever elusive "treasure."

This really was turning into a circus.

Disgusted with the whole damn thing, Jake forgot about watching the too-stupid-to-breathe-on-their-own defendants and turned his attention back to Gina.

While she talked, her voice drifting through Jake's awareness like a cool wind, a strange sensation settled over him.

He was being watched.

He felt the power of a steady stare as surely as if someone's index finger were jabbed into the center of his back. The small hairs at the back of his neck stood straight up.

He'd listened to his instincts for years. And those instincts had saved his butt more times than he liked to think about.

Slowly, carefully, he shifted position just enough to turn his head to the left. From the corner of his eye, he checked out the few people sitting behind him.

Bad situation from the get-go.

He didn't like having people behind him. Maybe it came from life in the Palermo family, but he felt a hell of a lot safer when people were where he could keep an eye on them. But here he opted to sit directly behind Gina, to protect her, and that left *way* too many seats at his back.

He picked out the two teenagers and dismissed them. Lounging on the bench, they looked as bored as only teenagers could get. The middle-aged woman hadn't moved—or changed her used-up tissue for a new one.

But the swinging door into the courtroom was swinging. Did that mean someone new had been here and then left? Or did it mean someone here had slapped that door to throw him off? He shifted his gaze to drift across the *harmless* bunch he'd already considered and dismissed.

And he wondered.

"Mr. Tortelli," the judge was saying.

At the familiar name, Jake turned his attention back to the court. The young thug at the defendant's table was a long way from Chicago. Rico Tortelli had the face of an angel and the personality of a rattlesnake. Both had served him well so far in his career of choice. Hell, *everybody* was looking for that stupid treasure.

"We don't approve of bar fights in Sunrise Beach," the judge said. "You will make restitution to the club owner and in addition pay a one thousand dollar fine."

Chump change to a guy like Tortelli. The creep grinned, then had the nerve to wink at Gina as the jailer walked him out of the courtroom.

"Well, Ms. Palermo," the gray-haired judge said, with a relieved and tired sigh. "That's it for today's festivities. See you tomorrow, same time, same place?"

"Yes, Your Honor." Everyone in the room stood as the end of session was announced and the black-robed judge slipped off the bench and into his chambers.

Jake stood up, too, pushing his sense of disquiet to the back of his mind for the moment. Leaning across the barrier separating them, he asked, "So how many treasure hunters today, total?"

She swung her hair back out of her face to look at

him. "Five, not counting Mr. Barfight." She shut her briefcase, then curled her fingers through the handle and picked it up. Walking through the gate, she fell into step beside him, ignoring the people still in the room. "This is getting more and more nuts every day, Jake."

"Tell me about it." He checked the hall before allowing her out into it, then ushered her through the door. "That last guy, Tortelli?"

"Another knee breaker?"

"Oh, yeah." He shot her a look and shrugged. "The guy loves his work, too. Surprising it was only a bar fight."

"See?" she said, waving one hand to keep time with her own words. "This is what I mean. My nice little town is all of a sudden looking like Vegas in the fifties."

Jake came to a stop just outside the door to Gina's office and looked down at her. "I know. But I spoke to your father yesterday. He said he's trying to spread the word about the no-treasure thing. So maybe…"

"Maybe." She held the briefcase in front of her body like some sort of leather armor. "The truth is we have no idea how to convince these idiots that there's no reason to stay here."

Anger flickered in her eyes, and he couldn't blame her. Frustrating as hell to come up against something you didn't have a clue how to fight. *Damn it, Jimmy, did you know what you were starting with all that talk about a treasure?*

"I have to get back to work," Gina said, snapping Jake out of his thoughts.

"Don't," he said suddenly, giving in to an impulse he should have tried to bury.

"What?"

"Don't go back to work." Remembering the eerie sensation he'd experienced in the courtroom, he thought maybe it was a good idea to get the hell outta Dodge for a while. Whoever had been watching him and Gina might still be around. Why give them another opportunity to reach her? "Take the rest of the day off."

"Right." She choked off a laugh. "And do what?"

Think, Falcone. Think.

Then it hit him.

He shrugged and shoved both hands into his pockets. "Show me around. Try to convince me that 'paradise' is better than Chicago."

"That wouldn't be tough," she said, smiling with one corner of her mouth.

Damn, a smile did amazing things for her eyes. Just to see it again, he teased her. "Hey, I love Chicago. Convincing me that the Land of Constant Sun is a better bet could take some doing."

She was waffling. He could see it in her eyes. He gave her another verbal nudge.

"How anyone could prefer this—" he waved a hand toward the closed glass doors and the sunlit world yonder "—over Comiskey Park, Vienna hot dogs and Lake Michigan is beyond me."

She took a long, deep breath and blew it out. Jake

was pretty sure he could actually *see* tension sliding out of her body. Then she smiled and all he could see was the liquid warmth in her eyes.

"Okay, Falcone," she said, holding out her right hand. "You're on. In one glorious afternoon, I will prove to you that Southern California is the best place to live in the world."

He took her hand in his and shook it. "Deal. But you're gonna have to show me some amazing things to pull this off."

"No problem," she said, and grinned.

Hell.

Nothing was going to be more amazing than that smile.

as she pulled up the zipper. Too many snacks lately. Nervous eating. In times of stress, she always reached first for chocolate. But much more reaching and she'd be out shopping for a new wardrobe. She walked to her dresser and opened a drawer. Pulling out a dark green, cropped tank top, she slipped into it, then stood back and stared at herself in the mirror.

Her hair was a wild tangle around her head and she thought for a second about subduing it in a ponytail. Then she realized she and Jake would have the same hairstyle, so she opted for loose, messy curls. High spots of color dotted her cheeks and her eyes looked way too excited.

"Chill out, Gina," she warned her reflection sternly. "Jake is not Prince Charming and you're certainly not Cinderella." She scowled at the woman in the mirror and hoped she was getting through. But she sincerely doubted it.

Prince Charming or not, Jake Falcone was a formidable presence.

"Hey, you ready?" Jake knocked on her bedroom door. "Or are you one of those women who take forever to—"

Gina walked over and threw the door open, cutting him off in midsentence. Oh, he looked even better in jeans than he did in black slacks and dress shirts.

His jeans were worn, broken in, and looked great on him. His open-collared, black—naturally—pullover shirt displayed a small V of his chest, and Gina swallowed hard. She remembered all too well just how tan his chest was. How broad and well muscled.

How his skin felt beneath her hands. She sucked in another breath. His black hair, pulled into the familiar ponytail, made her hands itch to free it. She wanted to see him as she remembered him from that night a year ago. Wild.

Dangerous.

Naked.

"You look…" He paused and ran his eyes up and down with a slow deliberation that set off both warning bells in the back of her mind and wildfires in her bloodstream. When his gaze locked with hers again, he smiled, and Gina's stomach did a quick somersault. Oh, boy.

He breached her defenses.

Leaning one shoulder against the doorjamb, he said, "Well, let's just say jeans never looked so good."

"Thanks."

"You're welcome."

She inhaled sharply and blew it out again. "You look good out of uniform."

Frown lines erupted between his arched brows. "Uniform?"

"The black slacks, white shirt, blue tie, black jacket."

He gave her a quirked smile again. "You don't approve?"

She threw his words back at him. "Let's just say jeans never looked so good."

His eyes went dark and hot for one split second,

but it was enough to melt her knees again. Gina locked them just to keep upright.

A second or two ticked past as they stood in the doorway to her room, neither of them willing to move along just yet.

"Are we actually having a civil conversation?" she asked.

"Amazing, huh?" he agreed, then reached out and took her hand. Gina got zapped instantly by something that felt a lot stronger than static electricity. He felt it, too; she saw it in his eyes. But he didn't mention it, just folded his fingers around hers and challenged, "Okay, California Girl, show me your world."

I'll show you mine if you'll show me yours, she thought.

Oh God.

They covered a lot of territory.

They hit a sand castle competition in Seal Beach, and a surfing contest in Huntington Beach. They dropped by the Sawdust Festival in Laguna Beach, the tide pools at Dana Point and then finished up by going for Mexican food at a restaurant that advertised the world's biggest margaritas.

They sat on the restaurant's patio, perched high on a cliff overlooking Dana Point Harbor. Below them, waves crashed relentlessly against the jetty built to stop the more powerful sea surges, then, subdued, slapped against the cliff face, sending spray high into the air. The steady swell and retreat of the ocean sounded like a heartbeat and thundered, low and powerful, beneath the voices coming from the tables surrounding them.

A spectacular sunset dazzled the sky, streaking the few clouds with shades of deep purple and blood-red. The surface of the ocean sparkled in the dying light and reflected the colors shimmering above.

"So," Gina asked, lifting her margarita glass in both hands, "what do you say? Southern California growing on you?"

"Good beaches," he conceded.

She took a long sip of her drink, then swiped her upper lip with her tongue. He followed the motion and felt his whole damn body straighten up and shout *Hallelujah.*

"But there's so much more," she said, and set her drink down so she could tick off points on her fingers. "Things we didn't have time to get to. There's Disneyland—"

"Please, no," he said.

She laughed. "Knott's Berry Farm. They have an Independence Hall there, too. And there are museums and the tar pits and Hollywood and Beverly Hills and there's Exposition Park, the observatory, the Center for the Performing Arts and the Hollywood Bowl with their summer concert series and—"

"How many more points are you going to hit?" he interrupted quickly when she took a breath.

"I could go on all night," she said, and tipped her head to one side. The ends of her hair brushed her shoulder, and Jake wanted to reach out and do the same. Instead, he rubbed his fingertips together, remembering just how silky her skin felt to the touch.

"You don't have to," he said, chuckling at the competitive gleam in her eyes. "I surrender. Southern California isn't *exactly* the hellhole I thought it was."

"Ooh," she said, shaking her head. "Big concession."

"Hey, that's a lot, coming from me."

"What is it about Chicago that makes it so great?" she countered with her own challenge.

"What's not to like? Big city, lots going on. *Our* river actually has water in it," he teased, and leaned back in his chair, keeping his gaze fixed on her face. "We've got the Cubbies and the White Sox...."

"Angels and Dodgers," she countered.

"We've got the St. Patrick's Day parade."

"Year-round golf."

"Snow."

"*No* snow."

"Vienna sausage vendors."

"Churros."

He laughed now. "Cinnamon-sugar Mexican pastries do *not* compete with Vienna sausages."

"Who'd want to?" She leaned forward, pursed her lips around the straw in her glass and took another long sip of the frothy drink. "Nope. Admit it, Falcone, I did it. I showed you just how great this place is and you can't deny it."

Jake just stared at her. It had been a long afternoon, but he wished it wasn't ending. She'd done her best, showing him all the beauty that could be found on the California coast. But if he was to admit the truth, nothing she'd shown him could compare to Gina herself.

And the fact that California had *her* was enough to let her state win their little contest. But he couldn't exactly say that, now could he? Instead, he took a sip of his beer and smiled.

"Okay, I admit it. You convinced me."

"Yes!" She lifted both hands high in the air in a victory salute, and the action raised the hem of her already-cut-off tank top. Jake's mouth went dry and his fingers tightened around the cold, wet bottle of beer.

"Oh, look..."

She spoke and he had to force himself to come up out of the delicious daydream looking at her exposed skin had thrown him into. "Hmm? What?"

She shook her head, lifted her left hand and pointed. "Look."

He did. The setting sun was almost down. Half of it already swallowed by the vast ocean, the upper half glowed like a ball of fire and sent ribbons of golden light streaming across the surface of the water. The scattered clouds overhead were banners of brilliant color against the darkening sky.

"Isn't it gorgeous?" she whispered, as if they were in a church.

Jake shifted his gaze to her face. "Absolutely."

She turned her head to catch him staring at her, and her eyes went soft and smoky. A soft wind tousled her hair and carried the scent of her perfume to him.

Jake drew it deep inside and held it, in the same corner of his heart where he kept the memory of their one night together.

Back at her house, Gina was glad he stayed outside to make some calls on his cell phone. Ever since she'd caught him staring at her in that I'm-starving-and-you're-a-steak kind of way, her nerves had been jumbled into knots. She needed a few minutes—okay, hours, but she'd settle for minutes—alone. She'd always loved her little house on the rocks. She'd considered it cozy.

Now, with Jake in it, it just felt *small.*

Too small.

The flowered curtains draped across the windows closed the room in. The narrow hallway and tiny spaces gave her no room to maneuver. Nowhere to go to keep a safe distance between her and the man who was slowly, inexorably, destroying her defenses.

They shared the one bathroom, and seeing his shaving gear on the sink and his soap and shampoo in the shower felt *intimate.* They were living in each other's pockets here, and it couldn't go on forever without exploding in their faces. Something had to happen. Something had to give.

And she had the distinct feeling it was going to be *her.*

"Get a grip, Gina," she said, leaning toward the bathroom mirror as her fingers grabbed the cold edge of the porcelain sink. She met her own gaze and kept her voice stern. "If you give in, there's nothing but trouble headed your way. And if you don't..." She paused, bit her bottom lip and inhaled deeply. Unfortunately, that one deep breath brought her the scent of Jake's shampoo from its uncapped bottle. Quickly, she grabbed it and twisted the lid on fiercely. "If you don't give in, you'll always regret it and always wonder what 'round two' might have been like...." She slammed the shampoo bottle onto the edge of the tub and looked into the mirror again. "*But* you won't have your heart ripped out of your chest, so that would be a good thing."

Right. Good. She could do this. She just wouldn't think about how much fun the day had been. About how he'd tried to keep a solemn, disinterested expression on his face when they'd explored the tide pools. About how he'd laughed when that rogue wave slapped into them, giving them both an icy shower. About how he'd held her chair for her at the restaurant and how he'd looked at her and how his eyes had flashed in the last lights of the dying sun.

"Oh, yeah. This is gonna work," she muttered, and stomped down the short hall to her bedroom. She hit the light switch on the way in, and instantly the bedside lamps flicked on, casting soft, golden haloes onto the wide bed and the hardwood floor. The sheer white curtains fluttered like peppy ghosts in the breeze slipping beneath the open window. Gina stripped off her tank top, unhooked her bra and tossed it onto the bed—then froze.

Open window?

She didn't leave the window open.

She *never* left the windows open.

She shot a quick, startled look at the fluttering curtains, and as they lifted again in their wind-tossed dance, she saw a face. Watching her.

Gina screamed and called for help. "Jake!"

He heard her scream all the way at the back of the house. Jake hung up on his boss and took off at a dead run. Slamming through the kitchen, he kept going, through the hall, bypassing the living room and heading straight for her bedroom, following her shouts.

"Jake!"

"I'm here!"

She was wearing her jeans and clutching her tank top in front of her naked breasts. With her free hand, she pointed to the window. "Someone was there. Watching me. Looking in, and when I screamed, I think he took off. Or she. I think it was a he, but I don't know, it—"

As she babbled, Jake shoved the curtains aside, pushed open the window farther and climbed out. Nothing. Nobody. There wasn't enough light to look for footprints, but then he'd probably obliterated them already, anyway. He moved away from the window, farther into the shadows, and strained to listen. From far off, he heard the whine of an engine and recognized it as a motorcycle.

Whoever the Peeping Tom had been, he was gone now.

Damn it.

"Did you see anything?" Gina materialized beside

him. She'd climbed out the window right behind him, and he'd been so focused on finding the intruder he hadn't even noticed. She stood close enough to him that he felt her body trembling. He glanced at her. She'd pulled her tank top back on without bothering with the bra, and her nipples stood at attention beneath the thin fabric.

"No," he said, draping one arm around her shoulders to pull her even closer to him. "Whoever it was, he's gone."

She sighed and turned her face into his chest, leaning on him, drawing strength from him. Silently, he wrapped both arms around her and just held on for a long minute, letting her heart—and *his*—regain a normal beat. God, hearing her scream had taken about ten years off his life.

And in his line of work, he couldn't afford that.

But she was all right. Shaken, but okay. If she'd been hurt... Oh, he didn't want to think about that. Not while he was holding her, soft and warm and pliant.

He had to wrap this up.

Things were getting too weird.

Maybe it was time to talk to the sheriff. But not right now. Right now, Jake wanted to make sure Gina was okay.

"Come on," he said, and started for the back door. "Let's get you inside."

She nodded and walked with him, still holding on for all she was worth. When they stepped into the kitchen, Jake paused long enough to turn and lock the door behind them. Then he guided her not to her bedroom, but into the living room, where she could sit and relax and try to forget about—

"Shit."

"Oh my God." Gina straightened up and away from him, then took a step farther into the room. They hadn't seen it before. She'd gone straight to the bathroom, and when he'd come in, all he'd been able to think of was getting to her.

So the living room was a complete surprise.

Her Peeping Tom had been busy.

The sofa cushions had been knifed and searched, and cotton batting lay across the floor as if some freak snowstorm had blown through the room. Tables were upended and the bookcases emptied. Books and magazines were scattered across the braided throw rugs. Even the TV had been tipped over onto its side and the table it usually rested on was listing on three legs. Knickknacks were shattered, pictures ripped from their frames and tossed aside and her matching overstuffed chairs had been sliced open and searched.

"Who would…?" she murmured, walking into the room and accidentally kicking a picture frame. "*Why* would…?"

"That damn treasure," Jake growled, from low in his throat. "They're still looking for Jimmy's treasure and they think *you've* got it."

"Me?" Gina turned in a slow circle, mouth open, eyes wide as she surveyed the destruction of her little nest.

"Yeah." He bit the word off. "We probably surprised the guy. That was your peeper."

"He did all this," she said, spreading her arms wide to encompass what was left of her house, "then stopped to spy on me?"

"Looks that way," Jake stated tightly, and silently congratulated himself on being able to form words despite the red haze of fury nearly choking him. "Probably considered you stripping a bonus."

"Why is everything so nuts?" she demanded, and kicked a throw pillow across the room. "Why is my nice, neat little world imploding?"

"You won't be hurt," he said. "I won't let you be hurt. So don't be scared."

"I'm not scared," she said, then sucked in a gulp of air and admitted, "Okay, I *was*. When I saw that creep staring at me, I was plenty scared. But I knew you were here. I knew you'd come."

"Unfortunately, not fast enough, though." He hadn't caught the guy and that really fried him.

"But if you hadn't been here…"

He looked into her eyes and caught a quick glimmer of lingering fear. He didn't like it. "I was."

She nodded, swallowed hard and nodded again. "I…" She shook her head, tried to speak, then stopped. A second or two later, she tried again. "I don't even know what to do, what to say. Except I want that guy caught."

"He will be."

"Damn right he will be." Stalking around the room, she looked at the devastation and muttered darkly under her breath. Then, louder, she said, "They even broke this!" Grabbing up a twisted metal frame and shaking loose the jagged glass shards, she held up a photo of herself and her father.

"It can be fixed," Jake said, keeping his voice a lot calmer than he felt at the moment. He hated seeing her like this, but angry was better than scared.

"It shouldn't have to be fixed." She slammed it back onto the bookshelf where it belonged. It teetered and fell over, and that motion only seemed to feed the fury inside her. She'd known this could happen, of course. She just hadn't believed it actually would. "They wrecked my house!"

"Yeah, they did."

"Looking for a treasure that doesn't exist."

"That's true, too."

"Quit agreeing with me."

"Yes, ma'am."

She stopped, inhaled sharply, deeply, and blew the air out in such a rush the curls near her forehead ruffled. "You're trying to calm me down, aren't you?"

It was better than feeding her fury with his own. Damn it, just standing here doing nothing was killing him. He wanted someone to pummel. Someone to pay. But she was more important. "Is it working?"

She looked at him. Really looked at him, then nodded abruptly. "Yes, damn it."

"Good. Getting mad is okay, keeping calm is essential."

"Essential." She nodded again and took a step toward him, stepping on a torn book and staggering slightly as it gave beneath her foot. She scowled down at it, then seemed to forget about it as she looked at him. "You know what else is essential here, Jake?"

He shook his head, staring into her eyes, drawn by the storms swirling in those whiskey-colored depths.

"I think you are," she said, and his body went on alert.

"Gina…"

"In the last week, my godfather's died, my town's been invaded and now my home has been trashed." She threw her hands wide and let them slap against her thighs when they fell. "I've been calm. I've been logical. And you know what? It hasn't helped."

"You think this will?"

"I think we need to find out."

"Dom'll kill me."

"If you talk about my father at this particular moment in time, *I'll* kill you."

"It's complicated, Gina," he said, trying to talk her down, despite the fact that his instincts were screaming at him to grab her, no questions asked.

"It doesn't have to be. For tonight, it doesn't have to be."

Chapter 7

"It's crazy," he said, and moved closer, one slow step at a time. "All of it. Us. The treasure hunters. The peeper. It's all crazy."

"Uh-huh," Gina said, her gaze locked with his. She couldn't look away. Couldn't break the connection humming between them.

It had always been there, just below the surface. She'd tried to ignore it. Tried to overcome it. But the feelings he created in her just wouldn't be denied. Not now. Not tonight. Not after walking into her home and finding it ransacked. Not after realizing a stranger had been there. Walking through the cozy little rooms. Going through her things. Destroying her memories, her personal belongings...her illusion of safety. If she'd been home alone… If she'd walked in on whoever had done this…

A bubble of fear swelled inside her, but she fought against it. She didn't want to be afraid. She wanted to be *grateful*. Grateful to be alive. And here.

With Jake.

"I shouldn't be anywhere near you," he murmured, and closed the remaining distance between them, his gaze moving over her features hungrily.

Gina breathed deeply, evenly, trying to steady her erratic heartbeat. But he was so close. So solid. So strong. So…*Jake*.

"Nothing's changed since last year," he said, his voice strangled as if he was fighting the urge to grab her. "We're still—"

"I know." And she also knew that pain would be waiting for her, sometime soon. The pain of losing Jake again. Of watching him walk out of her life. He didn't want to change and she couldn't. Their "twains" would never meet. But that didn't alter one undeniable fact.

She loved him.

God help her, she loved a gangster.

Fate really did have a sense of humor.

He was so close now she felt the heat of his body reaching out to her. And the cold she'd carried inside for more than a year melted in the warmth of his eyes.

"We'll probably regret this," he murmured.

"But we'd regret it more if we didn't."

"Oh, yeah." He reached for her and she moved

into his embrace and the decision was made. No more thinking. No more questions. Just need and the demand to satisfy it.

She tipped her head back and looked into his eyes as he slowly lowered his head to come within a kiss of her lips. He stopped just short of the magic and whispered, "You sure?"

"Yes." This was the one thing in her life she was suddenly, absolutely, certain of. "You?"

"I've been sure since the minute I saw you again." Then he kissed her and Gina's mind short-circuited. His mouth came down on hers and claimed her as thoroughly as he had a year ago.

Every touch was familiar, yet new, exciting. Her blood raced and her heartbeat quickened until she thought she might strangle with it. She couldn't draw in a breath and she so didn't care. His hands stroked her body, fiercely, possessively, up and down her spine, exploring her, discovering her all over again.

She groaned, went up on her toes, wrapped her arms around his neck and held on tightly—preparing for the roller-coaster ride she knew was coming.

He parted her lips with his tongue and swept into her warmth. She welcomed him with a sigh and gave herself up to the amazing sensations that only Jake could create. She met his caress with every stroke. He took and she offered more. She sighed and his arms tightened around her, like bands of steel, as if he was never going to let her go again.

He groaned, tore his mouth from hers and looked

down at her as he struggled for air. His gaze moved over her face, his fingers dug into her waist and she pushed herself even closer to him, wanting, needing, to feel. To be devoured. To become a part of him.

Without a word, he bent and picked her up, cradling her close to his chest as he turned and headed for her bedroom. Her hands stroked his chest, and even through the fabric of his shirt, she felt his heart pounding, crashing against his chest.

In seconds, he was laying her down on the bed. Then he stepped back, slammed the window closed and drew the curtains.

Gina came up on one elbow. "Thought you said the peeper was gone."

He crossed the floor, hit the light switch and plunged the room into darkness. Moonlight seeped through the curtains, shadowing the room with a soft, pale light that allowed Gina to just make him out as he came close.

"Yeah, well," Jake said as he tore his clothes off, "this is just in case he comes back looking for the late show."

When he joined her on the bed, Gina opened her arms to him. Her hands scraped across his face, defining every feature, then slipped to the back of his neck. With a flick of her wrist, she pulled the band off his ponytail, freeing his thick, black hair so she could spear her fingers through the mass. Then she looked up at him and whispered, "I don't want to think about that. Here, now, it's just us. Nothing else exists.''

''Just us,'' he agreed, and skimmed his palms up beneath her tank top. She shifted, helping him, and he pulled it off of her, tossing it over his shoulder to land on the floor beside the bed.

He filled his palms with her, his thumbs and forefingers tweaking her nipples, pulling at them gently until she moved and shifted beneath him as if she were lying on a bed of coals, looking for comfort. ''Jake…''

''Yeah, baby,'' he whispered, then dipped his head to taste first one nipple, then the other. He nibbled at her and suckled until she rocked on the bed, moaning his name, clutching at his hair, his shoulders. Pulling him closer, tighter, more firmly against her, she arched into his mouth, wanting him, *needing* him, to take more of her. To give more. To race with her into the crashing release she knew was waiting for them.

Eager, hungry for him, Gina reached for the waistband of her jeans, but Jake's hands stopped her. ''No,'' he said softly, his breath dusting her skin, ''let me.''

He undid the button, slid the zipper down, then slowly, agonizingly slowly, began to pull her jeans over her hips and down her legs. His mouth trailed after the fabric, moving along her skin like damp heat. Gina writhed beneath him, moving with his touch, his kiss, feeling the buildup of fire within until it nearly consumed her. Her need reached out to him and fed the flames devouring him.

Jake had wanted to go slowly. To savor being with her again. But need flashed through him and he surrendered to it. It had been too long since he'd been with her. Too long since he'd felt this...*alive*. Quickening his pace, he pulled her jeans off and paused only a moment to smile at her red lace panties before disposing of them, too. He let his palms slide up her legs, remembering the feel of her, memorizing this moment and storing it along with the images of that night a year ago.

Because he knew, even as he loved her, even as he stroked her body, that he couldn't claim her heart. He knew that night would end, tomorrow would come— and the wall that stood between them would still be there.

But for this one moment, for this small slice of time, she was his. And he closed his mind to the rest, determined only to enjoy what they had. To make the most of a few stolen moments out of a lifetime. What they could make together, here, in the moonlit shadows. She sighed and moved under his touch. His heart slammed against his ribs, his blood thundered in his ears.

"Jake," she sighed, and lifted both arms in open invitation. He went to her, covering her body with his, needing to be closer, to feel her heart beating in time with his. He relished the brush of her nipples against his chest. Her skin felt like warm silk and he couldn't seem to touch enough of her. A soft groan slid from her throat and dropped right into his soul.

She moved into him, opening for him in a silent demand, a silent plea. Jake bent his head and kissed her, his hair falling forward to shutter them both. He claimed her as he had a year before, restaking his territory. Mouths mating, breaths mingling, they came together in a silent dance where words weren't needed. Where only passion reigned and reason had no place.

He moved against her, increasing the already unbearable tension shimmering between them. She shifted beneath him, spreading her legs, welcoming him. And he couldn't prolong the waiting. He had to have her. Had to be in her. He entered her with a sigh and then stayed perfectly still, savoring the connection between them. The wonder of being a part of her.

"Jake," she said, her voice coming on an exhaled breath. "Jake, please…"

He stared down into her eyes and felt himself falling into the warm amber of her gaze. Then he moved within her and she responded, shifting with him, moving in that rhythm that only lovers share.

The world held its breath.

Time stopped.

And in the shadow-filled bedroom, two hearts came together as two bodies tumbled over the edge of oblivion.

* * *

An hour later, the sheriff and his deputy were grimly assessing the living room. While the deputy sprinkled fingerprinting powder on the shattered remnants of Gina's home, Sheriff Reynolds faced Jake.

"You should have called me in right away."

The cop looked furious and Jake couldn't blame him. Maybe they should have called right away. It would've made more sense than what had actually happened. But given a choice now, he wouldn't change a thing.

"Gina was upset," Jake said, his gaze shooting to her, following the deputy as he worked. They'd had to call the cops in, whether he liked it or not. Gina hadn't been anxious to have more people poking around her house, but she was willing to do whatever she had to do to catch whoever was responsible for the mess. And as a D.A., she knew the police had to be notified and a report filed.

Hell, Jake would be making his own report, later.

"I don't know what you're up to, Falcone," the sheriff was saying, and Jake swung his attention back to the man watching him. "But I don't trust you."

One black eyebrow lifted. "Is that right?"

"Yeah." Reynolds shifted, so that his back was to Gina. "See, ever since you guys hit town, I've had nothing but headaches."

"You guys?" Jake repeated, stiffening slightly.

Reynolds noted his reaction and shook his head. "Don't play dumb with me. I'm not impressed."

A flicker of admiration spurted to life inside Jake, though he hated to admit it. Local cops were usually more of a pain than anything else. But Reynolds hadn't backed down from the bunch infiltrating his city. He'd locked them up and hauled them to court. And now he was facing Jake and looking as though he'd like nothing better than to lock *him* up, as well.

"It's one thing for me to spend most of my time tossing idiots in jail for trotting through backyards with metal detectors," he said. "It's another when my friends start getting hurt."

Jake shifted, planting his feet in a fighting stance, and unconsciously folded his arms across his chest. "What's your point?"

"My point is..." he glanced over his shoulder toward Gina, still heckling his deputy "...whatever else you're up to, I figure you care about Gina. Want to see she's safe."

"Yeah? So?"

"So, you make some calls. You talk to whoever it is you know who can get these guys the hell outta my town."

Jake scowled at the other man and swallowed back his own frustration. Jake was worried about Gina. Reynolds was worried about a whole town. "I'm working on it," he said.

"Work harder."

The police had no leads on her break-in.

So Gina spent the next two days studying the faces

of everyone around her. Even the familiar ones. The ones belonging to people she'd trusted. People she'd known for years.

And she didn't like it.

Her sense of safety was gone.

Okay, maybe it *had* been an illusion. After all, she wasn't an idiot. She dealt every day with criminals. She knew all too well that the world wasn't an easy place. That anyone and everyone was a potential victim.

But she'd never really believed it could happen to her.

Break-ins were things you read about in the newspaper. Or on court dockets.

They weren't something you actually had to *live* with.

Just being alone in her own house was a little creepy now. She half expected someone to jump out at her from behind a door every time she walked down a hallway. Her nerves were stretched to the breaking point, and having Jake there was only making it worse.

On the one hand, she'd hate like hell to be alone right now, jumping at every creak and moan her old house made in the night. On the other hand...Jake being there created a whole different sort of tension.

Two days ago, their relationship had shifted. They'd gone from wary adversaries to wary lovers. And though they hadn't made love again since that night, that didn't change the fact that each of them wanted it to happen. But neither was willing to take another step down a road that was already filled with land mines.

There were no happy endings here.

There were no easy answers.

Just confusion.

And the promise of pain.

Gina went through her days in a sort of haze. She did her job, but took no joy, no satisfaction in it anymore. Her mind was too wrapped up with her heart, and her heart was just too bruised.

The phone on her desk rang and she pushed her thoughts aside, picked up a pen and answered it. "Gina Palermo."

"Hi, honey."

She dropped the pen and leaned back in her chair, relieved that this wasn't a work call, demanding concentration. "Hello, Dad."

"How are things out there?"

Gina smiled, despite the turmoil in her brain. "You say 'out there' like I'm on Mars."

"Might as well be," he said cheerfully.

Gina's hand tightened on the receiver. "You sound just like Jake. Nowhere but Chicago, huh?"

He ignored that question and asked one of his own. "How is Jake? He taking good care of you?"

Instantly, images filled her mind. Jake looming over her. Jake bending to kiss her as his body slid into hers. Jake showing her the stars all over again.

"Uh..." She sat up straight to grab up that pen

again. "Sure, Jake's doing...*fine.*" Oh yeah, that sounded convincing.

"Is there something you're not telling me?"

Plenty. "No, Dad. I'm just busy, is all. Everything is all right. Well, except for the treasure hunters."

"It'll blow over."

"I hope so. Our jail isn't very big, you know."

He chuckled and Gina smiled.

"Trust me, honey," her father said. "Nothing stays the same forever."

Jake kept his gaze locked on the doorway to Gina's office, twenty feet away. He didn't like being even this far from her, but some things couldn't be helped. "What did you find out?" he asked.

Freddie "The Lip" Baldini wheezed out a laugh that ended in a harsh, broken cough. The little guy shook all over for a minute, his too baggy suit shivering and shaking along with him as if it had a life of its own. When he was finished, he wiped his ever present hanky across his thick bottom lip and smiled.

"I been asking around, just like you told me."

"Yeah?" Jake swallowed his impatience. For Freddie, telling the story was half the fun. And if he was interrupted, he'd only start all over again.

The skinny man lifted one finger and pointed to his very generous nose. "I got ways of finding things out. I know how to listen."

If he could actually hear with that nose, Jake

thought, the man would be picking up conversations in Philadelphia.

"So I asked around. To see what's what."

"And...?" Jake flashed another quick glance at Gina's office. No one had gone near the front of the building. He and Freddie were standing in the skimpy shade of a tall, thin-as-Freddie palm tree, and the longer they stood there, the longer someone had to get to Gina.

"It ain't one of our guys," Freddie said, and two bushy gray eyebrows lifted as he waited for Jake's response. He didn't wait long.

"Our guys? You mean no one from Chicago was behind that break-in?"

"Nope." Freddie wiped his lip again, gave a cautious look around at the empty front yard of the courthouse, and shivered a little at being so close to a house of justice. Then he looked back up at Jake. "Nor the rock, neither."

Okay, now Jake was confused. He had figured the rock thrower and the peeper were the same person— and he'd have been willing to bet that that person was here for Jimmy's treasure.

Sure, Gina might have made enemies. But come on. Half the mob had descended on Sunrise Beach. What better suspects could a man ask for?

"You sure?" he demanded, giving Freddie a look that told him he'd better have his facts straight.

The little guy just tapped the side of his nose. "Da

nose, knows," he said solemnly, then chuckled again, sending himself into another paroxysm of coughing.

Jake waited until Freddie was himself again, then he asked one question. "Do you have a name?"

Freddie gave him a sly smile. "Do you have my money?"

Chapter 8

Freddie's information had really paid off.

Jake pushed the hulking blond skateboarder down onto a wooden bench set against the beige wall in the police station. "Stay," he ordered, then winced and touched one finger to his split lip.

Damn kid.

He slanted a glance at the blonde, slouched on the bench and muttering to himself. *Not really a kid, either,* Jake thought. He looked a lot younger than twenty-two. Must be the dark tan and all the skateboarding.

Or maybe it was the breaking and entering that kept him young. Little bastard.

"Can I help you?" A short, brunette deputy came

out from behind her desk and walked toward him, keeping an interested eye on the blonde.

"Yeah," Jake said. "I want to see Sheriff Reynolds."

"He's—"

"Reynolds!" Jake glanced around the small, but efficient looking station. A bulletin board took up one wall, with community announcements tacked to it, along with sheafs of brightly colored bits of paper and the occasional Wanted poster. Four wide desks cluttered the main room and three closed doors led off to God knew where. Probably jail cells. But at the moment, Jake didn't care. All he was interested in was getting this wrapped up.

A split second later a door flew open, the sheriff stepped through one of the doors—apparently his office—and demanded, "What in the hell is—" He broke off as he caught sight of Jake and the blond hulk sitting close by.

Waving his deputy off, Reynolds approached, shot another look at the tall, muscular kid and took in Jake's blackening eye and split lip. "What happened to—"

"He wants to make a confession," Jake said, then turned a dark eye on the blond guy who'd sucker punched him when confronted about the rock-throwing incident. Damn punk had gotten in two or three good hits before Jake had hit him back. Maybe he shouldn't have waited so long, he thought, running his tongue over a tooth that felt a little loose.

"What happened to him?" the sheriff asked.

"He fell," Jake said, keeping a straight face even as he shot the blonde a look daring him to challenge the statement.

"On you?" Reynolds asked, smothering a chuckle.

"Funny." Hell, it was embarrassing to admit that a younger man had taken him by surprise. But Jake's split lip and sore eye spoke for themselves.

Shaking his head, the sheriff glanced at the younger man. "So I'm guessing this is Jeff Doyle."

Surprised again, Jake stared at him. "How'd you know?"

"It's my job to know," Reynolds said. Then he added, "Fingerprints from Gina's place. The guy's not exactly a rocket scientist. His prints were all over everything." He slanted a look at the sullen blonde. "Isn't that right, Jeff?"

"So you already—"

"One of my guys went to his house this morning, but he was gone. Guess he was off...*falling.*"

"Yeah. Guess so." Jake scraped a hand across the back of his neck. Good to know that at least there was evidence to hold the guy, more than just his confession. Jake probably should have figured the police would follow up and do their job. But he hadn't been able to wait. With Freddie's information, Jake had headed right out to Doyle's place.

The guy had hassled Gina.

Endangered her.

Made her afraid.

And Jake had wanted a shot at him.

He glowered at the tall blond skateboarder. The

same guy who'd nearly run Jake over his first day in town…the same one who'd sat in the back of a courtroom observing Gina…the one who'd tossed a rock through her window.

Reynolds crooked a finger for his deputy. Without taking his gaze off the blonde, he said, "Read him his rights, Kathy, then throw him in a cell."

The tiny brunette came forward, grabbed the guy's upper arm and dragged him to his feet. "Come on, Slick," she said with a smile. "I've got a nice room all picked out for you."

"But why?" Gina paced the length of her office, stopped at the windows overlooking the front of the building, then turned around to face Jake again. "Why would this Jeff Doyle want to hurt me?"

Jake perched on the edge of her desk, watching her pace. He licked his split lip, touched it gingerly, then shrugged. "Apparently you put his baby brother in jail."

"What?" *Doyle,* she thought. *Doyle.* But it was no use. She'd been working hard at her job for three years. She'd sent her fair share of criminals to jail and it would have been impossible to remember them all. Reaching up, she pushed her hair back from her face and admitted, "I don't even know the name."

"No reason why you should," he said. "Doyle's brother stole a car, you gave him six months and Jeff thought that was a little harsh. So he pitched a rock."

"Lovely," she muttered, grateful that good ol' Jeff hadn't had a gun.

"Then he started hearing about the treasure," Jake continued, "and he heard bar talk, indicating that *you* were the key to the whole thing. So our friend Mr. Doyle decided that he could look for clues and mess with you at the same time."

"Unbelievable," she murmured.

"Oh yeah," Jake added, "he says he hadn't planned on peeping in the window, but when he saw you undress he thought, what the hell, you're still hot."

Gina did a slow burn for a long minute. The gangsters in town had thrown everything into chaos. They'd spawned the talk of the treasure and were ultimately responsible for this idiot ransacking her house. He wouldn't have bothered if he hadn't been trying to find the stupid treasure!

"Did you hit him?"

"Once."

"Thanks."

"No problem," Jake said, leaving his lip alone long enough to reach up to check the swelling around his eye.

"Are you all right?" Gina looked at him and felt her heart squeeze in her chest. He'd gone out and found the bad guy. He'd defended her honor and come away from the field of battle beaten but not bowed. And she loved him for it. She loved him for lots of reasons, none of which changed the facts still standing between them.

"Yeah, I'm fine."

"I'm glad...." she said, walking toward him, her heels tapping on the wooden floor.

He quirked a smile at her. "But..."

God, he knew her so well, she thought. Why was this all so hard? Why couldn't it have been easier? Why did he have to be working for her father and living the kind of life she hated so much?

Gina inhaled sharply. *"But..."* She had to say it. Had to say what had been nibbling at the back of her mind all morning. Ever since talking to her father. "This whole situation is your fault."

"Huh? *My* fault?" He stood up and looked down at her. "How do you get that?"

"The treasure, Jake. This is all about the treasure. Without it—" she threw her hands high "—that Doyle character would have been satisfied with pitching a rock through my window."

"Oh, and that's no big deal."

"Of course it's a big deal, but it's not... You know what I mean."

"I don't think I do," he said tightly.

Gina wasn't even sure where the words were coming from, but it was as if a dam had burst inside her and nothing could stop the onrushing tide. "Don't you get it? Even the crummiest criminal, the smallest, the pettiest of them are somehow magnified when they get around you guys."

Impatiently, he pushed one hand along the side of his head. "That's the second time today someone's said 'you guys' to me in that tone of voice."

"Do you think I like it?" she demanded, planting

both hands on his chest and shoving. He didn't budge. It was like pushing a mountain. A tall, dark, gorgeous, glowering mountain. "Do you think I like knowing that you're part of my father's world?"

"Gina..." He covered her hands with his, but she jerked back as if burned.

"God, I wish you were a...a plumber," she said, muttering wildly as she reached up to scrape both hands along her scalp, trying to keep her brain from exploding. "A computer nerd. *Anything* but what you are."

Frustration shimmered across his features, dazzled his eyes and left him defeated. "There's nothing I can do about that."

"You *could*," she countered, snapping him a look that flashed with her inner fury. "The real truth is, you *won't*."

He ground his teeth together, and Gina could almost hear them being crushed into powder. Well, she knew how he felt. Ever since he'd come back into her life, she'd felt it. The sense of impending doom. The beginning of the end. God, she sounded like a soap opera, even to herself. But the simple truth was she was in love, with someone she couldn't have. And the pain of that knowledge chewed at her relentlessly.

"Gina, if I could—"

"Don't even say it," she snapped, interrupting him before he could hold a carrot out in front of her, only to yank it away at the last minute. "Don't say you would quit if you could. Because we both know that's a lie.'' She wrapped her arms around her middle and held on tight.

Pulling in a long, shaky breath, she said, ''It just can't work, Jake. I'm a rule follower.'' She swallowed hard, then continued, ''If there's no traffic on Pacific Coast Highway at three in the morning—if I'm in the only car for miles around—I'll still sit there and wait for the light to turn green.''

He smiled, but his eyes gleamed with a sorrow she felt right down to her bones. She spoke again quickly, trying to say it all and be done with it. If she'd said these things to him last year, instead of just running away, then maybe she wouldn't be so miserable again *now*.

''I don't even *litter,* Jake. I never lie about my taxes and I keep off the grass when I'm supposed to.'' She took a step away from him and felt a chill she hadn't known in a year creep over her again. ''I could never live the kind of life most people only see in old gangster movies.''

Jake reached for her, but she stepped back, though the movement cost her. His hands dropped to his sides. ''I can't give you what you want, Gina. You know that. You knew it going in.''

''I know,'' she whispered. ''I *know,* but it doesn't make the pain go away.''

''If it's any consolation,'' he nearly growled, ''this is killing me.''

She lifted her gaze to his, and Jake was staggered by the sheen of tears glistening in her eyes. ''You know what, Jake? It doesn't help at all.''

* * *

Back at her house, Jake kept his distance. The place had been straightened up, but the sense of warmth in the house was gone. At least for *him*.

He hadn't meant to hurt her again. Hell, to hurt himself again. But there was nothing he could do about it. If he could change things, he would. For *her* sake.

Standing on the rocks behind the house, he stared out at the dark ocean and told himself that it was his job to keep her safe. Not happy. And if she hated him now, then maybe that was a good thing.

Waves crashed at his feet, thundering against the rock, sending spray into the swirl of wind pushing at him. Overhead, the moon pulsed in a black sky and even the stars looked a little dimmer.

A car engine thrummed above the roar of the sea, and Jake went on red alert instantly. Whipping around, he ignored the soft glow of lamplight streaming from the windows to lay across the ground in golden patches. Instead, he focused on the compact car pulling to a stop in Gina's driveway.

He drew his nine millimeter, and crouching low, ran across the gravel to come around the side of the house just as Gina stepped onto the front porch. Her hair twisted and flew in the wind. Barefoot, in a T-shirt and jeans, she looked impossibly young. Impossibly vulnerable. His heart clutched painfully in his chest.

"Get back," he ordered.

She didn't move.

Stubborn.

A tall, thin man with wire-frame glasses and a hairline that had receded to the back of his head stepped out of the car, clutching a small, brown package. He spotted Jake first and jerked back at the sight of the gun. "Hey—"

"Who are you?" Jake demanded, even as Gina stepped off the porch and walked toward them.

"Charles Simmons," the man said, his voice quavering, his gaze still fixed hypnotically on the pistol in Jake's hand. "I'm with Schuyler, Fitch and Hopkins, attorneys for James Miletti."

"Jimmy?" Gina said.

The man flicked a quick look at her, gulped loudly and nodded. "Yes. I, uh, have a package for a Ms. Gina Palermo."

"What kind of package?" Jake asked, and held out one arm to keep Gina back when she would have gone closer. His forearm brushed her chest and she stepped away from him. Her quick, instinctive movement stabbed at him, but he ignored the pain and concentrated on the nervous man in front of him.

"It's…excuse me, but could you point that somewhere else?" he asked.

"Nope."

"Jake…" Gina looked at him.

"Not till I know what he's got," Jake said, not even looking at her.

The man in question straightened up to his less than spectacular height, tugged at his tie as though he were strangling and said, "Ms. Palermo is the beneficiary of Mr. Miletti's will. I'm here to carry out his last request.''

He looked harmless, Jake thought. But then, so did a lot of psychos.

"It's all right, Jake," Gina said, and walked up to the man. "What is it?"

Simmons looked at her, but, not at all sure he was safe yet, kept darting glances at Jake. "I have no idea," he said. "This was left at our offices with instructions to deliver it to you within a month of Mr. Miletti's demise."

Gina took it, ran her fingers over the brown paper and said quietly, "Thank you for bringing it."

"Of course," the man said, backing away toward his car again. "Uh, there was also a small amount of money, a few stocks. I'm afraid he didn't leave much." He handed her a thick envelope. "It's all in here."

Gina looked at him and held the package and envelope tightly to her. "Thank you again."

"Yes. I, uh, of course. And now, good, uh, good night." He hopped into his car, fired up the engine and threw it into reverse. Stepping on the gas, he skidded at the end of the driveway and raced off into the night.

Jake tucked the gun back into its holster and stood looking down at Gina. "Think I scared him."

"You have that effect on some people."

"Are you gonna open that?"

"Yes," she said, and smoothed her hand across the package again before tearing away the tape at the edges and folding back the brown paper. A picture frame, it was upside down when she opened the package. When she turned it over, she inhaled sharply. It was an old photo, one of her and Jimmy, taken at her high school graduation.

She blinked back tears. "Oh, Jimmy…"

Jake dropped an arm around her shoulders and she didn't move away. She was just too grateful for the warmth of him.

"There's a note," Jake said, and pulled it from the paper it was taped to.

Still staring down at the photo of herself and her precious godfather, she said, "Read it."

Opening the note, Jake read it. Then read it again. He couldn't believe it. After everything that had gone on, it had come down to this. A chuckle started low inside him and slowly, inexorably built until it pushed free. Shaking his head, he just stared at Gina as she looked up at him with tear-filled eyes.

"What's so funny?" she demanded.

"This," he said, holding the note out to her. And in the soft glow of the porch light, she read the note aloud.

"'To Gina, my only treasure. Remember me, Love, Jimmy.' Treasure?" she repeated, shifting her gaze to the photo again.

"That's right, honey," Jake said, still laughing to himself. "*You're* Jimmy's treasure."

It didn't take long to get the word out.

And with no treasure to be found, the Chicago contingent packed up and left Sunrise Beach within forty-eight hours. With everything back to normal, and life settling back into its pleasant, if too-familiar rut, Gina was forced to accept the fact that Jake would be leaving.

"It's for the best," she told herself, though even she didn't believe that. She already ached for him. She would miss him the rest of her life. And all she could see of the future was a long succession of years stretching out ahead of her, one following the next, each as empty and lonely as the one before.

She stepped out onto the back porch and stared at Jake, standing out on the point of rocks. His cell phone to his ear, he was so involved with his conversation he hadn't even noticed her. She took the opportunity to burn his image into her brain. She wanted to always be able to remember him like this. Tall and strong, his black hair whipping in the wind.

Then he hung up and turned to face her. Too far away to read his expression, Gina braced herself for their goodbye. She just hoped this was the last time. Because she didn't think she'd survive it again.

As he approached, he shoved his cell phone into his jacket pocket and scrubbed one hand across his face.

"Just *go,* Jake," she said abruptly. "I can't take a long goodbye."

"How about a long hello?" he asked.

She blinked at him and shook her head. "What?"

He looked off to one side, then shifted his gaze

back to hers. "I was just on the phone with my boss and—"

"Dad wants you back in Chicago."

He smiled wryly. "No. I wasn't talking to your father. It was my real boss."

"I'm confused."

"Not surprising," he said, and stepped up onto the porch to stand directly in front of her. Reaching out, he ran his hands up and down her forearms, his thumbs stroking her skin just below the sleeves of her plain white blouse. "Look, I couldn't tell you this before. I wanted to, but I couldn't."

"Tell me what?" she asked, hardly daring to draw a breath.

"I'm not a gangster." He shook his head, sucked in a gulp of air and blew it out again. "I'm with the FBI."

"FBI?"

He grinned at her shock, but kept talking before it could wear off. "I've been working undercover with your father. Helping him to legitimize his business holdings." Jake shrugged. "Your old man wants to go straight. He wants to make you proud of him."

Proud? He wanted to…? Gina lifted both hands and rubbed her face briskly. It was just too much information. Too much to take in. "Dad's…"

"Getting out of the mob business," he finished for her. "He's got enough information stored away in a safe place to insure he stays 'healthy,' and within six months, he'll be totally legal."

"Legal. My father."

"Yeah. He's given us so much evidence, we'll be trying to make sense of it for years."

"You're FBI." She said it again, testing the sound of it.

"Yeah, I am. We're on the same side, Gina." His hands tightened on her arms. "We always have been."

"FBI."

He frowned at her. "Are you okay?"

She kicked him.

"Hey!" He let her go, bent down and grabbed his shin.

"You should have told me," she shouted as she shoved him out of her way and stormed down the steps. She didn't stop, just kept walking until she was out on the point, standing on the rocks with the waves crashing below.

Jake was just a step behind her. When he caught up, he grabbed her upper arm and swung her around to face him. "I *couldn't* tell you. I was undercover, remember?"

"You could have trusted me," she said, her voice snatched by the wind.

"I did. I *do*," he said, willing her to believe him. "But it wasn't my decision to make. I just now got the go-ahead from my superior."

"Why now?" she asked, trying to hear him over the pounding of her own heart. "Why was it all right *now?*"

Pulling her tightly to him, Jake threaded his fingers through her hair and tipped her head back until she was looking at him. "Because *now* is when I told him that I wouldn't let you get away again. *Now* is when I told him that the work at Dom's is nearly finished. They can send someone else in to wrap it up."

"But—"

Jake bent his head, kissed her into silence, then drew back long enough to say, "I want to marry you, Gina. I want to marry you badly enough to have requested a transfer to the L.A. office."

She grinned suddenly and felt her heart swell with the sweet sting of hope. Only a few minutes ago, she'd been wrapped in darkness, loneliness. Now everything had shifted again, and it was...*wonderful.* "You're willing to leave Chicago to be here with me?"

"For you, honey, you bet. On one condition."

"What's that?"

"Every summer, we go to Chicago for a Cubs' game—or two."

"That's it?" she asked, wrapping her arms around his waist and hanging on tight enough to keep him with her always.

"That's it," he said, lifting one hand to cup her face with gentle fingers. "I love you, Gina. Always have. Always will."

"Oh, Jake," she said softly, "I love you, too. So much."

"Then you'd better marry me fast." One corner of his mouth tilted into that quirky smile that tugged at the bottom of her heart. "Even though your father's going straight, that's one man I don't want mad at me.''

"Dad?'' Gina said, laughter filling her voice, her heart, her soul. "He's a sweetheart. *I'm* the one you have to worry about.''

"Trust me, baby. I do.''

Then he kissed her, and the wild, crashing surf sounded like a symphony.

CALLING AFTER MIDNIGHT

Linda Winstead Jones

With a special thanks to Steifon Passmore,
for his help, friendship and sense of humor.

Dear Reader,

There's something special about a man who dedicates himself to keeping a woman safe. In real life and in fiction, these are our heroes. Some heroes change the world, some touch one or two lives.

Eli Benedict is one of those heroes. Ronnie Gray is determined not to need a hero of her own, but when she finds herself in the middle of a mystery, she doesn't have much of a choice in the matter. As for Eli, what starts out as a job soon becomes much more.

Here's hoping you all have your own hero.

Happy reading!

Linda Winstead Jones

Chapter 1

Ronnie leaned close to the microphone and lowered her voice. Even though the entire radio audience could hear her, at the moment she was speaking only to the woman who'd called. "You're better off without him. I mean that, from the bottom of my own shriveled heart. It's better to live a thousand years alone that to let a man like that one back into your house. You deserve better."

It was well after midnight, and she was alone in the small radio station where she'd worked for the past year and a half. The booth was simple, easy for one person to manage. All the songs she played were programmed into the hard drive of the computer that sat before her. A touch of her fingertip, and the selected song began to play. To her right was a small window set high in the wall, giving her a limited view of the outdoors. From here she could look out to the tower, so she could periodically verify that the blinking light was functioning properly. To her left was another, much larger window. It offered her a view of a narrow, dimly lit hallway. She had her phone system, her computer, her microphone. In this room, it was just her and her audience.

"There's no romance allowed here," Ronnie said as she reached for the computer screen. "No sap, no crap."

Music began, playing to her audience and over the speakers that were placed throughout the station. "When God Fearin' Women Get the Blues" sounded throughout the room, down the hallway, into the offices.

She took a deep breath and leaned back in her swivel chair as the song played. In the beginning, this job at WPFT had been a temporary gig, something to pay the bills until she decided what she wanted to do next. But one night a caller had cried over the phone, and Ronnie had calmed the distraught woman and commiserated with her. She'd dug through the selections before her until she'd found something appropriate for a woman with a cheating, low-life boyfriend and a career had been made.

Ronnie Gray—Angel to her listeners—worked the overnight shift. From midnight to 5:00 a.m. she took calls from the brokenhearted and played music to suit the mood. There were no romantic ballads allowed on her show. Nothing peppy—ever. No songs of love and forever after. She worked for a station whose format was Hot AC, a combination of pop and adult contemporary, but during her show she played a little bit of everything. Rock, country, oldies…as long as there was no hint of sweet romance.

The station manager wanted to transfer her to the afternoon-drive shift, but she was fighting fiercely. He planned for her to make the move to a more popular time slot with a lot of promo. Television, billboards, the works. The very idea made Ronnie uneasy. What she liked best about this job was the anonymity. She wasn't going to be saddled with a stalker if she was anonymous. Invisible.

She'd been invisible since moving to Laurel, Georgia, and she liked it.

The phone rang again as the song came to an end, and Ronnie hit the button on her phone bank so the call would go out over the air. "This is Angel. Talk to me, baby."

Someone breathed once, hard. The hair on the back of Ronnie's neck stood up, in instinctive warning. She was about to disconnect, when a voice came across the phone lines. "It's me," a man said.

Her audience was primarily female, but she did get a few male callers. Men got their hearts broken, too. They just didn't like to share their pain the way women did. It took Ronnie a second, but she recognized the voice.

"Wayne, right?"

"Yes," he said, sounding pleased that she remembered his name from last night's call. "I just wanted to tell you, I took your advice."

"Good," Ronnie said enthusiastically. Wayne's girlfriend had been ignoring him, not answering his phone calls, basically acting as if he wasn't alive, according to him. "How'd she take it?"

"Not very well," Wayne said softly. "She cried."

That didn't sound like the woman Wayne had described last night, a girlfriend who was acting as if he'd ceased to exist. "Maybe she likes you a little more than you give her credit for."

"I don't think so," Wayne said hesitantly. "When I went to her place to pick her up, she didn't even want to come with me."

"Well, you're better off without her," Ronnie said. And the woman was probably better off without Wayne. He sounded a little creepy over the phone. "Good luck."

"Don't you want to know what she said when I dumped her?" he asked quickly.

"Sure," Ronnie answered as she went through the selections on her computer screen and pulled up the next song.

"She said, *'No. No. Please don't do this to me.'*" Wayne's voice remained flat, completely emotionless.

"Maybe you should give her a second chance," Ronnie said. "Sounds like she's sorry she treated you badly."

"She's very sorry," he said.

"Well, good luck to—"

"She screamed when I stabbed her the first time,"

Wayne interrupted, his voice not completely emotionless now, but excited. "When I stuck the knife in her chest the last time, she wasn't screaming anymore."

Ronnie froze, her heart thudded so hard that's all she could hear, and for a split second she saw Roger the way she had seen him last...dead on her front porch, covered with blood, those red roses resting in his lap.

"I killed her," Wayne continued, "just like you told me to."

Eli grumbled as he drove down the deserted street, fumbling with the search button on his radio and listening to the snippets of music go by. Country, rap, some god-awful noise he could not identify...was he really getting that old? Finally he found the station he was looking for.

A woman's husky voice drifted to him. She was responding to a listener, apparently, talking not about the earlier call that had Eli out at two in the morning, but about a cheating boyfriend. There was something about that voice that grabbed him; it was like he knew the woman in the radio, like she was an old friend or an old lover. That voice was undeniably sexy.

She probably had a mustache and seven kids.

He shouldn't be here. The police had dismissed the complaint saying the confession had been a prank. They'd written off the caller as a nutcase who wanted to make a splash on the radio, but the station manager was not convinced. He'd decided to call in someone private. Since Eli was on duty tonight, he was the one who'd taken the call. He'd been dragged out of bed when he hadn't been asleep an hour and a half. Mondays were tough enough without being wakened by the shrill ringing of a telephone right in the middle of a fairly decent dream.

Eli Benedict had once been a detective in the Major Crimes Division in a big city. Nashville. He'd left that job and come here to Laurel to start his own business with Dale, an old friend and another ex-cop, four years ago. The money was better, there were no political hassles, and since Eli had never been good at taking orders, he definitely liked being his own boss.

Still, this was degrading. Divorce cases were bad enough. They didn't always remind him of his own messy divorce, but now and then something hit home. Checking out some rich guy's new significant other wasn't exactly fun, either, but this… He *did not* hold hands with radio personalities who panicked over crank phone calls that came in the middle of the night.

That's what he was supposed to do, right? Hold her hand and tell her everything would be fine.

The woman on the radio laughed lightly in response to something her caller said, and that husky laugh was sexy as hell.

She probably had warts. Lots and lots of warts.

"This is Angel," that voice said. "Laurel's own Miss Lonely Hearts. And here's something special for my last caller. 'You Give Love a Bad Name.'"

Bon Jovi blasted over Eli's radio as he pulled his pickup truck into the station parking lot. One car, a gray sedan, was parked in a space near the front of the building and under a street lamp. Another had been pulled haphazardly to the station's main entrance. As Eli walked toward that door, it flew open and a small, obviously excited man poked his head out.

"Are you Benedict?"

Eli nodded, and the little man opened the door wide. "Thanks for coming so quick. Do you want to talk to Ronnie? Contact the phone company and see if they can tell us where the call came from? Just tell me what you need from me, and you've got it."

Already, the man was giving Eli a headache. Eli stepped into the dimly lit reception area, and the little man locked the door behind them.

"You're the station manager?" Eli asked calmly.

"That's me. Carl. Carl Gamble. We spoke on the phone." Carl belatedly offered his hand, and Eli shook it. "I was listening to the show when the call came in and I phoned the police. They sent someone to take a statement, but they didn't take me too seriously, you know?"

He could understand why the cops had dismissed Gamble's rantings. He was one of those extremely intense little guys who made a big deal out of everything. His eyes were too bright. His hands too jittery.

"Ms. Gray didn't make the call to the police?" Angel's real name was Ronnie Gray, according to the information Eli had collected during the initial call from Gamble.

Carl, who stood a good half foot shorter than Eli, shook his head. "No. She says it's just a prank, most likely. A sick prank, but still…'' He shrugged his bony shoulders. ''She's not worried, but I really don't like leaving her here alone, you know?''

The song that had been playing over the speakers in the front room ended, and Ronnie Gray, aka Angel, returned to the air to take another phone call. Man, her voice was working its way under Eli's skin, reminding him that it had been more than a year since he'd been involved in a semiserious relationship, which to him meant he'd seen the same woman more than three times. Worse, it had been more than three months since he'd had a woman in his bed. He'd finally come to the conclusion that women were just too damn much trouble. Too bad he couldn't seem to live without them.

Ronnie Gray's voice filled the room; filled the dimly lit hallway Carl led Eli into; filled Eli's head.

She was probably ninety years old.

Carl stopped before a wide uncovered window that looked into the studio where Ronnie Gray worked. All Eli could see of the woman at the console was the back of her head. Dark-red hair had been pulled up into a thick ponytail and fell down past her shoulders. She continued to talk to her listener, oblivious to her audience in the hallway.

Eli almost cursed aloud. Ronnie Gray wasn't ninety. And he'd bet his brand-new pickup truck that she didn't have warts or a mustache, either.

She touched the computer screen with a long, slender finger, and a new song drifted through the speakers overhead. ''Nobody Knows You When You're

Down and Out.'' Okay, she definitely had a theme going for herself, here. That done, she spun her chair around, coming to an abrupt stop when she saw Carl and Eli standing there. After a second's hesitation, she jumped from her chair and stalked to the door.

After she'd joined them in the hallway, she rolled her eyes and turned on Carl. ''I told you not to call the cops! First the uniforms and now this guy. I have better things to do than answer questions all night.''

''Ronnie, sweetheart…'' Carl began.

''It was a crank call.'' She turned her eyes to Eli.

Nope. No mustache. No visible warts. She was drop-dead gorgeous, in fact. And with a figure like this one…he doubted she had seven kids at home.

''What makes you think he's a cop?'' Carl asked in a high-pitched voice. ''He's not wearing a uniform. He could just be, like, my brother-in-law or something.''

''If it walks like a cop and talks like a cop, it's a cop,'' Ronnie Gray said with obvious disdain.

''He hasn't said a—''

Ronnie interrupted him. ''Look, I just have a couple of minutes before I'm back on the air. Carl overreacted. I'm sorry, but you've wasted a trip.'' She looked Eli up and down critically, taking in the rumpled suit and loosened tie. ''Go back to bed.''

It was exactly what he wanted to hear; the call was some pervert's idea of fun, nothing more. And the way Ronnie Gray stared him down—on the surface she didn't seem to be alarmed.

But her fingers trembled, and her eyes were restless. She wasn't as calm as she'd like him to believe.

"Ex-cop," he said as he looked her over. Jeans, T-shirt with the station logo and call letters, well-worn tennis shoes. Diamond studs in the ears. Classy. Smart. He knew all that in a couple of seconds.

"Then why are you here?" she snapped.

"I hired him," Carl said brightly. "I mean, the cops didn't take me seriously, but you never know. There's some wacko out there and I think we need someone to look into it for us."

Ronnie Gray rolled her eyes again.

"I'd like to hear the call for myself," Eli said, ignoring her dismissive reaction. "You do have a tape?"

"Of course there's a tape, but it's not necessary for you to listen to it. Carl can tell you exactly what the caller said."

"I'd like to hear the tape. I'd also like to ask you a few questions, if you don't mind." Even if she did mind, he wanted to get to the bottom of this as quickly as possible so he could put this nuisance call, and Ronnie Gray, well behind him. If it walked like trouble and talked like trouble, it was trouble.

Ronnie Gray tried to stare him down, but since he was a foot taller than she was and outweighed her by at least seventy-five pounds, probably more, she didn't have a chance of winning. He stared right back.

"I get off at five in the morning," she said. "You're welcome to come back then, I suppose."

"I'm not going anywhere," he said. "Mr. Gamble

here has hired me to keep an eye on you until this blows over.''

She huffed and glared at the station manager, who answered with a sheepish shrug.

"Great,'' she muttered. "Just great.''

Eli couldn't help but wonder, as she returned to her booth, why a woman who looked like Ronnie Gray was working the late-night shift at a small radio station, why she was a low-rent Miss Lonely Hearts... and why she was so adept at spotting cops.

Chapter 2

Cops—*ex-cops*—weren't supposed to have bedroom eyes. The broad shoulders and long legs she could live with. The morning stubble on Benedict's square chin did not affect her at all. The fact that he managed to look appealing in a rumpled suit wasn't really all that remarkable. The black hair, which was a tad too long to be conservative and slightly mussed, she could handle.

But Eli Benedict shouldn't have bedroom eyes. Hazel. Sleepy. When she looked directly into those eyes, determined to let him know that she was not impressed, she shuddered to her bones. It just wasn't right.

Ronnie and Benedict sat in Carl's office, listening to the tape of the disturbing call for the third time.

Did he think he was going to hear something new this go-round?

She'd managed to avoid Benedict for the past few hours, but he'd definitely been present. Pacing in the hallway, staring at her, listening to every word she said. Carl had left the P.I. here as her bodyguard, while he went home for a couple of hours. They refused to listen to her when she insisted that she did not need any man to baby-sit for her.

Benedict watched her as he listened to the recording of the call, those hazel eyes of his hooded and piercing. Finally, he turned off the tape recorder and leaned back in Carl's chair.

"If you're so sure this is a prank, why are you scared?"

"I'm not scared," Ronnie snapped.

"Bullshit," he growled. "If I said boo, you'd jump straight up out of that chair."

"I'm tired," she said tersely. "Yes, the phone call was disturbing, but that doesn't mean I'm frightened."

"You think it's a joke of some kind."

"Yes," she said softly.

"Why?"

Ronnie felt the fear she tried to hide wash through her, like a wave of icy water in her veins. She had an answer for that question, she did. She just wasn't sure she wanted Eli Benedict to know what that answer was.

"Why?" he asked again, more softly this time.

"If it's not a sick joke, then I'm responsible for a woman's murder," she whispered. Her fingers trembled, so she clasped them tightly in her lap. Not again, she could not go through this again. She would never forgive herself for her part in Roger's gruesome death. To be put through that hell again…

"Did you instruct him to kill her?"

"Of course not!" She looked up, straight into those annoyingly attractive eyes. "When he called Sunday night, I told him to…to…" The words caught in her throat. "To get rid of her." For a woman who made her living with her voice, she sounded awfully tentative. Weak. "I told him to dump her, that he'd be better off without her in his life."

"I think it's a prank, myself," Benedict said, sounding almost reassuring. "Murderers don't normally call in their crimes."

Ronnie took a deep, calming breath. "I know."

"He was trying to shake you, and your audience," he continued.

She nodded.

"Unless a body turns up, there's really nothing we can do. Wayne is probably not this guy's real name, and even if it is—" he shrugged those broad shoulders "—we can't get the police to visit everyone named Wayne in the city and ask if he's recently done away with an annoying girlfriend."

Ronnie was relieved that Benedict believed it was a crank call, that she wasn't responsible for yet another murder. "Anything else?"

He reached into an inside pocket of his jacket, drawing out a business card he slid across the table to her. "Nope. I'll follow you home, make sure you're settled before I leave. If you'd like, I can arrange for one of my associates to watch your home during the day—''

"No," she interrupted sharply. "That won't be necessary."

"Mr. Gamble has hired me to keep an eye on things here, while you're working. I'll be back tonight, but if you think of anything else before then, or if you decide you want someone to sit with you outside your work hours, you can reach me at one of these numbers."

She stood, took the card with Benedict's phone numbers from the desk and shoved it into the pocket of her jeans. Anxious to escape, she turned her back on Benedict and opened the office door. Carl was waiting in the hallway. Behind her, the recording of the call started to play again. She trembled deep as she closed the door, cutting off the sound of that chilling taped voice.

"This is incredible timing," Carl said. "We can switch your show to afternoons starting on Valentine's Day. That's just three and a half days, so I need to get busy as soon as I get your okay. This story is sure to hit the papers. It's, like, free publicity!"

Ronnie glared at her boss before stalking away. "No."

"There won't just be radio ads announcing the change," Carl said as he followed her down the hall. "We're talking television, billboards, the local newspaper. You'll be a star!"

"No!" Her heart climbed into her throat. She just wanted to go home, crawl into bed and pull the covers over her head. Would she dream? Would she dream about Roger and rivers of blood and a faceless Wayne?

"Ronnie!" Carl called as she opened the front door.

"Move me to another shift and I quit," she said, walking out on him and his offer. A quick glance over her shoulder revealed that Carl was no longer alone. Benedict stood behind him, and the P.I. was watching her with those bedroom eyes.

"It's a ratings ploy," Eli said as he kicked back in his chair. "If I had any doubts about that, they died when the station manager almost salivated over the potential publicity. He probably had the newspaper on the phone before I was out of the parking lot."

Dale Merrill, Eli's partner and friend, shook his head. Dale had that "happily married" look. He was a little bit too well fed, his brown hair was neatly trimmed, and on too many occasions his eyes were red from lack of sleep. He also had a very contented smile. "If it makes you feel any better, they're paying top dollar for you. Now that he's met you, Gamble wants you and no one else. Did you get any sleep at all last night?" he asked.

"A couple hours," Eli said. "About an hour before the call. A short nap after I followed Ms. Gray home." He'd had time for two or three hours of sleep after his 5:00 a.m. departure from the station, but he hadn't been able to rest long or well. Ronnie Gray had been drifting through his tired mind, unwanted and persistent. Her voice, that face.

"You should head home early," Dale said.

"I will."

He'd go home, get to bed early, and he'd sleep like a baby—until it was time to return to the station. Midnight.

"Do you think Miss Lonely Hearts is in on the scam?"

Eli shook his head. "I don't know. Maybe. Probably." Still, she *had* seemed adamantly opposed to a move to a more popular slot; she had openly rejected the station manager's suggested publicity. What was she doing? Holding out for more money?

"What's she like?" Dale asked. "I've heard her a few times, when I was up with one of the kids and there was nothing on television. She sounds hot."

"She is hot," Eli grumbled.

"Exactly how hot?"

"Don't worry. I don't plan to get burned." He'd been burned enough. The job he loved and the kind of women he liked didn't work well together. They always clashed.

Dale grinned. "Speaking of getting burned, Karen has someone she wants you to meet. Friday is Valentine's Day. What do you say we all get together Friday night and—"

Eli silenced his friend with a glare.

"It was just a suggestion."

"Wouldn't you prefer a nice quiet Valentine's Day with your wife?" Eli asked.

Dale shrugged. "Romance is dead in my house. Dead, I tell you. Four kids will do that to you." He wrinkled his forehead. "I think they instinctively know when I'm about to make my move. One of them always throws up or has a bad dream or gets a sudden urge to sleep with Mommy and Daddy.''

Eli grinned. If anything could take his mind off Ronnie Gray, it was Dale's talk about his kids.

"Julie said 'Dada' last night.''

"She did?''

"Yeah, but it was 'Dada no-no.' I was reaching for something and she slapped my hand.''

"What were you reaching for?''

"Mommy.''

Eli laughed as the phone rang. Dale offered to answer, since it had already been a long day for Eli, but he waved off the overture and answered. "Benedict.''

The nasally voice of a close friend who kept him informed of anything juicy and important that was going on at the police station said, "Hey, Eli. How's it hanging?''

"Troy,'' he said with a smile. "What's up?''

"A body,'' he whispered. "We don't have an ID yet, but they found a woman's body in Archer Park a couple of hours ago. It's definitely a homicide.''

Murder wasn't commonplace in Laurel. It happened, but not often. Coming on the heels of Ronnie's phone call…it couldn't be sheer coincidence.

"How was she killed?'' Eli asked.

"Knife, I think. I heard it was pretty nasty.''

A knife. Ronnie's caller had talked about how his victim had screamed when he stabbed her. It wasn't looking good. "Thanks,'' Eli said as he stood. "If you hear anything else, call me.''

"Sure thing. Hey, my sister's going to be in town

this weekend. She just got divorced and she's really bummed. Are you busy?''

He'd dated sisters and cousins of friends before; it never worked out. Dating in general didn't work well for him, especially not these days. At thirty-four he was too old to play games, and dating was one big game. Besides, he'd discovered that "really bummed" new divorcées were not looking for a good time. They were looking for a man—any man—to pummel.

"I've got to work. Sorry."

"Okay," Troy said, not sounding terribly disappointed. "I'll let you know when I hear anything definite about the body."

"Thanks." He grabbed his jacket from the back of his chair and motioned for Dale to join him.

He had no proof that this newly discovered body was connected to Ronnie Gray's midnight call, but he didn't believe in coincidence.

Ronnie leaned over the rest-room sink and stared into the mirror. She looked awful and felt even worse. Her face was pale, there were circles under her eyes. And those eyes were red from crying. She'd hidden here in the ladies' room at the station to do her crying, because she had refused to break down in front of Carl, the cops who had insisted on questioning her and Eli Benedict.

Maybe Benedict and the cops were wrong. Maybe the body that had been found today had absolutely nothing to do with the call she'd gotten last night.

She didn't believe that. If she did, maybe she could stop her heart from pounding so hard.

Sooner or later she would have to get out there and face Benedict again. Now that the detectives who had questioned her were gone, he wanted to talk to her alone. That's what he said. What he really wanted to do was grill her.

She'd been through this before, when the detectives in Atlanta had questioned her about Roger's death. She knew the cutting looks that came with those accusations. She knew what the hatred felt like.

She couldn't go through that again.

The detectives who had questioned her earlier had been so nice. Respectful. Professional. That could change in a heartbeat. They would turn on her like a pack of wolves.

She splashed cold water onto her face and took a deep breath. No matter what, she didn't want Benedict to see that she was frightened of him and his questions. She had done nothing wrong. She had no reason to tremble this way.

Benedict was waiting for her in the hallway, too close to the rest-room door. Again he wore a dark suit; at least this one didn't look as if he'd slept in it. It was a power thing, she imagined. Why else wear a suit to sit in the station all night? He was very proper, very businesslike. His tie was loosened, though, and his hair was less than perfect. It was the tie and the hair that made her relax a little. The flaws made him human.

Carl stood behind the larger man, all but cowering.

"Are you all right?" Benedict asked sharply.

"Of course I am." Ronnie took a deep breath. "But I think it might be best if I cancel the show

PHAEDRA AND OTHER PLAYS

Racine

Phaedra, which Voltaire called 'the masterpiece of the human mind', is the greatest of the plays of Jean Racine (1639–99). In this sombre tragedy of the guilty passion of Theseus's queen for her stepson Hippolytus, Racine again chose a pagan plot to express that amoral ruthlessness which shocked French conservatives. (*Iphigenia* had similarly been based on Agamemnon's terrible conflict over his daughter's sacrifice.) But he was already swinging back to religion, and *Athaliah*, his final play, was built on an Old Testament story.

This new translation by John Cairncross renders the original French into modern English blank verse.

THE ROPE AND OTHER PLAYS

Plautus

The plays of Plautus (*c.*254–184 B.C.) are the earliest complete works of Latin literature we possess. Plautus adapted for the amusement of Roman audiences the Greek New Comedy of the fourth century. His wit is clever and satirical and his entertaining portrayal of slaves firmly set the style for the 'low' characters of Elizabethan comedy, of Molière, and many others. In this new translation E. F. Watling presents, in a form suitable for the modern stage, *The Ghost* (*Mostellaria*), *The Rope* (*Rudens*), possibly the best of the plays, *A Three-Dollar Day* (*Trinummus*), and *Amphitryo,* a cheerful story involving the gods.

THE JUGURTHINE WAR
THE CONSPIRACY OF CATILINE

Sallust

Sallust (86–*c*.35 B.C.), who held various public offices in Rome and later a governorship in Africa, supported the political group known as the *populares*. He was a friend of Caesar and an opponent of Cicero. His history of the war against Jugurtha, King of Numidia, and his account of Catiline's conspiracy in 63 B.C. are his only complete works to survive: they were written in the years after Caesar's assassination.

These narratives are more noteworthy for literary style than strict accuracy, and S. A. Handford's new translation fully preserves the dramatic and vivid qualities of the original Latin.

THE BARBER OF SEVILLE
THE MARRIAGE OF FIGARO

Beaumarchais

Beaumarchais (1732–99) was a man of immense wit and feeling and it is our loss that his two great plays are only known to us through Rossini and Mozart. It was Beaumarchais who brought fun back into the theatre and broke the convention of formality which had grown up since Molière. His dialogue was colloquial and his people real in eighteenth-century Paris. The humour, liveliness, and vigour depend on an interplay of character which was quite new to his audiences.

The Beaumarchais vivacity comes over well in this new translation by John Wood, who has also translated two volumes of Molière plays for Penguins.

ADOLPHE

Constant

In *Adolphe* Benjamin Constant (1767–1830), for many years the companion of Madame de Staël, puts down on paper an analysis of passion, recognized but unfelt, that remains unsurpassed in literature. A young man experiments with the love of an older woman: tiring of the passion he creates but cannot answer, he leaves her and she dies. Written in 1816 *Adolphe* remains a unique psychological romance.

This modern translation has been made by L. W. Tancock, who also translated *Germinal* and *Manon Lescaut* for the Penguin Classics.

THE PENGUIN CLASSICS

The Most Recent Volumes

tonight. I can play some prerecorded stuff. There's no need to—''

"No!" Carl snaked around Benedict and reached out to Ronnie. "Sweetheart, there was a mention in tonight's paper. The ratings will be huge. You can't just walk away."

Ratings! Oh, she was beginning to despise her boss. "I can, and I will."

"I wish you wouldn't," Benedict said in a soft, deep voice that cut to the bone.

She turned her eyes up. "Why? If some sick, murdering bastard is using me and my show to get his jollies, I don't see why I should accommodate him!"

He remained calm. "The victim that was found this morning has not been identified. The murder weapon was not at the site. All the police have is your connection to the man who called claiming to have committed murder."

"How do you know what's going on?" she snapped. "You're not a cop."

"I have connections. If we turn up anything concrete, I can have this studio crawling with cops in no time."

She didn't want to do this. She wanted to run, far and fast. Farther, this time. Faster. The last thing she wanted was to spend the night alone in this station, waiting for a murderer to call.

Benedict reached out and placed a hand on her shoulder. His touch was firm but gentle, nurturing and real. It was exactly the kind of touch she'd been avoiding for the past two years.

"Remember, I'll be here with you," he said. "I

had caller ID set up on your phone system. He calls, and we get him.''

Ronnie shrugged off his hand. She wasn't sure if she was more disturbed because she actually liked that comforting hand on her shoulder, or because she realized that Benedict had looked at her and known what she feared most: staying here alone. ''You think the idiot is going to call from home so you can have the police drive over to his house and pick him up?''

''Stranger things have happened.''

Carl stepped back, and held up both hands as if he was framing both Benedict and Ronnie. A strange smile crossed his face. ''I'm picking up on a vibe here. This would make great publicity. Seductive late-night radio host and grumpy P.I. The television stations would eat this up!''

Benedict turned a glare on Carl. ''There is no vibe, and I'm not grumpy,'' he growled.

''Okay, okay,'' Carl conceded. ''Woman in jeopardy and the dedicated private investigator who guards her. I like that much better.''

''Don't even think about it,'' Benedict snarled.

The light on Carl's face died. ''What? Are you married?''

''No,'' Benedict said succinctly.

''Engaged,'' Carl said with a shake of his head, as if he was trying to decide if that would be an obstacle to the plan he was formulating.

Again, Benedict answered with a precise, ''No.''

Carl turned his attention to Ronnie. He looked her up and down with a critical eye. ''Sweetheart, do you have a dress? Something—'' his fingers waggled

"—virginal. No!" he said quickly. "Not virginal. I want you in something so drop-dead seductive we'll have to have a fireman follow you around to put out the flames."

Before Ronnie could formulate a response to the station manager's insulting suggestion, Benedict took Carl's arm and practically dragged him down the hallway, toward the door. "Go home, Mr. Gamble. I'll call if I need you. And if the papers get wind of this, if there's a single sentence in the social column or the local section or at the bottom of the last page of the newspaper, I will hold you personally responsible. If television cameras show up, you're a dead man."

"Hey!" Carl protested. "You can't threaten me! I'm paying you!"

"Then let me do my job."

Ronnie stifled a small smile as she followed the two men.

"See you in the morning," Benedict said, all but tossing Carl out of his own radio station and locking the door behind him.

As soon as Sparky, the disc jockey who was on from seven to midnight, was finished, Ronnie and Benedict would be locked in the station for the night. There was a very good alarm system, sturdy locks on the door…and she was so glad that she wouldn't be here alone.

"Am I?" she asked as Benedict turned to face her. For the first time she was glad that he was tall and broad-shouldered and strong. She was even glad that he wore a gun on his belt. He would stand between her and whoever was out there. It was a comforting thought.

"Are you what?"

"In jeopardy," she whispered. "Carl said I was a woman in jeopardy. Do you think this man who calls himself Wayne is dangerous? To me," she clarified. "Is he a threat to me?"

"Your boss is a jerk," Benedict said in a low voice.

"You didn't answer my question."

He didn't, for a long moment. Finally he said, "I don't know. It could be he's only using you for the publicity. But..."

"But what?"

He gave her a half smile. "Better safe than sorry. It can't hurt to have your own personal bodyguard sitting outside the door while you work."

She didn't want Benedict to know that his presence here was a relief for her, that she was already depending on him in a way she hadn't depended on any man for a very long time.

"Whatever makes you happy," she said as she turned her back on him. Sparky's sign-off song was playing over the speakers. In a couple of minutes she'd be on the air.

Chapter 3

Eli sat in the narrow hallway, his legs stretched out before him, his eyes on the window that gave him a wide view of the studio where Ronnie Gray worked.

He couldn't see Ronnie from here, which was just as well. He had to stand to get a really good look at her. When he watched closely, he made her nervous. Her chocolate-brown eyes kept cutting his way, her face went pale.

So he sat here where she couldn't see anything more than the top of his head and he couldn't see her at all and he listened.

Now that he knew the face that went with that voice, she sounded sexier than ever. A man could close his eyes and listen to that voice and think very, very bad thoughts. He could imagine her saying all sorts of naughty things, just for him. He could imagine her laughter as he tossed her onto the bed. He could imagine the way she would moan, with a voice like that.

And all he could do was imagine. Not only was she a client and therefore off-limits, she didn't like him. Or else she was afraid of him. Either way, imagination was the best he was going to get from Ronnie Gray.

Man, he was in bad need of a good night's sleep, if he was allowing his mind to wander this way. He had managed to grab a couple of hours before heading over here for the night, but it hadn't been enough. Not nearly enough.

He stood slowly. If he continued to sit here, he would likely fall asleep in the chair and dream about Ronnie Gray. He discarded his jacket. Even though it was cold outside, it was plenty warm in the station. The heat was running full blast. He rolled up his sleeves and loosened his tie as he watched the woman in the booth.

Ronnie's attention was on her caller at the moment, so he was free to look his fill as she leaned into the microphone and basically told the woman her boyfriend was an ass. In spite of her sassy banter and half smile, he could tell she was shaken.

And with good reason. The body they'd found this morning…it hadn't been pretty. Murder was never pretty, it was never clean and nice and simple. But some were more violent than others. Some gave him the chills.

He'd tried to assure her that she wasn't in danger, but he didn't really believe that assurance himself. Something about this case—*everything* about this case—stunk to high heaven.

Ronnie ended her conversation and introduced a Joe Cocker song. As soon as the music began to play, the phone on her console rang.

He read her lips. "Talk to me, baby," she said with a come-hither smile.

Eli couldn't hear the caller, since music was playing over the speakers instead of her new call, so he stepped cautiously into the booth. Ronnie's smile disappeared quickly, and she cut her eyes in his direction. She punched a button on the phone and replaced the receiver, and the voice she'd been listening to drifted from the intercom on her desk. The voice was clear for the two of them to hear, with the strains of "Night Calls" playing in the background.

"...you think I was kidding?" he asked. "Did you think I wouldn't actually carry through with your instructions?"

Eli gave Ronnie a sign to keep the man talking, and checked the caller ID. Pay phone. As he stepped into the hallway he heard Ronnie say, "I didn't tell you to kill that woman."

Eli nodded, assuring Ronnie that he would be right back, and closed the door on the soundproof booth as he dialed a number on his cell phone. The cop on the other end was waiting for his call, and he gave her the number that had come up on the station caller ID.

That done, he clipped his cell phone back onto his belt and reentered the booth.

"She was very attractive," the man who called himself Wayne said dreamily. "Not as beautiful as you, of course, but appealing in her own way. I do prefer your red hair to her more common brown, but she did have her own attributes."

Ronnie's face went paper white. "We've never met, have we?"

"Have we?" the caller teased. "Maybe. Maybe not."

"I don't know anyone named Wayne."

"Maybe that's not my real name."

"You didn't kill anyone," Ronnie said in a challenging manner. "You're just a pathetic little man who has to make up stories because you're too much of a wimp to get out of the house and actually do anything on your own. You sit there and listen to the radio and pretend. You're nothing."

The song that was playing ended, and Ronnie reached out to punch an icon on her computer screen. Another song began without introduction.

"Aren't you going to put me on the radio tonight?" Wayne asked.

"No," Ronnie said. "I can't."

"Why not?"

"You know why," she said, her voice growing heated. "I don't need every nutcase in the city calling me, believing I'll let them have my audience."

"You think I'm bluffing."

"I know you're bluffing."

"Tell the cops to look under her arm." The caller severed the connection abruptly.

"You did good," Eli said. "You made him mad, and that might have meant keeping him on the line a few minutes longer. I spoke to a detective, and at least two patrol cars are on their way to the location of that pay phone. They'll get him," he assured her.

"Was there anything under her arm?" Ronnie asked in a shaking voice.

"I don't know. I have a few contacts at the police department, but I'm not exactly in the loop."

"Can you find out?"

"Sure," he said.

"Now?"

He almost told her they should wait until morning for an answer, but one look at Ronnie's face and he knew she couldn't wait that long. She was two seconds away from losing it.

"Why not?"

"Well?" Ronnie asked as she stepped into the hallway and closed the booth door behind her. She was playing three songs in a row; she had ten minutes and thirty-four seconds before she had to be back at the microphone.

She had to tilt her head back to stare up at Benedict. She'd never cared much for large men. They were usually bullies. Eli Benedict was definitely a large man. He had to be a couple of inches over six feet, and from the set of his broad shoulders it appeared that he worked out. Not to excess; he didn't have oversize arms and a thick neck. But he was definitely in shape. His body was hard, sculpted. Just what she *did not* need.

Right now, Benedict didn't look happy. He'd had time to get an answer for her, if he had the kinds of connections he claimed to have. What had been under the murder victim's arm? For some reason, he didn't want to tell her what had been found there. His mouth remained closed; his eyes guarded.

"Come on," she snapped. "I don't have all night."

He studied her for a moment. His expression softened a little. "What's your middle name?"

"What does my middle name have to do with…"

"Just tell me."

"Irene," she said.

"I'm guessing the Ronnie is short for Veronica?" She nodded.

He moved one step closer. Too close. One step, and he was too deep into her personal space. Something about the way he slanted toward her made her respond with a involuntary quiver. Her mouth went dry, her pulse beat too quick. Benedict's fingers twitched a little, and he lifted his hand. Oh, no. Did he think he might have to *catch* her?

"The initials VIG were carved under her arm."

Even though she had known from his physical response that what was coming would be bad, Ronnie swayed slightly. Benedict reached out to steady her with one big hand. He gripped her upper arm, firmly but with an unexpected gentleness. And he held on. She wanted to shake the big man off, to let him know that she did not need his comforting hand or his support or the concern in his eyes. She didn't move. It would be foolish to shake him off and sink to her knees because she could not stand. Another moment, that's all she needed. Maybe two.

"The police haven't made the connection to you yet," he continued, "but they will. It won't take long."

She lowered her eyes and let her head drift toward Benedict's shoulder. She wouldn't touch him, she wouldn't even think of laying her head there and closing her eyes and trying to forget what he'd said. But something about moving closer was...nice. She needed to be close at the moment.

The grip on her arm changed, gentled. Benedict laid his other hand on her shoulder. A thumb rocked, mindlessly caressing.

"Do you think I know him?" she whispered.

"Maybe," Benedict replied in a gruff voice. "He knows you, that doesn't mean you know him."

Ronnie nodded. Now was no time to panic. She didn't have time to panic! She couldn't fall apart... She couldn't cry. Not until later, when she was alone.

"The cops will be investigating the murder," Benedict said in a surprisingly comforting voice. "My job is you. Just you. Now that we know there's more to this than a prank call, you're my top priority."

She nodded again. It was all she could manage right now.

VIG. In her mind she could see the initials carved into some poor woman's flesh. On the air, she was

Angel. She used the name Ronnie for everything else these days. Whoever this was…he knew her. He'd tapped into some very personal records, maybe seen her driver's license… He *knew* her.

"I'm just a voice on the radio," she said. "Just a voice. Why is this happening?" She lifted her head and looked Benedict in the eye, hoping for an answer that made sense.

He didn't have an answer for her. As if she were shrugging off a heavy overcoat, she finally forced herself to break the hold Benedict had on her. That done, she turned away quickly, afraid that those eyes might see too much.

Eli wanted to curse, loud and long. By the time the cops had arrived at the pay phone, *Wayne* had been long gone. The phone and the booth had been wiped clean, so there were no prints to work with. There was nothing in the area to point them in any direction. They were back to zero.

All he could do was watch Ronnie Gray, keep her safe, make sure she *knew* she was safe. Finding the caller wasn't his job.

Watching Ronnie Gray was not a chore. She was the kind of woman who could very easily work her way under a man's skin. He didn't think the subtle seduction was deliberate, but the woman had a way about her that made him itch. A tilt of her head, the way her fingers fluttered when she reached for a cup or her computer, the gentle working of her throat… No, watching her was not a problem.

Shortly after 4:00 a.m., other employees began to arrive at the station. The janitor, a stooped, older man who let himself in and got directly to work, arrived first. His only response to Eli's presence outside the booth was a nod of his gray head before he got to work. He wore a gray uniform with the name Frank embroidered on the pocket.

A receptionist walked through the front door fifteen minutes after the janitor. She was a tall, solidly built, plain woman who looked as if she could take just about any man in a fair fight. She pursed her lips at Eli when she saw him standing there, and then she made coffee.

Next, the morning crew arrived. Two chattering, inane, not-very-funny deejays arrived within five minutes of one another. Chuck and Jesse. Chuck was tall and thin, and his stringy hair was in bad need of an introduction to shampoo. Jesse had a wide mouth set in a perpetual smile and eyes that darted this way and that, taking in everything. They made a few cracks about Ronnie having her own personal Sir Galahad parked outside the booth, until Eli gave them a glare that shut them up. Dweebs.

Carl Gamble arrived at fifteen before five. Did the man never sleep? He was like a ferret, or a hummingbird, always in motion.

He was paying the bills at the moment; that didn't mean Eli had to *like* him.

At five to five, Ronnie introduced the Joan Jett version of "Love Stinks," and left the booth, making way for the morning crew to take over. The shorter of the two deejays, a grinning Jesse, made a blatant pass at Ronnie as he passed. She ignored him.

As Eli and Ronnie walked toward the reception area, the station manager held his squared hands up, framing the two of them as he had last night. "You need to ditch the suit and get a leather jacket," Gamble said. "And could we have the gun where it's a little more visible?"

Eli glared at the little man. "Don't even think about it," he growled.

Gamble dropped his hands quickly. "You can't blame a man for trying."

"Yes, I can." He led Ronnie into the parking lot, anxious to get out of the small building. A stiff, cold breeze slapped them in the face.

Ronnie was digging in her purse for her keys when Eli laid a hand on her arm. "Let me drive you."

"I don't need a baby-sitter," she snapped.

"I think maybe you do."

She dropped the keys and looked up at him. It was still more dark than light. Lamplight illuminated her face, not sunlight. She was one of those women who belonged to the night, sultry and secretive, beautiful in a pale sort of way. A primal urge made him want to wrap his arms around her, keep her warm and safe. If he wasn't careful, this would turn into something much more than a *job*.

"I don't know what to do," she said softly, as if it was an admission she was not comfortable making; not to him, not to anyone.

"Better safe than sorry," he said. "Let me drive you home."

She smiled crookedly. It was the kind of smile that might do any man in, even a self-professed bastard like Eli Benedict.

"Sure," she said. "And then what? Are you going to sleep on the couch? Follow me everywhere I go? Become my shadow?"

He stared at her for a moment before answering. "Yeah."

Chapter 4

Ronnie was surprised she'd slept as long as she had, considering what the last couple of days had been like. Six hours of good hard sleep took some of the edge off; she hadn't slept much at all yesterday.

She pulled on her robe and belted it, then headed for the kitchen. On her way to the coffeepot, she had to pass through the living room. Eli Benedict was stretched across her couch, which was much too small for him. His shoes were on the floor, the top buttons of his shirt were undone. He slept like a baby. A great big macho baby.

In the past year and a half her house had been her refuge, every bit as much as the late-night radio show. She'd tried living in an apartment at first, but there was too much noise during the day. This little house on a large lot near the edge of town was quiet and secluded.

There hadn't been any men sleeping on her couch.

She'd tried very hard not to like Benedict. He was an ex-cop, for one thing, and she'd had enough of cops to last her a lifetime. On top of that, he was too good-looking. Guys who looked like he did were conceited, they expected women to fall at their feet. He was also well into his thirties and unattached. There was something wrong with a man who reached a certain age and hadn't settled down. Maybe he was divorced, in which case he came with way too much emotional baggage.

These were all reasons for her to steer well clear of him, but...

Benedict hadn't pushed her the way a cop would have. He had insisted on sticking close to her, without making a big deal out of it. Yes, he was good-looking, but he didn't act the way some men did, when they expected all women to love them and fall victim to their charms. He was much too real for that.

And in truth, she herself had reached a certain age and was unattached. She couldn't very well hold that against him.

"Good morning," he growled from the kitchen doorway.

Ronnie turned, startled by his greeting.

"Good afternoon," he said, correcting his mistake.

"Sorry," Ronnie said. "I didn't mean to wake you."

He nodded and walked into the kitchen, moving slowly and cautiously; like a man who'd just woken up. His jaw was dusted with a morning beard, his hair was mussed, his eyes were sleepy, still. Big men weren't supposed to look cute. Somehow he managed.

"I smelled the coffee," he said, pushing his fingers through his black hair and straightening some of the disheveled strands. It curled a little, she noticed. Not a lot, just at the ends. Again, cute. And very bad news.

She pulled two large mugs from the cabinet and poured. "What do you take in your coffee?"

"Nothing." She heard the squeal of a chair on the kitchen floor, and when she turned around, Benedict was lowering himself into that chair.

Ronnie sat across from him with her own cup of black coffee. "What's next?" she asked.

He took a sip of the hot coffee before answering. "The police will probably be calling today."

"Because of the initials," she said, her voice remaining soft. Deep down, she shuddered.

Benedict nodded his head. "Yeah. They'll put two and two together before long, if they haven't already."

"I can't tell them anything new."

"Yeah, but since they didn't take you seriously the first time, they're bound to have more questions."

Ronnie stared into her coffee. Maybe six hours wasn't enough. What she wanted to do right now was crawl into bed, pull the covers over her head and stay there. "I can't do this again," she whispered.

"Do what?"

She looked Benedict in the eye. She hadn't told anyone in Laurel about Roger. Maybe some of them remembered the story; it had been on the news, after all. But she'd changed. She was no longer Veronica Michaels, murdered sportscaster's widow; she was Ronnie Gray, and she stayed out of the limelight. Not only did she not want people to look at her the way they had in Atlanta, she didn't want to relive that horror in any way, not even in a short retelling. It was best to leave that time buried; the deeper the better.

But if the police did a little digging into her background, they'd find everything. They'd ask questions. She didn't want Benedict to hear the news from a stranger.

"Two years ago, my husband was murdered." She stared into her coffee again. It was safer than looking into Benedict's eyes. What would she see there when he knew the ugly story? "Stabbed," she said, her voice little more than a whisper. "Roger and I had been separated for months and were in the process of getting divorced, and still, I can't seem to forget what he looked like, that…last time." Blood and roses. "The police caught the murderer. He was a homeless man I used to help on occasion, and he and Roger argued now and then. If you could call it arguing.

Usually Roger just yelled at Gordon until he went away.'' She shuddered. Something within her wanted to reach out and grab Benedict's hand. She ignored the urge, but her fingers trembled.

"That night there was a scene in the parking lot." Over a cookie. Such an inconsequential little thing, hardly worth a moment's anger, much less murder. "The next morning the police found the knife Gordon used to kill Roger in his shopping cart." She took a deep breath, trying to push the panic deep. "For a while, though, the police thought I did it. They thought I'd killed Roger and planted the knife, or hired someone to do it for me." She shuddered again, remembering Gordon's pathetic cries proclaiming his innocence. "I found Roger's body on my front porch. We'd been apart for months, there were so many people who knew how I hated him, and so of course…" She choked on her words. "The way the investigators looked at me, the way they questioned me and pushed for the answers they wanted…I can't do that again. I'll run if I have to."

"This is different," Benedict said in an unexpectedly soothing voice. "There's no reason for the police to suspect you of any wrongdoing."

She finally lifted her head, no longer afraid to witness Benedict's reaction. "Why is this happening to me again? Am I a freak magnet? Did I do or say something to set them off?"

Unexpectedly, Benedict laid his hand over hers. His gentle grasp was warm, strong and comforting, and she did not pull her hand away. "You didn't do anything wrong," he assured her. "I know that. Deep down you know it just as well as I do."

"But the police…"

"Will have to come through me to get to you."

No wonder Ronnie was so scared. This wasn't the first time she'd been touched by violence. Most people managed to live a lifetime without ever encountering anything so brutal, and in the span of two years it had happened to her twice.

Dale was looking into the details of her husband's murder. There was probably no connection, but the cop in Eli wouldn't let it lie unexplored.

It was after midnight, again, and he stood in the hallway of the radio station and watched Ronnie work. You wouldn't know, to listen to her voice, that she was shaken, but he could see it in her face, in the way she held herself before the microphone.

"Just two days until Valentine's Day," she said, her voice husky and low, sexy as hell. "I usually have Friday night off, but this is a special occasion. Those of us who have no Valentine, who *want* no Valentine, will spend it right here. I expect you all to keep me company Friday night. To get us all in the mood, here's Chris Isaac and 'Things Go Wrong.'"

She touched her computer screen and the song began to play over the speakers and over the air. That done, she leaned back in her chair and swiveled in his direction. She almost seemed surprised to see him standing there. Did she get so lost in her own little world when she worked that she forgot the turns her life had taken in the past couple of days?

He'd been right when he'd predicted that the cops wouldn't waste much time before questioning her again. They'd showed up at her house late in the afternoon, notepads in hand. The detective in charge, Norris Page, had wanted to put a couple of officers in the radio station during Ronnie's shift, but she'd been so instantly and obviously dismayed that Eli had suggested he keep the cops informed of anything, as he had last night when the killer had called.

Eli figured it was the thought of getting overtime approved, never an easy task, that swayed Page.

So far, all had been quiet tonight. It was almost three in the morning, and Wayne hadn't called.

When ''Things Go Wrong'' was done, Ronnie gave a quick introduction to a couple of songs, cued them up and headed for the hallway.

With the door to the booth halfway closed, she leaned against the wall. ''I don't think I ever really thanked you.''

''For what?''

''For keeping the detective and his buddies out of here while I work.'' She gave him a crooked smile. ''Maybe it doesn't make sense, but I still get a little wiggy around cops.''

''I used to be one,'' he reminded her.

''I know.''

''You're going to let it slide?'' he teased.

"This time," she said softly.

He knew how brutal an investigating detective could be when he got his teeth into something like a juicy murder. What had they done to her? Ronnie was delicate, gentle. Whatever they'd done…she still had scars.

When the phone rang, she practically jumped out of her skin. She walked into the booth, her eyes on the ringing telephone. Eli followed her. Before she answered, he made note of the phone number. Not a pay phone, he observed, but a cell phone.

After taking a deep breath, Ronnie reached out and snagged the phone, one finger jabbing at the intercom button as she answered. "Talk to me, baby," she said in a husky whisper.

"You're not alone tonight, are you?" he asked.

Eli stepped into the hallway to make a quick phone call, listening to Ronnie's conversation as he gave the waiting operator the cell-phone number that had come up on the caller ID. He didn't have much hope that it would do the police any good. Only an idiot would make this kind of call on his own cell phone, and while the authorities could pinpoint the exact location of the call, it took time and equipment they didn't have here in Laurel. All they'd be able to do was trace the caller to a certain section of town, by the cell tower he was drawing his signal from.

"Why do you say that?" Ronnie asked calmly.

"I can hear him," Wayne said.

"You can't hear—"

"In your voice," the caller interrupted impatiently. "I can hear him in your voice. You're not alone."

"My voice hasn't changed," she assured him, her eyes on Eli as he returned to the booth.

"Yes, it has," Wayne said angrily. "I can always tell if you're happy or sad. Bored or excited. You usually sound so lonely. Like you're not only alone in the studio, but alone in the world. It makes me want to wrap my arms around you and hold you close, because I'm lonely, too."

"We're all alone," she said.

"You're not," he responded angrily. "Not tonight."

The song ended, and Ronnie cued up another one.

"Again," Wayne sighed, "you're not going to put me on the radio. I do so like an audience."

"I bet you do," she said tersely.

"Temper, temper." Wayne tsked into the phone. "You have an audience, why shouldn't I?"

"Because I'm a deejay and you're a psycho?" Ronnie snapped.

Her caller laughed, but the laughter was short-lived. It died, and was replaced with a dejected sigh. "I understand that you're concerned, but did you really have to take him to your home? Tell me, is the big lug ever going to let you out of his sight? How on earth will I ever find the opportunity to introduce myself if he's always—"

Ronnie quickly disconnected the caller, and for a moment she stared at the phone as if it were alive and was about to bite. Her face went white. She covered her mouth with one trembling hand.

When she glanced up at Eli, her dark eyes were wide and terrified.

"He knows where I live," she whispered. "And he knows about you. He knows you were at my house today, that you're here now."

Eli nodded and stepped toward her, offering a comforting hand she recoiled from. He didn't take it personally; she was withdrawing from everything, trying to disappear.

"Benedict," she whispered. "He's watching me."

Chapter 5

By the time they pulled into the driveway of Eli's house, it was full light. They'd talked to the police, played the tape of the caller's threat and answered a few more questions. As he'd said he would, Benedict had placed himself between her and the cops.

He'd not only handled the police and their questions, he'd arranged for someone from his agency to drive her car off the station parking lot. When she needed it again, it would be waiting in the detective agency parking lot. He also placed himself between her and Carl—who was much easier to scare into backing down than the cops.

After Roger had been killed, there hadn't been anyone to stand before or with her; not really. She'd had friends who said they supported her and never believed the accusations, and a supportive family. Her mother and father had flown in, her brother and sister had each driven down to visit with her.

But no one had ever physically stood between her and the police. Benedict did just that. For that, she could forgive him for being handsome and lifting weights and being single.

That done, he'd driven her to her house to pack a bag. They hadn't been there long. She was very aware of the fact that the caller, the killer, knew where she lived. Could she ever sleep here again? Would the house she loved ever again be her haven?

Benedict's place was a surprise. First of all, it was a very nice house, larger than hers and in a better neighborhood. Somehow she had expected an impersonal apartment, something dark and anonymous. All the houses along this street were well maintained. There were no eyesores, and none of his neighbors used their yards as parking lots for rundown cars.

His rambling ranch was painted a very pale shade of gray-green. There was a nice wide porch along the front and left side, and lots of windows. The house had a slightly modern feel to it, unlike her more traditional home.

The second surprise was that the place was well furnished. There were even pictures on the walls.

"Sit," Benedict ordered, leading her to the sofa. He had her bag in one hand and supported her with the other. "I'll make us some coffee and something to eat."

"Coffee?"

"Decaf," he clarified. "Like it or not, you need to get some sleep."

She shook her head as Benedict left her to go to the kitchen. He had promised her, more than once, that no one was following them. But what if he was wrong?

Soon she heard the gurgle of a coffeemaker. A moment later, the aroma reached her. Decaf or not, the coffee smelled like heaven. She closed her eyes and took a deep breath. The simple joy of a familiar and comforting aroma didn't last long. It didn't matter what Benedict gave her to drink; she wasn't going to sleep. Not ever again.

The killer said he had been drawn to her voice. All this time, she'd thought she was invisible. She played songs for and comforted brokenhearted women…and the occasional man. She had never suspected that she was putting herself out there again, that she was drawing some psycho to her simply by speaking.

"Here you go."

Her eyes snapped open at the sound of Benedict's voice. He was coming toward her with a cup of coffee in his hand. She took it, cradled the warm mug. It was going to be a chilly day. Even though the heater in this house was running, she still felt the cold.

"Bacon and eggs coming up," he said with a small smile.

"I don't want anything…"

"You need to eat," Benedict said, and then he turned away before she had a chance to argue.

She watched him walk away. He'd discarded his

jacket and rolled up his sleeves, and still wore a gun in a belt holster. The sight of him soothed her, somehow. Like it or not, she was beginning to depend on Eli Benedict far too much. She barely knew him, and the last thing she wanted in her life was a man…but the idea of going through this without him made her shiver more deeply and surely than any February chill.

After eating a decent helping of bacon and eggs and downing three cups of decaf, Ronnie stepped into the shower. While she was in the bathroom, Eli made a few phone calls. Dale first, a friend at the police station next.

They'd managed to trace the cell-phone number to a teenager who swore her phone was in her room, when she was confronted early this morning. When she couldn't find it and the officers had her retrace her steps, she decided she had last used it at the mall.

The girl's parents were afraid someone was running up a huge bill and they'd be responsible. Eli was very sure that the stolen phone had already been disposed of.

He was trying not to let Ronnie see, but this case worried him as much as it did her. Since he'd installed caller ID at the station, they'd had one call from a pay phone, the second from a stolen cell. What next? This guy was being careful, and last night he'd made it very clear that he was fixated on Ronnie.

She walked into the living room, hair down, robe belted tight. Eli reacted in a way any man might when a beautiful woman dressed for bed walks toward him. His insides tightened, his mouth went dry. There was something about those chocolate eyes in a pale face, the delicate hands, the dark-red hair. He had never known anyone quite like Ronnie.

And the last thing she needed right now was a horny guy making a move on her. She was much too vulnerable.

"The guest room is made up for you," he said.

"What about you?" she asked softly. "Aren't you going to bed?"

"In a little while. I have a few phone calls to make, and I want to grab a quick shower. You need to go on to bed."

She sat on the opposite end of the couch and curled her legs beneath her. "I don't know if I can sleep."

"Sure you can."

She shook her head. No thick ponytail for Ronnie this morning, just long red hair that was perfectly straight and looked wonderfully soft falling over her shoulders and down her back. "Not yet." She had a way of looking at him that told him something was going on in her pretty little head.

He'd been spending too much time alone with Ronnie Gray. That's why he had the urge to reach out and wrap his arms around her, to hold her, to promise her he'd make everything right. That's why what he really wanted to do was lie down with her, hold her close, make her forget about the man who was making her life hell.

That's why he was content to stay here and stare at her, certain that it was very right that she sit here on his couch, in her robe, with her hair down and her dark eyes pinned to him.

"Is it my fault?" she asked quickly.

"No," he assured her. She looked so fragile, he couldn't help but reach out and lay his hand on her face, cupping her cheek. "Absolutely not."

"He said it was my voice. With Gordon, it was my hair. Whenever I saw him, he always said something about how he loved my hair."

Eli dropped his hand. "You have a great voice. Your hair is beautiful. I personally think you're outrageously beautiful and sexy. That doesn't mean I'm going to go out and kill someone."

She flinched.

He wished he'd found another way to assure her that this wasn't her doing. "You know what I mean," he added in a gentler voice.

"I just don't know what to do next," she said, ignoring his awkward confession. "I've done television and radio, and neither worked well. Where can I go, what can I do, so I'll be safe? So the people around me will be safe?"

"Ronnie, you can't run and hide."

"What choice do I have?"

He rose from the couch and offered her his hand. After a moment's hesitation she took it, and he pulled her to her feet. "Come on," he said gruffly. "You're going to bed."

"I can't sleep," she insisted as he drew her toward the hallway.

"Of course you can," he said as he led her to the spare bedroom. It was a room rarely used. His sister had used it once. His parents two or three times. The third bedroom had been converted to an office, so he had little use for this one.

It was coming in handy today. Another night on the couch and his back would be worthless.

He drew back the covers and released Ronnie's hand. She unbelted her robe and shook it off. Beneath she wore a perfectly decent nightgown. Flannel. Flannel was perfect for February, but it wasn't supposed to be a turn-on.

Ronnie crawled into the bed and he raised the coverlet to her chin. "Sleep," he commanded.

"I don't think I can."

She was more tired than she knew. Her sleepy voice was telling.

"Don't worry for a few hours. You need to rest. Who knows, maybe the cops will have the man who called in custody before you go back to work tonight."

"Do you really think so?"

He couldn't lie to her. "No, but anything is possible."

Eli started to pull the door closed behind him, but Ronnie stopped him with an urgent, "Wait."

He paused in the doorway, doorknob in his hand.

"Leave the door open," she said. "Please."

He nodded and did as she asked.

* * *

When Ronnie woke, it was late afternoon. The day was gray, so the light in the room was muted already, even though they were hours away from full darkness. She jumped out of bed, turned on the lights and closed the door so she could quickly get dressed. Jeans and a station T-shirt, thick socks. No shoes.

She glanced into the master bedroom as she stepped into the hallway. The covers were rumpled, but Eli wasn't in the bed. She found him in the living room, sitting in a fat leather recliner and leafing through a book. No suit today, just a pair of jeans and a dark-maroon T-shirt. No shoes or socks, even though the room was cool. The casual outfit suited him.

He smiled at her, and she felt a strange rush of relief.

"Didn't you sleep?" she asked.

"For a few hours," he stood, book in his hand. "I woke up with an idea."

"What kind of idea?"

He walked toward her. "I don't know if you're going to like it or not."

"Try me."

Benedict looked her in the eye. He was judging her, somehow, studying her very closely. "The woman I hear on the radio is strong, she takes no crap from anyone."

Ronnie felt herself blush; her cheeks grew warm. "That woman is fiction, like a character an actor plays."

He shook his head. "I don't think so. I think that strength is a part of you. That's why it makes me so angry to see you afraid this way."

"Anyone would be afraid if they were in my shoes," she said defensively.

Again, Benedict shook his head. "Maybe. Probably." He shrugged. "Okay, I'll give you that one. I just don't want you to be scared anymore."

"It's not that easy."

"You could get mad, instead."

"I am mad."

"I want you to get royally pissed," he said as he stepped closer.

"I am!"

He shook his head. "No, you're scared. You're letting this weasel make you want to run and hide, and a woman like you should never run. Especially not from a weasel."

"So, I'm supposed to get mad and that will make everything all right."

His smile grew wide. "Ever taken a self-defense course?" he asked.

"No."

From just a few feet away, he tossed the book he held to her. She caught it and glimpsed at the title. *Fighting Dirty.*

"You're about to get a crash course."

Chapter 6

Ronnie hadn't expected to spend Thursday afternoon rolling across Eli Benedict's living-room floor.

After he'd fed her a sandwich and a glass of iced tea, he'd pushed all the furniture back against the walls of the large room and spent better than an hour giving her the crash course he'd promised. She now knew where to hit an attacker and how, in order to do the most harm. Benedict had also had her on the floor: dropping down, rolling away and getting to her feet quickly. Now he was making her practice her punches.

"I don't want to hit you," she said for the third time.

He smiled. "You're not going to hurt me."

"Then why are we doing this?"

"Practical training."

"There's nothing practical about this," she insisted.

He took a step toward her. Somehow that simple move was threatening and exhilarating at the same time. Ronnie knew she needed to stay far, far away from men like this one. She didn't move, not to step back, not to move forward.

"Okay," Benedict said smoothly, "I want to see for myself exactly how hard you can hit when the time comes."

She made a fist, the way Benedict had taught her, and hit him in the stomach. It was like punching at solid rock.

He shook his head in apparent dismay. "First of all, you bent your wrist. What did I tell you?" He grabbed her forearm and ran the palm of his hand along her arm from her elbow to her hand, where she obediently made a fist. "Keep this straight, so you'll have a little power in the punch. Otherwise you're going to hurt your wrist. And don't try to punch a man in the stomach. You can't hit hard enough to do any damage. If you go for the midsection, use your elbow."

Benedict continued to hold her. Ronnie stared at his hand against her pale skin, so large in comparison to her unthreatening fist. "I understand that," she said, unable to raise her head to look him in the face. "But I'm not going to strike you in the eye or the throat or the...anywhere else you told me to go for if I have to defend myself."

It had been a long time since she'd been this close to a man. Benedict's heat radiated off his body and touched her, his large body hovered over hers. It was almost as if he were wrapped around her, but that was impossible. He was just trying to teach her how to hit an attacker if she had to. Anything else was simply her imagination kicking in.

Maybe not. Benedict's fingers rocked over her arm, warmly caressing. Was his heart in his throat the way hers was? No, of course not. This was probably his idea of comforting her, since she was such a dismal failure as a fighter. But still, his hand remained on her arm, and she liked it. She wanted to fall against him, bury her face in his chest, and stay there.

She hadn't wanted to hold a man, any man, for a very long time.

He dropped his hand, and Ronnie glanced up. The smile was gone, the bedroom eyes sexier than ever.

"Time for a break," he said in a soft voice. "Since you're determined not to hit me, I'll see if I can round up a dummy or a punching bag for you to work on this weekend."

She nodded once, trying her best to dismiss the unexpected wave of feelings that had just rushed through her. "Thanks, Benedict."

His smile came back. "Maybe you should call me Eli."

"Eli. What kind of name is that for a tough guy, anyway?" She returned his grin. "Sounds like an old man's name."

"My grandfather likes it."

Knowing that he had been named for his grandfather made Eli suddenly more human, more real. "The name suits you, I think," Ronnie said thoughtfully.

His eyebrows lifted slightly and he leaned toward her. She didn't lean back.

"Are you calling me an old man?"

"I would never be so rude," she said innocently.

"Then I misunderstood."

Ronnie nodded. Eli was so very close. In the past two years—no, longer than that—no man had stood this close to her, so near she felt as if he were touching her. She hadn't allowed anyone to get this close for a long time, but she didn't step back, and she didn't push Eli away.

"Ronnie," he said softly, his face coming nearer. "Would you panic if I kissed you?"

She held her breath and considered the possibilities attached to that unexpected question. "Yes," she whispered.

He backed away, nodding gently. "That's what I was afraid of."

Eli moved the living-room furniture back where it belonged, while Ronnie took a shower to wash off the sweat she'd worked up during their self-defense class. He could hear the water running, pictured her standing beneath the spray. Naked.

This was not good. He needed to get Dale to relieve him for a while. Maybe one of the part-time employees, or Brandon, who was so good they'd just put him on the payroll full-time so no one else could steal him away. He'd been spending too much time with Ronnie Gray, if she'd already been able to work her way under his skin. And she was definitely under his skin.

The problem was, he didn't trust anyone else to keep her safe. She needed him. He was the one to place himself between her and the psycho who was fixated on her. There was no way he could hand the job over to anyone else.

His phone rang as he was moving the recliner into place, and he answered the cordless phone that was lying on the coffee table.

"Benedict," he answered curtly.

"Whoa," Dale said. "What's your problem?"

"You called me," Eli snapped.

"Yeah, I know. You just sound…mad. Is the deejay getting on your nerves?"

"You could say that," Eli muttered.

"Want me to get Brandon to—"

"No," Eli interrupted. The shower quit running. All was quiet from the back of the house. Ronnie was now stepping out of the shower. He could picture that as easily as he had pictured her standing under the water. "I got this one."

"We have an ID on the murder victim," Dale continued without further comment. "Allison Wayne, twenty-two years old, lived right here in Laurel."

Wayne. He heard a muted roar from the bathroom. Ronnie's hair dryer. "Why did it take so long to ID her?"

"She lived alone, no family in the area and according to her co-workers she used to take off now and then for a couple of days with no warning, so they weren't worried about her at first. No one got concerned until they heard about the murder on the news.''

"Where did she work?"

"She was a waitress at a coffee shop about two blocks from Miss Lonely Hearts's radio station."

Eli sat in the recliner. "Ronnie knew her," he said in a lowered voice. "Somehow, Ronnie knew Allison Wayne, and this guy saw them together, and…damn. This is getting uglier and uglier."

"Don't I know it."

Ronnie walked into the room, slightly damp from the shower and dressed for work. She wore jeans and a station T-shirt, white tennis shoes, her diamond studs. Eli stood, phone in hand.

"Let me call you back." He disconnected before Dale had a chance to respond.

"Sit down," Eli said gruffly as Ronnie walked toward him.

"I'm fine…"

"Sit."

She perched on the edge of the couch, and he sat beside her. Not too close. He didn't want to alarm her any more than he already had.

"There's a coffee shop just a couple of blocks from the radio station," he said. "Do you ever go there?"

"Most nights I stop on my way to work and have coffee, maybe a sandwich. Since all this started, I haven't been by, though. Why?"

Her face remained serene, untouched by pain and horror. He was afraid that wouldn't last.

"A woman named Allison Wayne worked there. Did you know her?"

Ronnie started to shake her head, then stopped. "Oh, that could be Allie." Her already pale face went white. "You said *did* I know her. Past tense." He watched the expression on her face change as she put two and two together. "Wayne?" she whispered. "Her last name was Wayne? No." She shook her head gently. "Tell me she's not dead."

"I'm sorry."

She trembled from head to toe. "Eli, she was just a kid."

"Yeah."

"Why would he... Why her?"

Ronnie locked her deep-brown eyes on his face. She probably thought he couldn't lie to her when she looked at him this way. She was right.

"Is she dead because I liked her? Did he kill her because we were friendly?"

"I don't know."

"Yes, you do," she whispered. "Somehow, this is my fault."

She looked as if she was about to fall apart, so he scooted closer and wrapped one arm around her. Instead of pulling away, as he'd thought she might, Ronnie laid her head on his shoulder.

"It's not your fault," he said. "You're going to have to stop saying that. Nothing you said or did compelled this man to commit murder. He's a sick bastard, and the police will find him.'' He stroked her hair. ''They're going to want to talk to you again. Did Allie say anything to you about a man who'd been bothering her? Did she have an old boyfriend who was giving her trouble?''

''We talked, but not... I can't remember. Not right now. She's dead?''

''Relax.'' He stroked his hand up and down her arm. ''Later on, when your head is clear, maybe you'll remember something that might help the police.''

Ronnie nodded, and her head brushed warmly against his shoulder. ''They don't know I'm here. Maybe we should call Detective Page.'' She shuddered deep, and he held her closer. Tighter.

''We will. When you're ready.''

''What if I'm never ready?''

He leaned back, but Ronnie didn't lift her head from his shoulder, and he didn't move the arm that held her. They just drifted back and settled in. He had a feeling they might be here for a while.

Neither of them moved. Ronnie eventually calmed down. Her breathing slowed, her heartbeat returned to normal, the trembling subsided. The light outside the window dimmed gradually, until they were left in a large room dimly lit by the bulb over the sink in the kitchen and the distant bathroom light Ronnie had left on.

Ronnie felt right, here. She felt so good. But he knew why she rested so easily in his arms, why she stayed.

Eli just wanted to hold her once when she wasn't afraid. He wanted her to fall against him because she liked the way they felt together. He wanted her to rest in his arms because it felt good, not because she was looking for a place to hide.

When this was all over, he'd ask her for a date. Maybe. He had lousy luck with women, to be honest. Ever since his divorce, and that had been more than six years ago, he'd absolutely hated the whole dating scene. It was so phony, so unbearably contrived. He wanted a woman to sleep with, nothing more. The whole flowers/candy/courting thing was a crock.

He'd never thought of it before, but he would have made a prime candidate for a caller to Ronnie's show in the past few years. Love stinks. When had he gotten so cynical?

He didn't realize that he continued to stroke Ronnie's hair until she lifted her head to look him in the eye.

"I believe in being totally honest," she said softly.

"So do I."

"This is probably just...the situation."

He didn't have to ask what *this* was. "Probably."

"Everything seems more emotional at the moment."

"Yeah."

"More...intense."

"Definitely."

"I can't call my family," she said. "I don't want to drag them into this."

"I can't blame you."

"So that leaves you, Eli," she said, her voice lowering to a whisper.

"Yes, it does."

"You and me, and if it feels like it's us against the world...that's just temporary. Right?"

"Maybe."

The two of them against the world. It made perfect sense for her to feel that way; he was protecting her, standing guard. Keeping her safe. They'd been together almost constantly since this crisis had begun. It made sense for Ronnie to feel this way, but why did he get the same sense of attachment?

Eli tried to convince himself it was dedication to the job that made him feel this way. He didn't quite buy it.

"A woman shouldn't trust her feelings when she's in such an emotional situation, no matter how real they seem." She was almost breathless, her eyes were so deep and dark they were unreadable.

He shook his head. "No, she shouldn't."

Ronnie tilted her head slightly. "I haven't trusted my feelings, my gut instincts, for a very long time."

His gut was churning right now. Did Ronnie have any idea what she was doing to him?

"If I kiss you, will you panic?" she whispered.

He held his breath for a moment. "Maybe. Maybe not." As Ronnie's lips came toward his, he drifted down to meet her. "There's only one way to find out."

Chapter 7

In truth, Ronnie had started hiding a long time ago; the late-night caller who was making her life hell had only exacerbated the situation. Her job, her secluded home, the way she led her life…they were all attempts to keep everyone at a distance.

She didn't want to keep Eli at a distance. In fact, she couldn't hold him close enough.

Eli kissed her in the near dark of his living room. His mouth worked some kind of magic as he held her with sheltering arms. When she'd decided that she needed this kiss, that she wanted it more than she'd ever wanted anything, she'd expected it to be awkward. Brief. Not as wonderful as she'd imagined it might be. It would be a cold dose of reality, a reminder that she no longer needed or wanted a man in her life. The kiss wouldn't be memorable or stirring. After all, it had been more than two years, almost three, since she'd kissed a man this way.

No, she had never kissed a man this way. The kiss didn't end, it went on and on until she was exposed, vulnerable, *open* to Eli in a way she had never been to Roger or anyone else. He reached deep inside her with this kiss. He touched a part of her that had been dead...no, not dead. Sleeping. Numb. That should scare her, at least a little, but the sensation of his mouth against hers was so intense she couldn't make herself back away.

She certainly didn't want to be frightened of this.

His tongue swept across her bottom lip, his fingers raked up her spine to plunge into her hair and hold her mouth against his. She parted her lips and her tongue danced with Eli's. Her body throbbed in time with her heartbeat. She forgot everything else and got lost in sensation.

She slipped her hand beneath Eli's untucked T-shirt, rested her hand on his warm, hard skin. His reaction to her touch was immediate and fierce. He deepened the kiss, and a discernable quiver passed through his body. She felt it in his mouth and in the flesh she caressed with gentle fingers.

To make a man like Eli Benedict quiver, that was no small feat.

Ronnie was not normally a bold person; she never had been. She went no further than resting her hand on Eli's bare skin, reveling in the warmth of his flesh while they kissed. When her hand felt comfortable here, easy and right, she rocked her thumb back and forth. Eli's answer was to lift her shirt, rake his hand up her side and caress one breast. His thumb brushed over a silk-covered nipple, and she felt that caress to her very core. Desire coursed through her body. Need settled in deep and gently throbbed.

Everything faded until there was only this; the kiss, the way they touched, the primal way her body reacted to his. It was right that they were lost in the near dark, where nothing was clear. There was only Eli.

She took her mouth from Eli's, but didn't back away. Instead, she kissed his throat, then trailed her lips to the side of his neck to rest there beneath his ear. And then she raised her mouth and whispered, "Make love to me, Eli."

He stroked her hair, raked one hand down her side. "I don't want you to ask because you're scared."

"That's not why." The way Eli held her, the way he kissed…she had no doubt that he wanted her as much as she wanted him. And still, he offered a way out, a chance to take back her bold command. "You make the world go away," she confessed. "From the first time I saw you, that's the way it's been. When you're with me I don't see anything else. I need that now. I need you."

He caressed her cheek and kissed her quickly, his mouth brushing against hers and then slipping away, his fingers lingering against her face.

Without another word, Eli began to undress her. He took the hem of her T-shirt in his hands and lifted it over her head, tossing it aside. He worked the clasp of her bra easily, then slipped that garment off her arms. It joined the T-shirt on the floor.

He touched her; cupped her breast and kissed her deep, caressed the already hard nipple with his fingers as he took his time arousing her. He lowered his mouth to her breasts, one and then the other, kissing and sucking until she ached for him.

Ronnie's breath caught in her throat, and still Eli lavished attention on her breasts. She threaded her fingers through his hair, held on tight, and closed her eyes. A deep shudder worked through her body.

Eli suckled a nipple deep as he unsnapped and unzipped her jeans. He worked them down just far enough that he could slip his fingers between her legs. When he touched her she moaned and arched into him. When he thrust those fingers against her, rocking and caressing, she almost came apart then and there.

Eli raised his mouth to hers and kissed her, and Ronnie kissed him back with a desperate passion she had not known was possible. Every nerve in her body felt exposed, more alive, hungry. He knew just how to touch her to keep her on a fine, sharp edge.

He very slowly withdrew his hand from her jeans, lifted his head to look her in the eye.

"Not here," he said hoarsely.

Ronnie nodded, and Eli stood. He took her hand, helped her to her feet and then swung her up into his arms.

"You're carrying me to bed," she said with a smile as he went down the hall.

"Yes, I am."

He dropped her gently onto his bed, and she laughed lightly. Amazing that she could laugh at a time like this, but it was joy that bubbled up inside her. Not fear, not apprehension. Pure joy.

Eli made short work of her socks and shoes, jeans and panties, and then he undressed himself quickly before joining her on the bed. He took a condom from the bedside drawer, sheathed himself and tossed back the sheet Ronnie had partially concealed herself with.

"I want to see you," he whispered.

She nodded, lying before him completely bare and wanting. He stared at her and stroked his hand over her body. Down her ribs, across her hip, over her thigh.

They still had only the distant light of the bathroom down the hall to illuminate them. It was enough. Eli Benedict had a great body…she had never doubted that for a minute. But to see it reclining next to hers, sculpted and hard, long and bare, aroused and strong…it made the throb in her body increase.

He parted her thighs gently and touched her intimately once again. Her body shuddered in response, and she arched up and against his caress. He found the nub at her entrance and circled his fingertip there, gently but not too gently. Again, he found that fine edge and kept her there. There was nothing else in the world but this, but them, but the pleasure he promised. Ronnie reached for this man who made the world fade. With her mouth, her arms, her legs, she drew Eli to her and surged against him. She wanted to be wrapped around him, she wanted him inside her.

He entered slowly. Even though she was anxious to have him completely within her, she knew this way was right. With every second that passed he was more a part of her. She held her breath and closed her eyes and savored the sensation of Eli's first gentle thrust.

When he held himself deeply and completely inside her, she felt the beginning signs of fulfillment. A flutter. A sharp pulsation. It was too soon, she wanted more, but her body would not be denied. Eli moved within her, no longer easy or slow. He made love to her until she cried out and surged against him as her body found release. Her inner muscles were still contracting when he drove deep and trembled all around and inside her.

Eli hovered above, keeping his weight from her and yet staying close. Their heated bodies were tangled and joined. She could barely breathe, and neither could he. There were no words, not for a moment like this one.

He kissed her; her mouth, her throat, her mouth again. Her heart pounded against his chest, her legs trembled.

"Why don't you take the night off?" he whispered, dipping his head down to kiss her again. "We can stay here."

"It's tempting, but I can't." She reached up and touched a strand of hair that had fallen over Eli's forehead. "I wish I could. I wish I could live here in this bed," she whispered.

"Sounds like a plan to me." He smiled down at her.

No, she had to go to work. Not only did she have to wait for the man who had killed Allie to call, she had to tell her audience that there was no such thing as happily ever after. Tomorrow was Valentine's Day, and that meant she had to be on duty to tell her brokenhearted listeners that love was a lie, that it was a sad fiction perpetrated by people who peddled cards and red roses, that there was no such thing as that one perfect person who might just show up on your doorstep one day and make everything good and right.

The problem was, for the first time in years she wouldn't believe what she said.

Sex had muddled his mind. That was it. That explained everything.

It was true that something about Ronnie Gray had moved him from the moment he'd first heard her voice. After all, that voice was gut-wrenchingly seductive. Add the face and the body and the way she sometimes looked at him...it was no wonder she had done him in.

Eli stood in the station hallway watching Ronnie as she spoke to her latest caller. He'd stepped into the booth just long enough to check the caller ID. It was a home phone number, complete with the name Waters, T. L. He'd waited until Ronnie answered the phone and Ms. Waters began to speak about her ex-boyfriend the jerk.

He could've remained in the booth with her. There

was a chair by the door. Before tonight he'd stayed out of the booth because she'd obviously wanted him to stay as far away as possible. Now that she didn't... he wanted the space.

Tonight he hadn't even bothered with a suit. Dale was always insisting that they had to convey a professional image, but this case was no longer professional in any way. He wouldn't try to dress it up to look that way.

He liked Ronnie Gray too much. It wasn't just the voice, or the body, or the big brown eyes, or the fact that she needed him... It was the whole, luscious package.

Ronnie Gray was a forever woman. Not a one-night stand, not a fling, not a casual-sex buddy. Ronnie deserved everything a woman could ever get from a man.

Right now he wanted to give her everything. Scary thought. It was the sex, he decided once again. He could still feel her on his skin, taste her, smell her body and his coming together. It would be enough to make any man think twice.

Ronnie finished with her caller and punched up a new song. "Baby Did a Bad Bad Thing." While the song played over the speakers she swiveled around to face the window and him, and she smiled.

It was a bad idea, there were a hundred reasons why he should steer clear of Ronnie from here on out...and all he wanted was to make the world fade again. For her, and for himself.

Chapter 8

Even dressed in jeans and a T-shirt, Eli looked as solemn as he had when she'd first seen him standing in the hallway with his arms crossed over his chest and his jaw clenched. Their eyes met, she smiled at him. After a moment, he smiled back. A little.

The smile didn't last. His head snapped to the side. He slipped his gun from its holster. Ronnie stood, ready to join Eli in the hallway, but he waved her back and headed toward the reception area.

She held her breath. Had he heard a noise? Was someone at the door? From the booth she could hear nothing. Her heart lurched. Surely the man who called himself Wayne wouldn't come here!

Even though he had silently ordered her to hang back, Ronnie ran for the door. If he was going to face

down a psycho, she wanted to be there. It was bad
enough to realize that someone she knew had been
killed by this nutcase. To imagine that Eli might be
in danger wrecked her heart.

But as she stepped into the hall she saw him coming, Detective Page and two uniformed officers trail-
ing behind him. Eli's gun had been holstered, but he
looked none too happy.

"Ms. Gray," Page said. "Just the woman I wanted
to see."

"Past your bedtime, isn't it?" she snapped.

"Yes," he grumbled. "It is."

Ronnie lifted a finger as the detective opened his
mouth to ask a question. She returned to the booth
and sat in her chair. One glance back proved to her
that Page was no happier than Eli.

"Here's a little something to get us all in the
mood," she said. She cued up a series of four songs,
swiveled around and stood in one smooth motion, and
returned to the hallway. When the door was closed
behind her, she said, "I have thirteen minutes and
fifty-four seconds."

The detective took a deep breath. "Is there somewhere we can sit and talk?" Ronnie glanced back at
the booth. Everything was running smoothly, and she
hadn't had any trouble with this computer system. "I
have a small office at the end of the hall." She waved
her hand toward the back of the building, and the
detective headed down the hall. Ronnie was behind
him, Eli behind her. The uniformed officers, who both

looked to be about twenty years old, brought up the tail end of the parade.

"You have an office?" Eli whispered.

"Yeah," she answered just as softly. "All the dee-jays do. I don't use mine often, but it comes with the job. Carl locks his office at night, so it's this or the reception area."

Her office was not much bigger than a decent-size closet, and sported a metal desk, a wobbly chair, one battered file cabinet and a dusty phone.

"Have a seat, Ms. Gray," the detective ordered.

"I'm fine, really."

"Sit," he said sharply. Detective Page was a vet-eran, gray-haired and haggard...and not more than three inches taller than Ronnie.

Ronnie glanced at Eli, and he nodded. Only then did she circle her desk to sit in the only chair in the room. The young officers waited in the hallway, just outside the open door. Still, the room felt crowded.

She sat there while Detective Page told her every-thing Eli had already found out. The initials. The fact that Ronnie knew the victim. She knew it all, and still the chills and the tears were real. Ronnie remembered Allie too well. The waitress had been such a sweet, optimistic girl. She deserved better than to die like this.

The detective perched on the side of the desk. "Is there anything you can tell me about Allison Wayne? Did she mention a boyfriend or a man who'd been harassing her? Did she tell you anything that might point us toward the killer?"

Ronnie shook her head. "No. Nothing I can think of." She took a deep, calming breath and looked the cop in the eye. "He called himself Wayne the first night he called. Did he know then that he was going to kill her?"

"Probably so," he answered, a touch of unexpected kindness in his voice.

"I don't want it to be my fault..." She went cold, down deep, and new tears welled up in her eyes.

"That's enough." Eli stepped around the desk and stood beside her chair to face Page. "Any other questions you have can wait until tomorrow."

"I'd like to stay here tonight," Page said, his eyes on Eli, not Ronnie. "In case he calls again."

"I've been keeping you informed," Eli said.

"I know you have, and I appreciate it, but I'd like to be here for the next call." He looked at Ronnie again. "With Ms. Gray's permission, of course."

He could get some kind of a court order, Ronnie imagined, if she didn't give her permission. She definitely didn't like the idea of seeing cops everywhere she turned, while she worked, and forcing them to go a more official route would buy her a little time.

But she thought of Allison Wayne, glanced at Eli's expressionless face and nodded her assent.

The detective didn't want to wait in the hallway, as Eli had done all week, so both men sat against the far wall of the booth while Ronnie worked. He wasn't about to leave Ronnie alone in the room with a cop. The two uniforms waited in the hallway.

Even though the cops in Atlanta had just been doing their job, Ronnie's fear was very real and certainly justified. He'd never been at the wrong end of an interrogation. He'd never been falsely accused. If he could make things better by stepping between her and the detective now and then, he'd do it.

Ronnie glanced their way often, not completely losing herself in her work as she usually did.

Had he really insisted, his second night on this job, that she stick it out? That she stay here and wait for the killer to call her again? He had. Right now he just wanted to scoop her up and take her out of here. He wanted to shelter her from everything: the good guys, the bad guys, the station manager who wanted to use this tragedy as a ratings booster. He wanted to protect her from everything but himself.

The phone rang, and both Eli and the detective stood. Ronnie glanced at the caller ID display, and then at them. "It's an Atlanta number," she said softly as the phone rang again. "Probably another cell phone." The detective scribbled down the number, as Ronnie answered and clicked the button to make this a call that was played over the intercom. "Talk to me, baby."

Strains of a depressing country tune played in the background as the caller breathed heavily.

"You sound so different tonight," he finally said.

Ronnie went pale, and Eli nodded to the detective. Page left the room, that scrap of paper with the cellphone number in his meaty hand. He handed the paper to the uniformed officers in the hallway, then returned to the booth to listen.

"Keep him talking," he mouthed at Ronnie.

"Why?" Ronnie asked the caller, her voice low and husky. "Why did you kill her?"

The caller laughed lightly. "I used to watch the two of you talking. You with your coffee, her with her smile. She did have a nice smile, didn't she?"

Ronnie closed her eyes and swayed in her seat, and Eli reached down to take her hand. She squeezed tight and held on. "That doesn't answer my question."

"Why do you sound changed?"

"I don't..."

"You do," he insisted. "Let's make a deal. I'll tell you why I killed that waitress, and you tell me why your voice is different tonight."

Ronnie glanced up at Eli, but it was the detective who nodded. They were trying to buy time. The longer they kept the caller on the phone, the better their chances were of tracing him.

"You first," she said.

The caller sighed. "She thought I was interested in her, in the beginning, since I always sat in her station. I almost always was able to take the chair you'd just left." He took a deep breath and exhaled slowly. "I thought she might make an interesting diversion until you and I could work our problems out. She kept turning me down." He sounded puzzled. "I sent her flowers, I left large tips, I tried to romance her...and she wanted nothing to do with me."

"So you killed her."

"Yes. When I want something and it's taken away, I have a tendency to lose my temper," he said calmly. "I've been patient with you. You needed time to recover from your ordeal in Atlanta."

Ronnie squeezed his hand tight. The detective glanced sharply at Eli, asking silent questions. Eli shook his head, and his eyes remained on Ronnie. She was about to fall apart.

The number that was playing came to an end. Ronnie didn't release his hand, but reached out and touched the computer screen to start another.

"What do you know about Atlanta?" she asked hoarsely.

"No. I answered my question. It's your turn."

Ronnie took a deep breath. "I don't think I sound any different tonight."

"You do," the caller insisted. "Something has changed, something more startling and momentous than last night's subtle distinction. It's as if the melancholy I always hear in you is...not gone but muted. I've always been able to hear the pain in your voice," he said dreamily. "And because I realized why you were hurting I stayed away. I wanted to give you time to heal."

Ronnie tipped her face back to look up at Eli, and he could see the terror there. Her eyes were so deep and dark against her pale skin, the hand he held trembled, and there was nothing he could do to help her. Not here, not now.

"What could you possibly know about my pain?"

"You haven't answered my question." The caller was finally losing his temper.

"I sound different tonight because I *am* different," Ronnie snapped. "I don't hurt so much anymore, I don't feel like I'll live the rest of my days alone. If you can hear that in my voice...good for you."

The caller took a deep breath. "A man," he whispered. "I waited too long, didn't I? You've...found someone."

"Maybe I have," Ronnie answered.

The caller did not respond immediately. In the silence, they heard something...the sound of a truck passing by. He was on the road. Would they be able to track him through the cell-phone towers he was using?

"It's him, isn't it?"

Ronnie didn't answer.

"You haven't called me Wayne tonight," the caller said.

"That's sick," Ronnie said. "To take her name and claim it as your own, that's not right. How could you be so cold?"

"I guess I need a new name." The caller sounded much too calm, but there was a quiet threat under the tranquillity. A layer of hate.

"I don't suppose you'd like to give me your real name," she said, challenging him. "Just between you and me."

The caller laughed. "Just between you, and me, and your Sir Galahad, and the cops. Do you think I'm stupid?"

"I think you're an idiot," Ronnie answered.

Again they heard the distant sound of a large truck through the intercom on Ronnie's console.

"I'm an idiot who managed to get away with murdering your husband," he said tersely. "I got away with murder once, twice... I don't see why I can't get away with it one more time."

"My husband?" Ronnie whispered. She didn't look up, she let the hand in Eli's go slack. "You killed Roger?"

"Surprised?"

Ronnie didn't answer. Eli suspected she was incapable.

A cold voice drifted from the phone. "I wish you had chosen me, Veronica. I do. I would have ended your pain. I would have made you happy again. You never gave me the chance."

Ronnie dropped Eli's hand and stood. "Who are you?"

"You can call me Gray."

Chapter 9

Ronnie buried her head against Eli's chest. They stood in the hallway, Eli leaning back against the window that looked over the booth. His arms were wrapped securely around her; they held her tight. Those arms and the steady beat of his heart kept her from falling apart.

The police were gone, having learned everything they could from the caller and the resulting questions about Roger's death. She didn't think anything they'd covered tonight would help. He'd probably called from another stolen cell phone, he'd been driving down the interstate…they'd never catch him.

And she was next.

It wasn't yet four in the morning. She had some preprogrammed music playing at the moment. She couldn't speak. Not to her audience, not to a broken-hearted caller, not even to Eli.

What would she do if he wasn't here?

He didn't try to make her talk, he didn't tell her everything would be all right. She was grateful for that; he didn't try to lie to her.

"He killed Roger," she whispered when she felt as if she could speak without crying.

Eli stroked her hair. "You don't know that. He might've said that just to upset you."

"No. I think he was telling the truth." She lifted her head, rested her chin against his chest so she could see his face. "I could never imagine how Gordon could kill anyone, but when the police finally said he did it...I accepted it as fact. It's true, Gordon was an alcoholic and he was mentally unbalanced, but I had never, ever seen him behave in a violent manner. That night, the night Roger was killed, Gordon gave me a heart-shaped cookie." She shuddered, and Eli's response was to hold her even tighter. "Roger knocked the cookie out of his hand and it broke on the asphalt. The police said that must've set him off. Roger was dead less than an hour later." She took a deep breath. "Gordon died in jail," she whispered. "There was no trial, no other suspects except me. He died, and it was just...over."

"Don't relive this," Eli ordered. "Not now."

"It'll be two years, tomorrow." She closed her eyes briefly. "No, today. It's well after midnight, it's officially Valentine's Day. I should be on the air right now, knocking the romantic holiday and putting down

heart-shaped candies and sweetly sentimental songs...
but I can't.''

Eli raked one large hand up and down her back.
"I'll get you out of here. I have a cabin a couple of
hours from Laurel. It's up in the hills, way off the
beaten track. No one will ever find us there."

"Just you and me," she whispered.

"Yeah."

Eli's suggestion sounded like a nice idea, a wonderful idea, but she knew it was nothing more than a
fairy tale. A fantasy. "And how long could we hide
in your cabin?"

Eli didn't answer. He knew as well as she did that
they couldn't hide forever.

"He's coming for me next," she said.

"He'll have to come through me," Eli said, his
voice dark and husky as he made his promise.

She shouldn't be leaning on Eli, figuratively or literally. He'd been hired to protect her; of course he'd
place himself between her and danger if he could. It
was his job. But was there more here? She sensed it.
Felt it to her bones. She never would've made love
with him if she hadn't known in her heart they had
something more.

"Why is it that one minute I think I hardly know
you?" she asked. "And the next, I feel like I've
known you forever?"

"I know what you mean," he said softly, and it
sounded like a confession. A reluctantly made confession.

She wanted to get her mind off the phone call, off

the anniversary of Roger's murder. The one person in the world who could distract her was right here.

"Tell me about Eli Benedict," she whispered. "Tell me something I don't know."

He shifted his body, realigned the arms that held her. He did not let her go. "I was born in a little town north of Nashville. My parents are perfectly normal people, and I have an older sister who was the bane of my existence until I was twenty-two."

"What happened when you were twenty-two?"

He grinned down at her. "I grew up, and suddenly she wasn't so bad."

"What else happened to you after you grew up?"

His smile faded. "I got married and became a cop. Unfortunately, I wasn't very good at either endeavor."

"I find that hard to believe."

"Ask my ex-wife," he grumbled. "She'll back me up on this one."

"How long were you married?"

"Three years."

"Divorced?"

"Six."

"Kids?"

"No, thank God."

"And you never got married again?"

Eli shook his head.

"What about…" she began.

"If you ever decide to give up radio, you should come to work for me."

"I should?"

"You're relentless. That's a good trait in a private investigator."

"I just wanted to know—"

He interrupted her once more, with a kiss this time. A long, slow, undemanding kiss that calmed and warmed her.

"You're changing the subject," she whispered against his lips.

"Yes, I am." He lifted her off her feet so her face was perfectly aligned with his, and then he kissed her again.

It was still dark outside when the morning personnel began to arrive. Eli stood in a position where he could see the reception area and the arriving employees, but could still keep an eye on Ronnie. She was back at her console, playing music, making cracks about Valentine's Day, taking one more phone call from a weepy woman whose husband hadn't yet come home.

The janitor, Frank, arrived first. He nodded at Eli as he headed for the closet at the end of the hallway, next to Ronnie's office, and dragged out his cleaning supplies. He went to work immediately, paying little attention to Eli or Ronnie as he began to clean. The older man hummed along with "Draggin' My Heart Around," then turned away, embarrassed, when he caught Eli watching him.

Frank hadn't been working fifteen minutes before Carl arrived. Today he beat the surly secretary to the station. Carl walked directly to Eli, nodded and smiled as if they were old friends. They stood side by side and watched Ronnie work.

"I could make her a household name," Carl whined.

"She doesn't want to be a household name."

"I don't get it," Carl said. "Everyone wants to be a star, right?"

Not everyone. Ronnie only wanted to be left alone.

Could he leave her alone when this was over and done? Not likely. Just when he'd gotten completely contented with bachelorhood, just when he'd let himself get comfortable with his life…boom, along comes Ronnie Gray to turn everything upside down.

Maybe. When this was truly over, when she didn't need him to stand between her and the rest of the world, would this thing between them fade? Or would it vanish immediately, in a flash, in a heartbeat.

The morning deejays arrived, annoyingly chipper as usual. He suspected they were on more than caffeine.

His first morning here, one of them—which one? he wondered as he watched them saunter down the hallway—had called him Ronnie's personal Sir Galahad. The caller had used those same words last night. Sir Galahad. A chill danced up his spine. Was that a coincidence? He didn't think so.

The man who was fixated on Ronnie would want to be near her. He watched her, he'd followed her on her way to work every night…even going into the coffee shop to sit in her recently vacated seat and flirt with her waitress.

Was he here? Right now, this very minute, was the man who'd killed Ronnie's husband and Allison Wayne watching them both?

Eli was in a rush to get her out of the station this morning. It had been a long night. Too long. She was anxious to get home herself, to fall into bed with Eli and let him hold her while she slept.

As soon as they were in the car and driving out of the parking lot, he flipped open his cell phone and began to dial.

"It's Benedict," he said in response to the voice on the other end of the phone. "Yeah," he said after a pause. "Too bad. A good detective doesn't need to sleep."

He glanced at her while the detective responded to that comment.

"I have an idea," Eli said more gently. "Run a check on the two morning deejays. Chuck and... and..."

"Jesse," Ronnie whispered.

"Chuck and Jesse. Carl Gamble, too, the station manager. Find out if any of them were in Atlanta two years ago."

Ronnie shook her head in silent denial. No one she worked with could have done these things. Chuck Landers and Jesse Greer weren't her favorite people, but to imagine that one of them might be capable of murder...

"Just do a background check on everyone at the station," Benedict snapped. "If you don't want to do it I can have my agency handle the job. I thought you might want to actually solve this murder.''

Ronnie heard the heated response from the detective on the other end of the phone as Eli ended the call.

''You don't really think someone I work with is...him.''

He glanced at her, and she saw the fire in his eyes. Yes, he did. ''Just a hunch.''

Ronnie shivered, drew up her arms to hug herself and hold in a hint of warmth as Eli made another phone call.

His first words were, ''Yes, Dale, I know what time it is. Just listen up. I want you to get on background checks for everyone at the radio station. Call Gamble and get a complete list of employees from him. And just because Gamble gives you the list, that doesn't mean you leave him off of it.'' He glanced at Ronnie. ''I suggested the same check to Page, but I don't think it's a bad idea to have both of us going at this from different directions.''

He ended that call and tossed his cell phone onto the seat between them.

''That cabin you suggested is sounding better and better,'' Ronnie said.

''Don't I know it,'' he grumbled.

For a few minutes, she watched his profile. It was strong, handsome...familiar, in a bone-deep way. ''You told me a little bit about yourself this morning.''

He glanced at her. "Too much? Have I already frightened you away?"

She smiled. "No. There is one question I never got to ask, though. You said you were a lousy cop. Why?" She'd seen him work, she had mentally compared him to every cop she'd ever met. He was extraordinary, by that comparison.

"I was actually pretty good," he admitted sheepishly. "Until the divorce. I was angry, and I started screwing up. Add to that the fact that I hate taking orders. When Dale suggested we start our own business…" He shrugged.

She nodded, understanding. He had run, too, but in a different way. Knowing that, she didn't want to push any harder for answers. "Maybe you have a few questions for me. Tit for tat, right?"

Eli returned his attention to the road. "You've been grilled enough for one lifetime, honey. But if there's anything you want to tell me, I'm all ears."

She'd been hiding for so long, she'd forgotten how to be totally open with another person. "You called me honey," she said.

"I did, didn't I." He frowned a little. "Is that a bad thing?"

"No, it's not." She liked the endearment, and it had come out of Eli's mouth so naturally, without pretense or forethought.

"I used to be very ambitious," she said, her eyes on Eli's profile. "Two years ago, an offer of all the promo Carl wants to do for me now…I would have been in hog heaven."

"But not now."

"Everything changed two years ago," she confessed. "Roger and I were separated, we were in the middle of getting a divorce, and he was worried about the bad publicity more than anything else." She laughed, and it was not a pretty sound. "He cheated on me, and from the very beginning he treated me like I was...a pet or a possession. Not a person, certainly not an equal."

Eli mumbled a low opinion of Roger's character, something vulgar and unexpected.

"I never got to be divorced," she whispered. "I became a widow before Roger signed the papers. The cops used that against me in the beginning. There was an insurance policy, and Roger owned a very nice house, and...I guess to them I looked very guilty."

"I'm sorry," he said gently. "They never should have treated you the way they did."

"By the time the investigation ended and they had a man in jail and charged with the murder, I was exhausted. Not just tired, but exhausted in my soul. I just wanted to hide from it all. So I came here, got a job working the overnight shift, and I did just that. I lived my life as obscurely as possible. There have been no friends to speak of, no life. Just...existence. I worked, I ate, I slept."

"You've been punishing yourself for something that wasn't your fault," Eli said angrily.

"No," Ronnie said quickly. "I've been protecting myself from being hurt again."

He pulled his pickup into the driveway of his home.

The sky was turning gray as he put the vehicle into Park, shut off the engine and turned to face her.

"Do you think you need to be protected from me?"

"No," she whispered.

"Good." He reached out and touched her face. "When this is all over, when the man who's doing this to you is caught and put behind bars, if I asked you to go to that cabin with me, would you say yes?"

She smiled. "Don't you think we should start slow? Maybe…go on a date first."

"No," he said succinctly. "First of all, it's much too late for us to start slow. Second, and just as important, I am not a good date. I hate dating. It's like this ancient ritual, and there are these secret codes and languages that no one ever bothered to teach me. Besides, I'm too old to date."

"Exactly how old are you?"

"Thirty-four. You?"

"Twenty-nine."

"Baby," he said accusingly.

"Old man."

"Quit beating around the bush and answer my question," he said almost harshly. "I'm not talking about dating. No games. No flowers, no candy, no dressing up everything nice and pretty when we know what we both really want. When this is over, if I ask you to go with me to a secluded cabin in the woods for a long weekend of mind-blowing sex, will you say yes?"

"Are you asking now?"

He stared at her. "See?" he said, shaking a finger in her direction. "This is like dating. I ask you a question, and you answer with a question, and I feel like I've lost something important in the translation."

She leaned toward him. "Yes," she said. "Is that uncomplicated enough for you?"

"It is. Thank you."

"Is it the answer you wanted?"

Eli paused for a moment, and while he hesitated, Ronnie held her breath.

"Yeah," he admitted. "That's exactly what I wanted to hear."

Chapter 10

The door slammed behind Eli and he spun the dead bolt until it snapped solidly into place. He switched on the light in the entryway, and then he reached for Ronnie.

He'd known yesterday, when she'd asked him to make love to her, that it had been a long time since she'd been with a man. He hadn't known then how long it had been—two years or more—and he certainly hadn't known that for her to come to him was such a momentous step.

Would he have stopped her if he'd known? No, he wasn't that strong. He wasn't that damn noble. He wasn't worthy of her trust and her passion, he knew that. But he didn't want to let her go. Not yet.

He began to undress her as they kissed, pushing off

her coat, unfastening her bra, unsnapping and unzipping her jeans. He needed her beneath him, around him. He wanted to hear her moan out loud, laugh and cry.

"I want you," he said as he lifted her off her feet and carried her toward the bedroom.

Her entire body shuddered in response, and that telling shudder only made him want her more.

When they reached the bedroom, he put Ronnie on her feet, there beside the bed, and set about finishing the chore. Her shirt came over her head, the band that was holding her hair back and up was discarded. And then he stopped.

"Ronnie," he said as he drew her bra off her arms and tossed it aside, "do you know what this is?"

"Of course I do," she answered softly.

He'd called her honey. The word had just slipped out of his mouth. He didn't call anyone honey. He didn't even know where the word had come from!

"It's strictly physical," he said. "This is hormones and tension and the intensity of the situation. We've been thrown into close quarters, I'm responsible for you, you're scared..." He tried to explain it to himself, as well as to Ronnie.

"Are you uninviting me?" she whispered as she reached out to unfasten his jeans. "Are you saying you don't really want me to go to your cabin for a long weekend of mind-blowing sex?"

Her touch and the word *sex* coming out of her mouth made him harder than he already was. "Of course not, I just don't want to mislead you."

"Would you like for me to sleep in the guest room?"

"No." The idea of letting her go now was torture...but he didn't want to lie to her. He didn't want her to think this was more than it was. An affair. A physical anomaly that would burn itself out, sooner or later.

Ronnie skimmed her fingers beneath the waistband of his jeans. "Eli, have you ever been a bodyguard before?"

"Of course," he said huskily.

"And your clients were sometimes women?"

"Usually."

Her fingers rocked back and forth, and she tilted her head in an angle that was endearingly sexy. "I imagine you've been in close quarters with frightened women many times. The situations were probably all intense."

"Yeah."

Ronnie rose on her toes and kissed his neck. "How many of them did you sleep with?"

She asked as if she knew the answer. He could lie and make up a number. He could tell her this sort of thing happened all the time. Instead, he told her the truth. "None."

"That doesn't make for a very convincing argument," she said, unconcerned.

He took her face in his hands and forced her to look him in the eye. "I don't want to hurt you."

"Then don't," she whispered.

Ronnie had been hurt enough, and she was so fragile. There were times when it seemed she was tough as nails, but beneath the facade she was delicate.

"Don't question what's happening to us," she said. "I'm not. At least, I'm trying not to. I can't explain it, I don't know what happened…and considering what's going on in my life right now I'm not ready to think of anything beyond today. But Eli, for the first time in a very long time, I *like* today. Thanks to you, I very much like today." Her fingers caressed his hips and slowly pushed his jeans and boxers down. "Don't worry, I promise not to ask you for a date."

She could hardly move. Every muscle in her body ached, and her eyes were heavy-lidded and sleepy. She smiled at Eli, who was stretched out beside her, every bit as naked and exhausted as she was. His hand stroked her, raking down her belly to rest between her legs and caress her gently. Her body responded as it always did when he touched her.

"What are you trying to prove?" she whispered.

"Nothing." He rolled onto his side and laid his lips on her shoulder for a gentle kiss.

"This is not nothing," she whispered as her legs fell apart and he caressed her deeper, harder.

"Maybe you should stop calling me an old man."

Had Eli really stood beside this very bed and tried to tell her their relationship was just physical? Maybe he was trying to prove it. She hadn't left the bed for ten hours, except for a trip to the bathroom. Eli had made love to her, and she'd slept a short while. She'd awakened to find him touching her again, teasing between her legs and kissing her breasts. He'd studied her with his hands and his mouth as if he was determined to know every curve, every inch of her body. He'd been so thorough she'd come twice that time. Once slow, once fast.

He'd cleaned and fed her, right here in this bed. And then he'd let her sleep for a while longer. Now she was awake again. Eli was aroused and so was she. The day had passed in a haze. A wonderful Eli-colored haze.

She reached out to touch him, to circle her fingers around his erection and stroke gently. They didn't need words, she was too tired for words…but she was not too tired for Eli.

He rolled atop her with a growl and guided himself to her. Eli loved her. He said it was sex, physical, something that would burn out when this was over…but there was more. She knew it and so did he.

When he was inside her, she didn't think about anything else. She couldn't. There was her body and his, passion, pleasure, and yes…love.

Eli knew her body so well already. He knew how to touch her, where, when. He lifted her hips, drove deep, and she shattered. She cried out, held him close while the waves washed through her. There was physical release, and pleasure, and the warmth that came from being joined with another human being, but there was also something new. Eli held himself deep inside her and found his own completion. He held her close and shook, he whispered her name, and then he came down to kiss her deep and long.

"I can't get enough of you," he said when he took his mouth from hers.

Was that why he kept waking and loving her? Did he think he could burn out this physical attraction he couldn't explain away? "That's a good thing, isn't it?"

"I haven't decided."

She wanted to argue with him, but she was too tired. Eli rolled away but kept his arms around her. She shifted to her side, rested her head on his shoulder and went to sleep.

The phone on his bedside table rang, and Eli sat up in a straight shot. It took a moment for everything to register. It was night, so the room was dark. Ronnie slept.

And he was a complete idiot.

"Benedict," he answered hoarsely.

"You're a genius," Dale said brightly.

"Huh?"

"A genius who sleeps all day, apparently," his partner added.

"How am I a genius, exactly?" Eli asked, swinging his legs over the side of the bed and pressing one hand against his temple. "And use small words."

"Jesse Greer lived in Atlanta two years ago."

"The morning Jesse?" Eli asked, coming instantly awake.

"Yup, only Jesse wasn't his name at that time. He

was a deejay on some easy-listening station that was just blocks from the TV station where Ronnie worked. And, get this, he was arrested twice for beating up his girlfriend.''

So, he was violent and he had changed his name. That wasn't proof, but it was more than they'd had this morning. "Do the police have him in custody?''

"No," Dale said, his voice less bright. "They went to his apartment to question him but he wasn't home. There's an APB out on him, though. They should have him soon.''

"Unless he got wind of this and has gone under.''

Still, the caller had a face. Maybe. How had he disguised his voice? Eli shook his head. Jesse made his living with his voice, of course he could alter it so Ronnie wouldn't recognize him when he called.

Ronnie stirred beside him, and he reached out a hand and stilled her.

"What is it?" she asked sleepily as she rolled up into a sitting position.

"Is that *her?*" Dale asked. "Oh, man. You dog. You are going to get burned.''

Eli ignored his partner's glee. "If you hear anything else, call me.''

He hung up the phone and turned to Ronnie. "Jesse," he said. "The morning guy. Did you know he lived in Atlanta at the same time you did?''

She paled. "No. Do you think he's…''

"Maybe," he said, not wanting to give her false hope.

She shifted toward him and cuddled. He had never

been much for cuddling, before or after. But he liked holding Ronnie. He liked that she came to him so easily, that she obviously found some comfort in this contact. She was naked, so was he...and yet there was nothing sexual about this. It wasn't hormones and, dammit, it wasn't temporary.

"Can we stop by my house on the way to the station?" Ronnie asked.

"Why?"

"I need to check my answering machine, and I'd like to pick up a few things. Five minutes, tops."

Eli headed for her house, reluctantly. Until they had a few more answers, he was going to play this close and safe.

Jesse. It was hard to believe that he might be the one. He'd started work at the station several months after she had, which did not work in his favor. But then, since the station had changed hands about the time she went to work there, a lot of the people had started then. Jesse had asked her out several times, but he'd never seemed pushy or weird. Just friendly. Nothing more.

If the people at the coffee shop could identify him as a frequent customer who'd paid special attention to Allie... The nightmare was almost over.

What would happen when this was settled? She'd be working alone at night, again. She'd be living in her own house. Maybe Eli would invite her to go away for that long weekend. Maybe not. Until they didn't have the case between them, she didn't know what would happen next.

"Five minutes," he said as he pulled into the driveway. She'd left the porch lamp burning, and had her keys in her hand as she approached the front door. Eli was directly behind her. Most days she loved the fact that her house was so far away from the neighbors. Tonight, the seclusion gave her the willies.

Inside, it didn't take her five minutes to check the messages on her answering machine and very quickly change her clothes. She was tired of jeans and station T-shirts, tired of making damn sure she never drew any attention to herself. She wanted Eli to notice her…when she was dressed and out of his bed.

She heard his cell phone ring as she stepped into a tall boot. A moment later she shook out her hair as she left the bedroom and turned off the light.

Eli was ending the phone call as she stepped into the living room. He heard her, and turned to greet her with a gruff, "They got…holy cow."

She ignored the last comment. "Jesse?"

"They've got him in custody."

Her heart hammered. "Is it him?"

"He asked for a lawyer right off the bat. That doesn't look good." His gaze raked over her from head to toe. "What time do you have to be at the station?"

"Five minutes ago."

He grumbled.

Ronnie grabbed her coat and slipped it on. "I guess

your job is over. If they have the caller in custody, I don't need a bodyguard.''

Eli shook his head. ''I need more proof than a couple of inconsistencies and a lawyer to let this one go.''

''It all makes sense, though,'' she said. ''Funny how when you look back, the pieces of the puzzle fall together in a way you never would have imagined.''

''Funny,'' he grumbled.

''You probably don't have to stay with me tonight if you have other things to do. I can lock myself in, and...''

''No way,'' Eli said as he locked the door behind them. ''Any woman who looks like you do definitely needs a full-time bodyguard.''

Chapter 11

"Valentine's Day," Ronnie said into the microphone. She turned her head, looked directly at Eli, and grinned. That smile grabbed him down deep. "Thank goodness it's technically over."

It was one-fifteen in the morning. No one was left in the station but the two of them. Ronnie had changed this week. Physically, she was more beautiful than ever. Her dark-red hair was down, falling around her shoulders, there was color in her cheeks and a smile twisting her shapely lips. Instead of jeans, tennis shoes and a station T-shirt, she wore a knee-length black skirt that hugged her hips, a white sweater that hugged the curves of her breasts and a pair of knee-high boots.

She was trying to seduce him with that look. And she was succeeding.

"For every woman who's ever wished for a knight in shining armor and ended up with a cold dose of reality instead..." Her smile faded. "Here's something to get you through the night."

She laid her fingertips on the computer screen, and "Where Have All the Cowboys Gone" drifted from the speakers.

That done, she joined him in the hallway. "What have you done to me?" she asked with a smile.

"You want a list?"

She blushed, but didn't back away. "You know what I mean. I was supposed to come here tonight and blast the very idea of romance and Valentine's Day and..."

Love. She didn't say it; neither did he.

"This was, without a doubt, my best Valentine's Day ever," he said.

"Mine, too," she said as she wrapped her arms around his neck.

They'd spent all day in his bed. There had been short breaks for food, sleep, even a little talking...but most of their hours in that bed had been spent in the pursuit of more physical and pleasurable activities.

He was still trying to convince himself that his attraction to Ronnie was purely physical. So why did the idea that this crisis might be over give him chills? He wanted her to need him, he wanted to be with her every day, all day.

Ronnie held her body against his. "When I first saw you, I thought you were a cop."

"And you hated me for it, if I remember correctly."

"*Hate* is such a strong word." She laid her lips on the side of his neck and let them linger. "It was suspicion, not hate." She nuzzled his neck. "I was wary of you," she whispered. "I'm not wary anymore."

It sounded very much like a confession. They were dancing close to an edge he had avoided for six years. "When I first saw you, I thought... Great. No warts."

Ronnie laughed, the sound warm and intimate against his neck. That laughter seeped inside him, touched him, broke down walls he'd spent a long damn time building.

She laid her mouth on his and kissed him, and he was lost. When this was over, he didn't want to lose her. A long weekend at the cabin? Not enough. He couldn't imagine ever letting Ronnie go.

The kissed turned in a heartbeat. It became deeper, more necessary. Ronnie was necessary. He rested his hand on her hip; she pressed her body against his.

Just like that, he needed to be inside her. "How much time?" he whispered.

Ronnie lifted her arm and looked at the watch on her wrist. "Nine minutes and forty-seven seconds."

She didn't have to ask why he wanted a time-count. She reached for his zipper, lowered it and reached inside to caress him. She found him hard, and she knew just how to touch him to drive him wild.

Eli spun Ronnie around and pressed her back

against the wall, and again she laughed. It was a low, husky, sexy laugh that didn't last long. He lifted her skirt, skimming it high one inch at a time, and snagged her panties with two impatient fingers. They came down quickly, and were kicked aside.

Ronnie closed her eyes when he touched her, and the expression on her face was the most arousing sight he had ever seen. Eyes closed, lips slightly parted, passion clear and open and only for him. He found her already wet, circled the sensitive nub in a nest of red curls until she moaned and swayed against and into him.

The hallway speaker was directly overhead, and the music blasted down on them as another song began. "Love Stinks."

Quickly sheathing himself he lifted her, pressed her back against the wall and in a heartbeat he was inside her. Ronnie was wrapped around him, she held him tight, and they listened to their bodies reach for release. They danced, in a way, there against the wall, holding on to one another with everything they had. His thrusts, her answering wave of motion. When she came, he felt her inner muscles contract around him, and she cried out softly. It was all the encouragement he needed to join her.

He didn't want to let her go. He wanted to stay here, inside her, for the rest of the night.

She feathered her fingers through his hair, glanced up at the speaker, and whispered, "'Love Stinks.' That's my signature song."

"I think you're going to need a new one," he said reluctantly.

She sighed. "So do I."

Ronnie ran into the booth with three seconds to spare. The phone was ringing, the last song she'd keyed in was coming to an end. She chose another number and answered the phone with a breathless "Hello."

Silence. Had the caller already hung up? No, she heard breathing. Familiar breathing that made the hair on the back of her neck stand up.

"Where have you been?" he whispered.

Ronnie glanced into the hallway, where Eli stood watching through the window. She didn't have to do anything; he read the expression on her face and hurried into the booth as she hit the intercom button on the phone and replaced the receiver.

"I've been right here," she said.

Eli checked the caller ID, saw that it was yet another cell call, and reached for his cell phone. Tonight he didn't bother to retreat to the hallway to make the call. He dialed from just a few feet away.

"No," her caller said tersely. "You haven't been right there. Not at all. I've been calling. The phone has been ringing and ringing and ringing. Where were you?"

"I was—"

"No! I don't want to hear it. Don't say it. You're out of breath, you answered the phone with a panting *hello* instead of your usual cool *Talk to me, baby*. I can use my own imagination and know very well what you were doing!''

It wasn't Jesse. Jesse was in police custody. "I was just going to say that I was in the hallway and couldn't hear the phone."

"I'm sure you couldn't."

"He's called her again," Eli spoke into his cell phone in a lowered voice. "He's on the line right now."

"Is that him?" the caller asked, his voice suddenly calmer.

Eli grabbed the phone so the voice on the other end of the phone would come directly to him, and Ronnie was glad. She didn't want to hear that voice again.

"Yeah, it's me," Eli said. "Come and get me, you sick son of a bitch. I've had enough of this. Crawl out of your hole and come talk to me, face-to-face, man to man."

Eli looked at her as the caller responded, hesitated, and then said, "No." With that, he hung up the phone.

He offered his hand, and Ronnie took it. A few minutes ago, she had been so happy. Even now, she could still feel Eli inside her, she could still hear those telling words falling from his lips. *You're going to need a new song.*

The phone rang, and Eli glanced down at the caller ID. It was the same cell-phone number that had just called. He lifted the receiver and then banged it down. Hard.

"You're not going to talk to him anymore."

Ronnie nodded her head.

"I never should've asked you to continue to work this week. It was a mistake. I'm getting you out of here and you're not coming back until he's caught, you hear me?"

Again she nodded, but this time she stepped in closer to him. He wrapped his arms around her.

"We'll take a couple of weeks at the cabin," he said in a calmer voice. "I have a feeling a long weekend won't be nearly long enough."

Chapter 12

After he hung up on the caller the second time, the phone stopped ringing. Ronnie keyed in a number of selections, then sat back and listened. She played commercials when they were scheduled and then noted the time in her log. She checked the blinking light on the radio tower now and then and noted that as well. Call letters were played at the top of the hour. She went through it all on automatic, rarely saying a word. Eli had suggested a couple of times that she get someone to fill in for the rest of her shift, but she refused. Softly and without room for argument, she refused.

Eli didn't leave the booth, but he didn't try to push Ronnie, either. He just wanted to make sure she kept it together until he could get her out of here.

Sometime after four, the phone rang again. Ronnie almost jumped out of her skin, until she glanced at the newly-installed caller ID. "A regular caller," she said with a half smile as she reached out to answer. "I recognize the name."

"This is Angel," she said. "Talk to me, baby." She hit the intercom button and replaced the receiver.

"What's wrong?" a woman's voice asked over the intercom. "You're so quiet tonight."

"Hi, Terri," Ronnie said familiarly. "Sorry there hasn't been much going on around here. I'm not feeling very well."

"Oh, I hope you're not getting that crud that's going around."

"Me, too. So, what's up with Stan?"

Terri sighed. "He wants me to take him back again."

"Are you going to do it?" Ronnie asked.

"I don't know. He seems really sorry this time."

Ronnie covered her eyes with one hand; she looked as if she was carrying the weight of the world on her shoulders. It struck Eli, for the first time, how seriously she took this job of hers. "I can't tell you what to do," she said softly. "You know what he's like. You know that better than anyone."

"Yeah, but what if he's it?" Terri asked. "I mean, what if no other man ever wants me?"

"If you keep hanging on to Stan, no other man is ever going to have a chance." Ronnie said. "You deserve better. You know you do."

"Play something special for me?" Terri asked.

"Sure. You take care, you hear?" Ronnie ended

the call, and when the last note of a twangy country song played, she leaned into the microphone and flicked her fingers across the computer screen. "Here's something for a special friend of mine."

"Unchain My Heart" began to play, and Ronnie leaned back in her chair. "I'm tired," she said.

"Of course you are," Eli said.

Ronnie spun in her chair to face him. "No, I'm really, truly *tired.* Tired of running, tired of hiding, tired of living like a hermit."

Eli wanted to make things better for her...and that was a new sensation for him. He'd known from the beginning that getting hooked up with Ronnie Gray meant trouble. He usually ran away from trouble, not willingly into it. He offered Ronnie his hand. She took it, and he pulled her to her feet.

He didn't know what to say to make her feel better, and he didn't get the chance to try. As Ronnie came to her feet, the power shut down. The lights flickered once and then went out. The only illumination came from lights outside the window and a small battery-operated emergency light in the wall.

Ronnie didn't waste any time. She released his hand and headed for the battery-operated light. There was a switch there beside the light, and she flipped it with a curse. "Backup generator," she explained. "It'll take a few seconds to kick in."

It was a very long few seconds. Eli peered out the window; lights were operational up and down the street. There were no pockets of blackness that he could see, and the street lamps continued to shine brightly.

"I don't suppose Carl forgot to pay the utility bill," he grumbled.

"Not likely." The board before Ronnie lit up once again, dim emergency lights high in the walls in the booth and along the hallway came to life. She ignored the few seconds of dead air, and when the computer rebooted she started a new song, then leaned back in her chair and relaxed.

Eli did not relax.

The phone rang, and Ronnie reached out to place her hand on the receiver. Eli lifted a finger and signaled for her to wait. He checked the caller ID, then nodded once and unholstered his gun.

"This is Angel," Ronnie said. "Talk to me, baby."

"You've been very subdued since we last spoke," the caller said.

Eli reached out and ended the call before Ronnie could say a word.

"What's wrong?" she asked as the phone rang again.

The same number came up. "Is there a lock on the booth door?" he asked, glancing toward the window that looked over the dimly lit hallway and switching off the safety of his pistol.

"No. What's wrong?"

"The call is coming from a station extension." Ronnie's face remained calm, as if the news simply did not register. "He's calling from inside this building."

Ronnie lifted the receiver before her to dial 911. "No dial tone," she whispered.

Eli stood between her and the door of the booth. He blindly tossed her his cell phone. She caught it in midair, dialed the three numbers and got an emergency operator on the line.

"What is your emergency?"

She almost choked on the words. "He's in the building. Send the police to WPFT. We're on Taylor Street."

Eli stepped closer to the door, a weapon in his hand. "Smoke," he said in a low voice. "The bastard set the building on fire." He turned to her. "Let's go."

"Send the fire department," Ronnie said as she rose to her feet. "There's a fire."

The emergency operator remained insanely calm. "Ma'am, what's your name?"

"Just send them!" She ended the call.

Eli took her hand and opened the booth door. The place was too dark. There were so many unlit corners where an intruder could hide. She and Eli could be walking down the hall toward the front door, and the man who'd murdered Roger and Allie could come up out of nowhere. It was the stuff nightmares were made of, and it was enough to make Ronnie instinctively hang back, even as Eli tried to lead her out of the booth.

Eli's cell phone rang, startling Ronnie so she dropped the phone onto the floor. It broke into two pieces. The battery went in one direction, the rest of the device went in another. She swallowed hard.

He looked at her, said nothing and nodded. Once they moved into the hallway the darkness would work for them, as well as for the man who had been tormenting her.

The smoke was not yet heavy. It was wispy and gray and tickled her nose, and it drifted toward them from the front of the building. What if there was fire between them and the front door? The building had a rear exit, but there were no emergency lights near that door; the entire area around her rarely used office was pitch black.

They hugged the wall, holding hands and inching toward the reception area and the exit. The smoke grew heavier, in growing clouds around them. Ronnie held her breath as she waited for the faceless man who had been calling her to appear. All remained quiet. Nothing moved, there was no warning sound.

Finally, she could see the front door and, through the windows, the parking lot beyond. Frank stood at the door, frantically working his keys in the lock. "Fire!" he called as he burst into the building.

"Get back!" Eli ordered sharply. "There's an intruder in the building!"

Frank just stood there, planted between them and the door. "I've got to put the fire out. And what happened to the power? It's not out anywhere else but right here."

Ronnie could see the front door, smell the cold fresh air that had come in with Frank. "The fire department's on the way."

Frank nodded.

The lights from the parking lot illuminated the reception area well enough to assure Ronnie that there was no one lurking in a dark corner. She let out a breath of pure relief and leaned into Eli.

She could see now that the fire truck wouldn't be necessary. Three fires were contained in small garbage cans, producing more smoke than flame. All they needed was a fire extinguisher, and there were several of those situated throughout the building.

"When did Mr. Gamble get in?" Frank asked as he walked toward the hallway.

"Carl's here?"

"I saw his car out back. He doesn't beat me here very often," the old man said as he disappeared down the hallway.

"Wait!" Ronnie called, turning away from Eli.

It was too late; Frank disappeared down the dark, smoky hallway.

"Come on," Eli said brusquely, dragging her toward the door.

"What about Frank? And Carl! They're both back there."

A hoarse cry from down the darkened hallway interrupted her argument and she spun around.

"Frank?" she called. "Carl?" There was no answer. Eli was intent on getting her out of the building. "You have to do something!" she protested as he pulled her into the parking lot.

"Remember, you're my job. My only job." He didn't look happy about that at the moment.

"We can't just leave them in there," she insisted softly. She knew Eli agreed with her; he just didn't like the bind it put him in.

"You sit in the truck, doors locked, and I'll take two minutes to drag the old man and Carl out."

Ronnie nodded, silently agreeing. Eli was about to run into the fire, literally and figuratively, and her heart kicked anxiously. It kicked for him and for the men in that building. Were Carl and Frank trapped in the station with the psycho who had been harassing her? Or was Carl the psycho? She couldn't believe the man she worked for could be capable of harming anyone.

"You know how to use that thing?" Her eyes were on Eli's gun as she jumped into the truck he unlocked for her.

"Yes," he replied softly, just before he slammed the door behind her.

Locked in the truck, she watched Eli reenter the building they had just escaped. Her heart leaped into her throat when he disappeared from view.

It was too quiet out here. Where were the police? The firemen? Just a few minutes had passed since she'd called 911. Each second seemed so long.

He came out of nowhere, pressing his face against the driver's-side window so unexpectedly that she screamed. "Frank," she whispered when the scream died. He looked grayer than usual, and when Ronnie's gaze drifted down, she saw that the front of his uniform was covered in blood. In the dark, the blood looked black. Her hand rested on the door handle...but she hesitated.

"Help me." Frank couldn't make any sound, but she read his lips.

She looked around sharply. There was no sign of

the man who had stabbed the janitor. Carl? Had Carl
stabbed Frank? They must have exited by way of the
rear door, missing Eli entirely. Another, more terrifying thought occurred to her. They hadn't *missed* Eli
at all. He was hurt. He bled, like Frank. Was Carl out
there just waiting for her to open the truck door? Or
was her tormentor a stranger?

In the distance, she finally heard sirens. The police
would be here in a matter of minutes.

She opened the door gently, trying not to throw the
injured man to the ground. "Get into the truck," she
whispered. "Hurry! You'll be safe here until the police arrive."

Frank grabbed her arm and held on tight, as if to
steady himself. He held on much too tightly for a man
who was so badly injured he could barely make a
sound. Ronnie tried to scoot over to make room for
him in the truck, but she couldn't move.

"Let's go," Frank said in a voice that was not his
own. Ronnie knew that voice; this was the man who
had been calling her after midnight every night this
week.

He dragged Ronnie from Eli's truck and toward his
own car. She fought every step of the way. Her heels
scraped across the asphalt and she swung out with her
free arm, trying to make contact. She did her best to
wrench her arm from his grasp. For an old man he
was strong; her struggling didn't affect him at all. Of
course, Frank probably wasn't an old man.

"Stop it right there!" Eli shouted.

Frank spun Ronnie so she was positioned between
the two men, facing Eli who stood at the station door,

her spine to Frank's sticky chest. "Back off," he ordered.

"No way," Eli said, gun aimed steadily in their direction.

"I'll kill her."

"I'll kill you."

She didn't know where the knife came from, but suddenly it was there, touching her side, slicing through her sweater. "I never really expected to get out of this alive."

Ronnie knew what that meant; he intended for them all to die. A man who was not afraid to die would do anything.

"Why are you doing this?" Ronnie asked breathlessly. If she was going to die, she wanted to know *why*. "This, the phone calls, Roger…Allie…why?"

"You don't remember me at all, do you?" he asked calmly.

She shook her head.

"When I first came here, I was afraid you might recognize me. The wig, the glasses, the way I hold my head so you can't see my face well… I went to so much trouble to make sure you wouldn't recognize me, but it didn't matter. You don't remember me at all."

"Who *are* you?"

He sighed. "You interviewed me once. It was such a special moment. Your eyes met mine, you smiled…" His voice drifted for a moment, as if he was lost in thought. "You were new at the television station in Atlanta then, and when my neighbor was murdered you were there to ask questions." The knife at her side moved up and down, as if he was caressing her with the sharp tip.

Eli took a single step forward, gun steady, and that made the man Ronnie knew as Frank tense and press the knife more threateningly against her. In those seconds, she remembered. She'd interviewed several neighbors after a young woman's murder. It had been Ronnie's first big story. Most of the people in that neighborhood had been married couples who stayed together as she questioned them, but there had been one man who remained alone. A nondescript man who said the woman who had been murdered was a very nice lady and he couldn't understand why people did such terrible things.

"Did you kill her, too?" Ronnie whispered. "Your neighbor. Did you kill her?" The police had never made an arrest in that case, though they had looked at the husband long and hard.

"Yes."

"Why?"

"Because I loved her so much." He sighed again. "I loved you more. So much, I would do anything for you. And I did. I killed your pig of a husband. I followed you here, I watched over you…I gave you time to accept what had happened and move on with your life…and you never even looked at me or remembered that special moment we shared."

Special moment? She had asked him two or three questions, and then she'd turned to another, more interesting neighbor.

"You should have loved me," he whispered.

Eli took another small step forward. "Drop the knife."

"Back off!" Frank shouted. "Or I'll—"

Ronnie swung her elbow up and back, putting everything she had behind the blow. Frank had not been expecting her attack; all his attention had been on Eli at the moment. On Eli and in the past, lost in a *moment* he had created in his own sick imagination. His grip on her loosened and she turned, backing up slightly and making a fist as she spun around. He drew the hand that wielded the knife back, but Ronnie was quicker. She swung up, punching him full force in the throat.

"Ronnie!" Eli shouted. "Down!"

She dropped down and rolled away before a surprised and gagging Frank could swing out with the knife. Eli fired. Twice.

As the police cars pulled into the parking lot, Eli ran to Ronnie, dropping down to his knees beside her and setting his weapon aside as a safety precaution, since the police were getting out of their cars armed and confused. He checked her out, with his hands and his hungry eyes, quickly assuring himself that she wasn't hurt.

When he finally spoke, he said, "Didn't I tell you to stay in the truck?"

Ronnie started to cry. She sobbed, lying there in the parking lot with Eli hovering over her. He laid his hands on her face for a moment, then scooped her up and held her close.

"I'm sorry," he whispered. He began to rock her back and forth. "That was a stupid thing to say. It's over, Ronnie. It's over. He's not going to bother you anymore.''

"Sir,'' one of the police officers snapped. "Put the woman down.''

"No,'' he grumbled.

"It's okay,'' she said, catching one officer's eye. "He saved my life, so please don't make him put me down just yet.'' The officers moved to a motionless Frank and lowered their weapons as the fire truck turned into the parking lot. Carl's familiar car pulled into the parking lot right behind the fire truck. He was *not* parked out back as Frank had said. Another lie, one of many, meant to confuse her.

Eli held her, and she grasped the front of his shirt with every ounce of strength she could muster. She closed her eyes, tried to make her heart stop pounding so hard. A deep breath, the scent and feel of Eli, and she was better. Not completely, maybe, but well on her way. She was fine, Eli was fine. Did anything else matter?

"I think it's about time we started that two-week vacation at my cabin,'' he said softly so no one else could hear. "You and me, Ronnie. No phones, no radios, no television. Just us. What do you say?''

She leaned her head back and looked him in the eye.

"No.''

Epilogue

Almost two weeks later

It was nearly three o'clock in the afternoon when Eli pulled into the station parking lot. His radio was set on WPFT, of course, and he listened to the new mid-day show. Angel had been moved to a new time slot, with a minimum of fanfare. From noon until one, the lunch hour, she maintained her old style—with a few changes in attitude. For the rest of her shift she stuck with the station's format. Maybe Carl and Ronnie were both happy.

He certainly wasn't. Twelve days without Ronnie was just too much. She thought they'd moved too fast, that things between them were too intense, that a true and lasting relationship couldn't be built in a matter of days.

She didn't much care for his argument that they were simply more efficient than other couples.

Her suggestion had been that they take a two-week cooling-off period. Cooling off. He hadn't wanted to cool off then, and he didn't feel at all cold now.

In her defense, she'd been sticky with fake blood at the time, and her heart had been beating too fast and too hard. The man who'd been tormenting her lay a few feet away, dead, after having confessed that he had killed because he loved her. How could she think straight with the memory of those twisted words in her head? That wasn't all. The man who was supposed to be taking care of her had left her alone in a damn pickup truck while he ran into a smoky building to rescue an old man who didn't need to be rescued and wasn't an old man. He should've known something wasn't right, he should've stuck with Ronnie until the police arrived. If anything had happened to her…he didn't want to think about what might've happened.

The man she'd known as Frank Horton did not exist, as she knew him. His real name had been William Stone. There had been a Frank Horton, in a town a couple hours south, but he'd been dead three years. Stone had taken his identity, bought a gray wig and a pair of glasses, and stooped his shoulders. No one had looked at him too closely, invited him out to lunch, visited him at home. He'd been practically invisible.

For more than a year, Stone had been working here with Ronnie. Watching her. Watching and obsessing. They didn't know why he had finally made his move after all these months. Maybe it was nothing more than the approach of Valentine's Day. After all, Stone had killed Ronnie's husband on that day, two years earlier.

No one stopped Eli as he pushed open the front door and walked through the waiting area. He wasn't good at waiting. He had no intention of waiting any longer than he already had. Ronnie's old signature song, "Love Stinks," was playing over the speakers, which meant it was the end of her shift. She stepped out of the booth and into the hallway right on cue.

Ronnie was a little surprised to see him, but she certainly wasn't shocked. She tilted her head to one side and smiled. "You're early."

"Just two days."

She looked good. Jeans, station T-shirt, white tennis shoes, red hair up in a ponytail…just as he'd seen her that first night. So what was so different about her now? Deep down, she had changed. There was color in her cheeks, a sparkle in her eyes. And she wasn't afraid anymore.

"I wasn't sure you'd come at all," she said, taking that first step toward him.

"You were the one who wanted two weeks, not me. Are you going to kick me out and make me wait another two days?"

She shook her head.

The station was crawling with people at three in

the afternoon. They weren't alone, as they had been for so many nights. It didn't even feel like the same building, with everyone bustling about.

"Why'd you switch to afternoons?"

"Midday," she corrected. "Ten to three." She shrugged her shoulders and kept coming. "I figured if I was going to date, maybe I should have my nights free."

"Date," Eli groaned. "I'm really not good at dating."

She did not seem disturbed. "That's too bad."

"Would you panic if I asked you to skip the dating process entirely and just marry me this weekend?"

"Are you asking?"

He took a deep breath as she reached him and slipped her arms around his waist. "Here we go again. I ask a question, and instead of giving me a straight answer you ask another..."

"Yes," she whispered.

He lowered his mouth toward hers. "See? We're very, very efficient." "Love Stinks" blared from the speaker over his head. "Honey, I still say you need another signature song."

Their lips were no more than an inch apart. "Are you gong to help me choose one?"

"'Makin' Whoopee,'" he suggested.

"Nice song, wrong era," she said with a wicked smile.

"'Love Me Tender?'"

Her grin widened. "Elvis?"

"Okay, okay. What's the rush, anyway? There are

lots of good songs to choose from. I'm sure you know more than I do. You think of something.''

"You're the one who keeps insisting that I need a new song," Ronnie argued gently.

"You do," Eli insisted. "Love *doesn't* stink. It used to, or at least I thought it did, but not anymore. Not since I met you."

Ronnie sighed as her lips finally touched his. "I love you, too."

* * * * *

THE BEST OF THE BEST™ — Here's How it Works:

Accepting your 2 free books and gift places you under no obligation to buy anything. You may keep the books and gift and return the shipping statement marked "cancel." If you do not cancel, about a month later we will send you 4 additional books and bill you just $4.74 each in the U.S., or $5.24 each in Canada, plus 25¢ shipping & handling per book and applicable taxes if any.* That's the complete price and — compared to cover prices starting from $5.99 each in the U.S. and $6.99 each in Canada — it's quite a bargain! You may cancel at any time, but if you choose to continue, every month we'll send you 4 more books, which you may either purchase at the discount price or return to us and cancel your subscription.

*Terms and prices subject to change without notice. Sales tax applicable in N.Y. Canadian residents will be charged applicable provincial taxes and GST. Credit or Debit balances in a customer's account(s) may be offset by any other outstanding balance owed by or to the customer.

BUSINESS REPLY MAIL
FIRST-CLASS MAIL   PERMIT NO. 717-003   BUFFALO, NY

POSTAGE WILL BE PAID BY ADDRESSEE

THE BEST OF THE BEST
3010 WALDEN AVE
PO BOX 1867
BUFFALO NY 14240-9952

NO POSTAGE
NECESSARY
IF MAILED
IN THE
UNITED STATES

BOOKS FREE!